Cheryl.

This one is going
to hurt...

EVEN IF
IT HURTS

USA TODAY BESTSELLING AUTHOR

MARNI MANN

Marni Mann (signature)

For Nina.
This one will always be for you.
Love you.

PLAYLIST

"Eyes on Fire"—Blue Foundation
"I Found"—Amber Run
"Pray You Catch Me"—Beyoncé
"Trampoline"—Shaed, Zayn
"Strange Love"—Halsey
"Say Goodbye"—Dave Matthews Band
"Impression"—Matt Woods
"At My Weakest"—James Arthur
"Haunted"—Beyoncé
"Dark Times"—The Weeknd, Ed Sheeran
"Finally Feel Good"—James Arthur
"I Care"—Beyoncé
"i can't breathe"—Bea Miller

PART ONE

That love ... was so wild.

ONE

MY HANDS SHOOK as I squeezed the envelope between my fingers, my eyes glued to the return address, scanning each of the lines over and over.

The letter had traveled so far to get here.

Just to give me an answer.

"Open it already," my best friend said from the other side of the small room.

Slowly, I glanced up at Molly while she sat on the end of the couch, holding a tall coffee to her lips.

We'd been roommates since we were freshmen. Now, two weeks into our junior year at Boston University, I was finding out my fate for next semester. Whether I'd be here or subleasing my room to study abroad in London.

"I'm so nervous; my hands don't want to move," I admitted, unable to take my eyes off the return address as though the words would change if I did.

University of Westminster.

It was a highly sought-after program at my college, making it extremely competitive. Almost everyone in my major had applied, all of us hoping the international marketing experience we would gain would be enough to set our résumés apart when we graduated.

"Girl, you got in," Molly said, her heels tapping the floor. "Stop stressing and trust me."

I slowly lifted the corner of the envelope and slid my finger across the top to break the seal. When the thin stack of papers was in my hands, I took a deep breath, and then I unfolded them.

My eyes immediately landed on *Congratulations*, and my mouth fell open.

"Molly, oh my God." I read a few more lines just to be sure and finally looked up at her. "I got in." My heart was beating so fast; I could barely get the words out. "I'm ... going to London."

She left her coffee on the table to rush over and hug me hard. "You've worked your ass off for this."

I was far from the smartest student in my major, and school didn't come easy to me. So, to compensate for my lack of straight As, I had to do all the extra things, like become a TA and volunteer and nurture my relationships with the professors in my department. I had known this program was going to be a long shot, but I'd had to try. That was why I couldn't believe I'd been accepted.

"I'm so ridiculously happy for you," she continued, squeezing me even tighter, "because I know how badly you've wanted this. But I'm devastated at the same time because you're leaving me for six whole months." Her voice softened, her emerald eyes a little teary. "Like seriously gutted."

Molly was an accounting major. There was no reason for her to study abroad. But we'd spent every semester and even our summers together, so this separation was going to be challenging in many ways.

I clutched her shoulders as firmly as she was holding me. "Me too."

When she pulled back, her hands went to my forearms, several pieces of her long chocolate hair landing on her lips. "Promise me something?"

I held my breath. "Anything."

"Since our freshman year, you've worked nonstop. You've sacrificed nights out, parties, football and basketball games, and you've always put school first. When you're in London, I want you to have the best time and experience it all—I'm talking about every bit that comes your way. I want you to put fun first."

Just because I'd gotten in didn't mean I could stop studying the minute I got there. I would have fun, the same way I did in Boston; I'd just have to find a balance.

"I'll—"

"I'm not done, missy." She smiled. "I also want you to grab ahold of the sexiest single British man you can find, and I want you to let him fuck your brains out."

My cheeks were so hot; they felt sunburned, and I couldn't help but laugh. "You're crazy. You know that, right?"

Her fingers grasped my arms as though she wanted to emphasize. "It's time, Chloe."

It hadn't been my plan to be a virgin this long, nor was it intentional. But I'd learned very early in high school that I didn't have time for it all. Something had to be sacrificed, and it ended up being boys.

I held her with the same force, so she knew how serious I was. "I'll go to England with the most open mind, I promise." As I pulled my best friend in for another hug, I was hoping some of the nervous energy would loosen.

But it was still very much there, matching the excitement I

had felt when I got accepted to BU, knowing then that my whole life was about to change.

The same way I knew right now.

"You're never going to want to come back," she whispered.

I hoped she was right.

TWO

FROM THE MOMENT I landed at Heathrow Airport, I saw similarities to New England everywhere I looked. In the narrow cobblestone streets and the architecture, even in the foliage.

It made me feel right at home.

And with help from my roommate, a junior from South Africa in the same program as me, we spent the first few days learning our way around the city and our campus and the area where our dorm was nestled. So, by the time classes started the following week, I was able to find the building with ease.

First thing Monday morning, I dressed in my warmest clothes and walked the three blocks, slowing when I reached the building. I unzipped my coat as I headed down the long hallway, entering the classroom from the back. It was smaller than I was used to with less than thirty desks, several already taken. I went for the middle row, hung my jacket on the back of the chair, and began to set up my laptop.

I was just opening a blank document onto my screen when I heard, "You've got a good twenty minutes before the professor says anything worth typing, so you might as well enjoy the scenery for a bit."

It had been spoken in my ear from the guy sitting behind me, a chair that had been vacant when I first sat down. I barely processed his words because I couldn't get past his voice. I was melting in it— in the depth of his tone, the grittiness that pushed through each syllable, and how all of it was wrapped in the most delicious accent.

I'd heard accents from the moment I stepped off the plane. His was no different, but it was his sound that stood out.

And it demanded all of my attention.

A heat suddenly moved through my cheeks, and I reached for the scarf around my neck, pulling it away from my skin. I continued to hold the material as I turned around.

I wasn't sure what I expected to see. It was impossible to envision a face out of just noise.

But what my eyes landed on ... I was not prepared for at all.

His eyes were a light blue, his hair a chestnut brown, and he had a short but unruly beard that covered almost half of the most handsome face I'd ever seen.

But it was his gaze that caused the air to leave my lungs and for my body to burst with tingles.

And as I took him in, swallowing his stare, I was never more thankful I had something to hold on to. I pierced the thin material with my nails and searched for my breath.

No matter where I looked, I couldn't find it.

Not with his eyes on me.

Not with my eyes on him.

I glanced away just to give myself a break. I wasn't gone for long. I couldn't be. And once I connected with his stare, all the air I'd gained back was gone.

He'd drained me.

Again.

And then he stretched out his hand in my direction with an urgency that told me he needed to know what I felt like and said, "Hi." There was a slight pause before he added, "I'm Oliver Bennett."

With the same curiosity, I clasped our hands, and I was transfixed by his strength, at the length of his fingers, and the size of his palm. His skin wasn't sweaty. It was just hot, warming me from the outside in.

"Chloe Kennedy." I was shocked at the sound of my voice. I had no idea where it had come from, but it felt right to give him my name.

"You're American ... I fucking knew it."

My brows rose. "How? You hadn't heard me speak."

"Ah," he sighed, but it was different than just releasing a breath. He did it gradually, his lips drawing in my attention as they widened into a smile.

One that was positively beautiful.

I focused on his grin until it became obvious.

Then, our gazes locked, and he added, "I could smell it on you."

I laughed, mostly out of nerves and not knowing how to respond and because I believed that a guy with a stare as experienced as Oliver's could smell it on me.

I glanced down, needing a break again, my chest so tight, as I was overwhelmed from his eyes.

I hadn't had feelings like this back at home. I hadn't ever been early to class, my schedule was far too tight to allow that, and I just hadn't had time for conversations like this one.

This moment taught me how much I had been missing.

"Where are you from, Chloe?"

I waited for the air to move into my throat before I could say, "A small town on the coast of Maine, but I go to school in

Boston. Or did." I laughed, and it was so needed. "I mean, I'm just here for the semester."

He said nothing for several seconds, the passion in his gaze intensifying, and my hand began squeezing the scarf with a whole new kind of force.

I didn't know why, but it felt like I was standing completely naked in front of him, baring my soul, and it was so hard to breathe.

I couldn't remember a time when anyone had ever looked at me the way he was right now.

"Have you been to London before?"

As I shook my head, I saw the other students begin to fill into the room, and I knew class would be starting soon. "First time to Europe."

"You're daring."

"It probably was a little crazy of me, but"—I inhaled and swallowed, and both were so difficult—"I'm here."

"Yes"—his eyes dipped and came right back—"that you are."

"Welcome to International Marketing, Planning, and Strategy," the professor said from the front of the class.

Except my back was to the teacher and I was facing Oliver.

I gave Oliver a smile, he returned it, and I reluctantly turned around.

Even though my hands were on the keyboard as I waited to hear something worth typing, my mind was on the gorgeous guy behind me. And while the professor lectured, I couldn't stop thinking about the way he had looked at me, how his lips had lifted when he grinned, how I could even feel his charm in the air.

How he was sitting only inches behind me.

It was those thoughts that kept my mind so busy that I

didn't hear the dismissal of class. And I didn't know until I saw the movement on both sides of me, telling me it was over.

I glanced back at my computer screen and saw I hadn't typed a single word.

This wasn't the way to start the first class of the semester, and I was so disappointed in myself.

I closed my laptop and reached for the bag on the floor, sliding my computer inside. I stood to put on my jacket, and just as I turned, anxious to see Oliver's face, I saw he was gone. I glanced toward the door, hoping to catch the back of him, but I didn't get that either.

I didn't know why; I didn't know how it was even possible.

But I missed him.

THREE

I WAS STANDING in front of the case of sandwiches at the market by our dorm. I wasn't sure how many times I'd read the short descriptions under each variety, but the more time I stood here, the thicker my tongue got.

I had officially survived my first night out in London, and I was positive it would be a while before I could stand the sight of another beer.

If we'd had something in our fridge back at the dorm, I wouldn't have forced myself out of bed. But my stomach couldn't wait for food to be delivered, and this was the only way to soak up all the alcohol, helping me recover from one of the worst hangovers in my life.

"Can I make a suggestion?" I heard from behind me.

It was that voice again. That accent. The one from two days ago that had come minutes before the start of my International Marketing class.

The one I'd thought about almost every moment since.

Out of all the times I could have run into him, I wouldn't have chosen now. Not when I hadn't showered and I was dressed in yoga pants, a wrinkled tank buried beneath my jacket, a messy bun on top of my head, and last night's makeup that I still hadn't washed off, hidden behind my aviators.

But at this point, there was nowhere to hide. So, I croaked, "Please," and hoped he could hear the embarrassment in my voice and offer me a cure. "I will try anything to make this go away."

He moved closer, and my entire body stiffened, a movement that ricocheted through my stomach, causing me to almost dry-heave.

He paused there for what felt like forever, and then I heard a laugh and, "You got pissed last night, didn't you?"

He'd smelled me.

I had no idea how I felt about that, and my stomach wasn't going to give me a chance to even think about it.

"Help me," I groaned.

"The cure isn't in that fridge."

I couldn't put it off any longer, so I gripped the strap of my purse that hung across my body, and I slowly turned around to face him. I was so thankful I'd remembered to put on sunglasses, so they not only hid the disaster that was behind them, but also the way I was gawking at him.

He had that careless look going on even though he was well groomed in an oversize hoodie and winter hat, gray jogging pants, and sneakers.

"Where is it?" I asked.

"Down the road a bit."

The thought of spending more time with Oliver was almost too much for my hangover. But I also knew there was no way I would pass up this opportunity. So, I tightened the scarf around my face and said, "Be easy on me. I feel like I'm going to die."

His hand went to my lower back, and he moved us out of the store. "Are you okay?" he asked once we got outside.

Even with the cold hitting me, I nodded, and he began to weave us around the large groups of pedestrians on the sidewalk, making sure I never strayed more than a few inches. We went over cobblestone walkways and through a long, narrow passage. Once we reached the end of it, we went down a staircase that dropped us not far from Buckingham Palace, and within a block, we were going into a pub. I'd heard the name from one of the girls on my floor, mentioning it was a place we should check out. But as soon as I got past the door, I was immediately hit with a stench my stomach hated.

I pulled my scarf up higher and said to him, "The smell of the beer—I can't." I pointed at the door, so he knew I was going back outside.

He put his hand on my shoulder, stopping me. "Don't worry; we'll go upstairs. It'll be much better up there."

He grabbed my fingers and brought me through another door, leading to an extremely steep staircase, and I squeezed him, using his help to get up.

"Better?" he asked at the top.

I took a quick sweep around, not seeing a single pint on any of the waitresses' trays, and lowered my scarf, carefully inhaling. "Much."

A hostess was standing a few feet away, and Oliver held up two fingers. She nodded, understanding the signal, and brought us over to a table by the window.

"Still or sparkling?" she asked, placing menus in front of us.

"Sparkling," he told her. "We're in a bit of a rush; would it be okay if we ordered?"

I appreciated him now more than ever, and so did my stomach.

"Go ahead," she replied.

"Could we have a traditional meat pie and chips and also the fish and chips? We'll share both."

She took our menus and left our table, and within a few seconds, someone else arrived to fill our glasses with the bubbly water. I brought the small tumbler up to my lips and swallowed. But it wasn't until the glass hit the rim of my sunglasses that I realized I still had them on.

The thought of taking them off, knowing what I looked like underneath, made me hurt even worse.

I set the drink down. "I can't believe you're seeing me like this." I slowly took off the sunglasses, running my fingers under my eyes to catch the fallen and smudged makeup. "I didn't think I'd see anyone I know ... and now, oh God, I'm just sorry you have to look at me in this state."

When my skin felt as clean as it was going to get, I looked up at him. And when I did, I felt all the air leave my body.

"Chloe ... you're absolutely gorgeous."

Heat moved across my face as though there were a vent in the ceiling above my head. But there wasn't. The room was almost too cold.

I pressed the back of my hand against my cheek, cooling the red that I knew was growing across it.

And before I needed to think of a response, he said, "Tell me about where you're from."

I was hoping the change in conversation would make my stomach relax, but the way he was smiling at me was causing just the opposite to happen. "I'm a junior at Boston University, and I live with my best friend, Molly, in an apartment in the city. I'm an only child. My parents are still back in my hometown, and they work at a processing yard."

"Processing?"

I took a drink, the smell of the food from the nearby tables actually making me hungry. "I'm from an area that's known for lobstering. It's Dad's job to weigh the lobsters when they come off the fishermen's boats. Mom's the bookkeeper, so she pays the lobstermen whatever they're owed."

"That's Maine life?"

I was so impressed he'd remembered where I was from.

"Pretty much." I shrugged and peeked out the window, seeing all the busyness below. "Home is quiet and casual, very slow-paced."

I glanced back at him. He was running his fingers through his beard.

I didn't know why I found it so fascinating, why I couldn't drag my eyes away, so I pushed myself to keep talking. "Boston is hectic and exhilarating. A lot like London. I think that's why I love it here already."

He made me want to move my own hands and wiggle in my chair and smile because I had no idea what else to do with my lips. But I did everything in my power to stay still.

"Tell me about you, Oliver."

"I'm in my final year. I've been living with the same mates since I started school here. I'm from Manchester, a city about two hundred miles away. I've got three sisters, and I'm the youngest. Mum is a nanny; Dad works at the bank."

"Three sisters?" I felt my eyes widen. "That explains a lot."

His head turned a little to the side, giving me more of his profile. "Why's that?"

I had surprised myself by saying something, and now, I just had to be honest. "I get the feeling you really know women," I admitted. "Makes sense, considering you've been surrounded by them your whole life. Your sisters trained you well."

It was no wonder he was so charming. How he'd learned to use his smile and his eyes to his advantage with three girls and a mother he needed to please.

When he laughed, it only proved my point further. "If you ever meet them, please tell them that." His hand went to his hair, brushing it back and forth, the longer locks landing in a messy pattern that looked absolutely perfect on him.

My heart was beating so fast in my chest; I could feel it in the back of my throat. "You're forgetting something really important."

"Yeah?"

His grin returned.

And I felt it ... everywhere.

I gripped my glass with both hands. "You can smell where people are from before they even speak," I said, referring to when we'd met in class.

He laughed again, but this time was different. It was deeper, and his eyes never left me. "Not with everyone, Chloe."

He said nothing else, and it was the unknown that was exciting. That was an advantage Oliver had—he knew when to stay quiet, making my mind explode with questions.

Before I had a chance to ask any, our waitress delivered two plates to the center of our table. One had several pieces of fried fish with peas that had been whipped into what looked like guacamole and a basket of fries. The other had a mini potpie with crust covering the top, the meat inside smelling so savory.

The waitress came back a few seconds later with more fries and a bottle of vinegar and said, "Can I get you anything else? Something else to drink perhaps?"

"No, thank you," I responded, and Oliver said the same.

"Eat up; you'll feel better," he told me once we were alone. "If you've never had chips with salt and vinegar, you're about to love it." He lifted the bottle and was drizzling it over both baskets.

"It's the way I grew up eating them."

Although the practice wasn't common in Boston, it was where I was from, so I didn't find it strange at all. I squirted some ketchup onto a plate and dragged a fry through it before popping it in my mouth.

"Mmm," I groaned from behind my hand as I chewed. "These are delicious." I lifted my fork and went for the peas next. I'd seen them on every menu since arriving in London, but I hadn't dared to order them yet. "Wow." I chewed, surprised by how rich they tasted. "These are great."

"First time trying peas?"

"This style, yes." I pointed at the fish and chips. "That I've had, of course." I moved to the pie, stabbing my fork about an inch back. "This one is completely new." Once I had the utensil all the way through, I pulled it toward me and scooped up the bite.

I didn't just connect with his stare as I surrounded the fork with my lips. I felt it deep within me, even as I chewed when I moved the deliciousness around in my mouth.

He was overwhelming my senses.

"What do you think?"

"The meat is more seasoned than I expected, and the shell is so buttery ... it might be my new favorite."

And I noticed the more I got down, the more my stomach began to settle. He was curing me, but each time I was around him, I seemed to get more worked up. The same thing happened every time I thought about him.

His teeth grazed his bottom lip, and then he smiled. "Just wait until dessert."

FOUR

"IS THERE anything you haven't done but want to?" Oliver asked as we approached my dorm.

He was walking me home after the pub, and I was stuffed from all the food we'd shared for lunch and the sticky toffee pudding we'd had for dessert.

"Hmm," I said as we slowed.

Before I'd left Boston, I'd made a list of things I wanted to see in London, and I hadn't checked many of the items off. And now that school had started, my life was just going to get busier.

I backed up a few inches, leaning my shoulder into the side of the brick building. "Probably sounds silly, but I really want to go on the London Eye. It seems like the perfect way to see everything I haven't gotten the chance to."

"You free Tuesday night?"

There was a numbness spreading through my entire body, and it wasn't because the wind was whipping past my face or that the temperature was far colder than I liked.

It was because this insanely attractive guy couldn't seem to get enough of me, and my body had no idea how to respond.

There was no reason to even think about my plans. Whatever they were, if I had any, they would be rearranged to make room for him.

But I still paused, my chest tightening, the longer I waited to say, "Yes."

He reached into his pocket and took out his phone, tapping the screen several times before he looked up. "What's your number?" I gave it to him, and then he added, "I'll text you the time I'm going to pick you up."

I slid my hands into my pockets so they wouldn't be fidgeting out in the open, and I flattened my back against the building. "Okay."

He reached forward, gently brushing the bottom of my chin. His warmth spread through me, my skin turning sweaty underneath these clothes. The numbness was gone, and I felt everything.

And I had no idea what to do about it.

"Get some rest, gorgeous. You'll feel better in a few hours."

His hand dropped from my face. Before I could open my mouth, he was gone, and I was staring at the back of his head as he moved down the block, disappearing around the corner.

I pushed myself away from the building and went inside, rushing up the stairs to the second floor and hurrying down the hall to my room. Seeing my roommate was gone, I sat on my bed and took out my phone. Once I saw the time, I quickly did the math, realizing it was just after six in the morning in Boston. There was no way Molly would be awake, but there was also no way I could go another second without talking to her.

"Someone had better be dying," she said after the second ring, her voice hoarse and raspy.

"You will be once I tell you what happened this morning."

She yawned. "All right, I'm up."

"Hi. I miss you." I kicked off my shoes, slipped out of my jacket, and climbed under the blanket.

"Ugh, I miss you more." She cleared her throat. "Your replacement is skinny without trying—the bitch—and so messy. And she walks naked from the bathroom to her bedroom even though I know she owns a robe. If she does it when I have a guy here, she's getting evicted."

I laughed, sinking further into the mattress. "She was the best out of all the options. You know I hated having to put anyone there."

"Babe, I'm just hungover and stabby and wishing you were here; that's all. Tell me your news."

I gave her a brief rundown of my night out and caught her up from the moment Oliver had come up behind me at the store to when he just dropped me off.

"My God," she said once I turned quiet. "I like him."

"I had a feeling you were going to say that."

"Chloe, you're going on a date. What in the hell are you going to wear? We need to video chat while you're getting ready, so I can help with everything."

"He's already seen me look like death, so I really feel like I have some making up to do." Still, despite how terrifying my appearance was, he'd never taken his eyes off me. *Oh God.* "How are you not here? And how am I going to get through this without you?"

If I were home, I would have climbed into her bed to have this conversation, both of us tucked under the covers, our heads sharing one of her extra-large pillows. It felt wrong to be away from her during a moment like this.

"Shh," she whispered. "If we go there, we'll ruin this, and this is way too big to let that happen. So, let's just pretend I'm there, okay?"

I pulled one of the pillows out from under my head and curled my body around it. "Okay."

"Here I was, worried you were going to study right through the semester, and it would be over before you even started enjoying it." Her voice began to rise, filled with excitement. "Looks like I can stop stressing about that."

I rolled onto my back, not feeling the same as her because fear was squeezing my chest. "Molly, I have no idea what I'm doing, and he's an expert. And I think I'm already crazy about him, and I'm petrified I'm going to make a complete fool of myself."

"Hold on. How do you know he's an expert?"

My eyes closed, and I saw a perfect image of him in my head. "He's so fucking hot—in that bearded, not-caring, throw-yourself-together kind of way. Don't you think someone that sexy with his smile is pro-level at this point?"

"Most definitely."

I put the pillow over my face. "I'm in so deep; I'm drowning before I even get wet."

"So, the boy has skills," she said as the room started to feel like a sauna. "That's not something to be afraid of; it's some-thing to appreciate. And you will, *trust* me."

I moved out of the fluffy feathers and used my hand as a fan. "I don't think I can breathe."

"Listen to me, Chloe. Stop thinking about how this is all going to play out and just focus on how ridiculously happy you are right now. It's not like you're marrying the guy tomorrow anyway. You're just going out and hooking up and losing your inhibitions. Sounds like the perfect night to me."

My knees bent, and I drove my toes into the mattress. "Oh God, I hope I survive this."

She laughed. "Take it from someone who lost her virginity to a guy who knew less than she did. It was dreadful from start to finish. I'd much rather have what you're about to experience."

Even if she had a point, it did nothing to settle me because if things continued between Oliver and me and I did what Molly was suggesting, I would have to soon tell him I was a virgin.

And that wasn't a conversation I was looking forward to.

But once we had it, so many firsts would follow—taking off my clothes, having sex with him, dealing with what the *after* looked and felt like.

It was a lot to process.

"This is heavy," I admitted, pressing my hand against my stomach, trying to soothe the feeling that was tearing through it. "I knew London was going to change me in many ways, but I don't think I realized how much."

"I did."

"Then, what's going to happen when I come home? What does that look like?"

Silence ticked between us, and then, "That's months away. Focus on how hard you're smiling right now and how dreamy Oliver is and how his beard is going to feel against your cheek when you guys are making out."

"Damn," I groaned. "Tuesday is, like, a century away."

She laughed. "Oh, babe, you've got it bad."

FIVE

Unknown: Hi, Chloe. It's Oliver.
Me: Hey you.
Oliver: Feeling better?
Me: I took a nap, and I'm human again, I think.
Me: Thanks again for brunch. I had a great time ... even if I looked half-dead.
Oliver: You looked perfect.

Me: Sitting in St. James's Park, and I swear you just ran by.
Oliver: Fuck, I didn't see you. I'll turn around.
Me: Don't. I have to head to class.
Oliver: Have a good day, gorgeous.
Me: :)

Oliver: One more night.

Me: *Feels like it's taking forever.*
Oliver: *That's because you're excited to see me.*
Me: *Ha! True ...*
Oliver: *Feeling is mutual.*

Oliver: *I'll pick you up at 7.*
Me: *Looking forward to it.*

Me: *Molly, I know you're in class, but Oliver is going to be here in five minutes, and I have so much nervous energy that I'm pacing.*
Me: *I've brushed my teeth twice, checked my makeup, changed my clothes again to only put back on what I was originally wearing. SMH.*
Me: *What if I make a fool of myself?*
Me: *I'm a wreck.*
Me: *He just rang. He's downstairs. I'll text you as soon as I can. Wish me luck. GAH.*
Molly: *I could not love you more than I do right now. You don't need luck. Just be you, babe, and everything else will fall into place.*

SIX

"DAMN IT, SWEET GIRL ..." Oliver said as I opened the door, his eyes dropping all the way to my feet. "You look absolutely stunning."

I hadn't forgotten that look in his eyes. I was just reminded how intense it was and how much I loved his accent.

"Thank you," I replied softly, silently thanking Molly for picking my outfit.

She'd paired the ripped black jeans with ankle boots and a sweater that hung past my shoulders and was snug around my waist. She insisted I wear my hair down and curled. She picked a bold lipstick with just some highlighter on my cheeks.

And it had paid off.

His hand went to his beard, and it was as long and shaggy as it had been the other day.

A winter hat covered his head, and his dark jacket and scarf made his eyes appear an even icier blue.

"I just have to grab my jacket." My palm loosened, my fingertips now holding the door. "You want to come in?"

He stepped forward, hand brushing mine as he clasped the

thick metal. The contact caused a spark to rush through me, and I left him there and went to my bed, where I had placed my coat. Once I had my arm through one of the holes, I turned around and saw him standing in the center of the room, checking out the whole space.

His eyes finally found mine. "Hasn't changed."

"You've been here before?" I put my other arm through the sleeve and worked on the zipper.

"I lived here my first year." He pointed toward the right side of the room. "End of this hallway, one floor up was where I stayed."

Even though he was only a senior, Oliver seemed so much older. Maybe it was because he was so close to graduating, and I still felt so far away. Maybe it was the maturity I saw in his face. But I felt so young in comparison.

"My three best mates I live with now, I met them here." He smiled, and I followed his gaze around the room.

It wasn't much to look at, certainly not like the dorm Molly and I had shared our freshman year before we moved off-campus. And because I'd only brought my personal items, the room wasn't decorated.

He adjusted his posture, arms crossing over his chest, a smile covering his deliciously handsome face. "Chloe ..." When his eyes traveled down my body, I no longer felt stable on my feet. "You're going to have one hell of a term."

Goose bumps began to rise over my skin.

Something told me Oliver was talking about what was going to happen between us.

And my body started to shake.

"Ready?"

I didn't know what I was answering, but I nodded, and then I lifted my bag off the chair and hung it across my body, meeting him at the door. I locked it behind us, and we went down the hallway to the first floor and out the lobby of the building. Once we stepped outside, his hand briefly touched my lower back. Then, his touch was gone, and we were walking in the direction of the Eye.

"What do you think?"

I glanced to the side he was on and slowed my pace a little, immediately noticing him do the same. "You mean, about London?"

"Sure."

"It's ... more than I expected."

We were at the end of the block, waiting for the light to change, and when I looked at him, his eyes were already locked with mine.

Boring through me.

The tingles threatened to explode inside me.

"You seem surprised by that," he said.

The surprise is you.

I took a breath, feeling the tightness in the back of my throat. "I am ..." My voice drifted off, as I was afraid to say any more.

A smile came across his face that was so beautiful. "But I think it's exactly what you've been looking for, Chloe."

I felt the warmth of his hand as it surrounded my fingers.

When the light changed, I waited for him to let go of me.

But he didn't.

He brought our hands down to his side, and that was where they lived for the next few blocks until we reached the ride. When we got to the front of the line to purchase tickets, Oliver wouldn't let me pay for those or for the glasses of champagne he bought us before we entered the capsule.

Once we got inside the pod, I took a seat and waited for others to join us. It was large enough to comfortably hold a decent amount of people, but so far, it was only us in here.

Because we'd waited in line for several minutes, watching the boarding process, I had seen how quickly the other capsules filled up, and I wondered why that wasn't happening to ours.

Then, the door closed.

Our pod began to lift in the air ... and I knew.

My body faced the River Thames, but my eyes were on Oliver's. "Why do I get the feeling you made sure we had this all to ourselves?"

In this intimate space, as we moved higher in London's cold black sky, Oliver stared at me with a look I would never forget. It was so strong; I had to remind myself to breathe.

"I hope this is everything you wanted." He clinked his champagne against my glass, his thumb briefly grazing mine. "Cheers, Chloe."

SEVEN

"WOW." I gawked, leaving my jacket behind while I stood from my seat and went over to the wall of glass.

Our capsule had only lifted a few feet from where we'd gotten on, but from here I could see around several buildings I couldn't before, giving me a whole different view.

My fingers pressed on the window, face so close to the glass that I was breathing in the coolness that leaked in from outside. "It's breathtaking up here."

I glanced over my shoulder, connecting stares with Oliver. He was sitting next to the spot I had just stood from, his legs crossed, foot hanging over the edge of his other thigh, arms spread across the back of his seat and most of mine.

And while he took me all in, I saw the intensity move across his face, and it was a good thing the wall could hold me because I wasn't sure my legs would.

Is this what I've been missing?

When my friends had described how they'd felt when they met their boyfriends, they never told me about the part where it became impossibly hard to breathe, where everything inside you felt like it was melting together. What they had described was an excited, anxious feeling that I completely understood from the few dates I'd gone on in the past, but those feelings weren't anything like this.

In fact, I had absolutely no idea what this feeling was.

I pushed through the tightening in my chest as our pod moved higher, and I tried to refocus my attention on the scenery. From up here, I could easily pinpoint Big Ben, Westminster Abbey, and the Houses of Parliament—landmarks I'd been walking by since I arrived that became more beautiful every time I saw them. I spotted a few of the adorable red phone booths, thinking of all the photos I'd taken with them and posted online. And just as I was glancing across the Thames, the air inside the capsule changed.

It warmed.

Thickened.

Because he was standing and moving closer to me.

My hands slid down the glass, needing a new piece of cold to hold on to as my body began to heat. I didn't turn around to meet him. I stayed, looking out the window, anticipating his actions, hypersensitive to every sound and swish of air. Tingles were shooting through my legs and around my chest, and as soon as he touched me, there was an explosion that I felt everywhere even though he was only holding my waist.

"Someone's ticklish," he whispered near my ear.

I wasn't. Not normally anyway.

But with him standing behind me, positioned so my back could rest against his chest, I felt the outline of his body and the zipper of his jacket and the thick buckle of his belt.

And it was setting me on fire.

"What do you think?"

My eyes closed just briefly while I searched for my breath,

and when they opened, the lights below were almost twinkling; they were so bright. "It's so beautiful."

My hands were still on the glass, and his were on top of mine, gripping me like he needed to hold on as well. "Not as gorgeous as you."

When he'd moved, he'd closed the separation between us, and the parts of his body that had just been outlined before, I could feel them in full detail.

If I'd thought I was exploding during any of the moments leading up to this, it didn't compare to what was happening in me right now.

"Look at me." His breath hit my cheek, his scent a combination of leather and lust, and his fingers loosened, giving me the ability to turn around. "I want to say this all to your face."

I was tingling in places I hadn't known could give pleasure, my heart was pounding, and emotions were bolting through me.

Slowly, I turned toward him, and it was as though his hands had been waiting for me because they immediately landed on my face and held me steady. And then his eyes roamed my face like he was looking at me for the first time all over again.

"God, this red hair." He lifted a chunk of it between his fingers, staring at my long auburn locks. "And these perfect lips." His thumb grazed over my pout, dragging back and forth across it. "And these wild honey-colored eyes."

Each word, each second his gaze was on me, was like a blanket of heat that spread farther over my skin, and I was basking in it. But the closer his lips got, the more this weight began to eat me.

The weight of the truth.

"Oliver ..." I said so softly, but it was as loud as my throat would allow. "I have to tell you something."

His eyes were making this so much harder. I clenched my fingers together, digging my nails into my palm.

"I have no idea how to say this." I could see his confusion; he didn't know what I was going to tell him, and my stalling wasn't making it easier on any of us. "Most of this is new to me."

"New?"

"Yeah ... I ..." This was so much harder than I'd thought. I'd never had to have this conversation before.

The few guys I'd gone out on dates with, it never moved beyond the basics with them. And that was because they just hadn't interested me enough.

But now, I was twenty-one with only three semesters left of college before I would be starting my career. And my body was more turned on than it had ever been before.

I was ready.

I'd been ready; I was just waiting for the right time.

I looked at his breathtakingly handsome face and admitted, "I have no idea what I'm doing, Oliver."

His thumb rubbed across my hip, each flick causing me to arch my back a little.

"I do." He glanced at my lips and then gradually back to my eyes. "You're seconds away from kissing me."

I shook my head. "I don't mean that. I mean ..."

His hands lifted up my sides, every inch emphasized. By the time he reached my neck again, my entire body was screaming. He leaned in, and we were as close as before but from an entirely different angle. His lips were almost on mine. I could taste the lust in his cologne, and I knew I couldn't hold it in for a second longer.

"I've never done more than kiss."

The recognition passed over his face. "A virgin ..."

"Yes."

He looked me over, his eyes giving me the compliments instead of his mouth. "How is that possible?" He held me tighter. "How has someone not worshipped you?"

"Because I wouldn't let them."

"And me?"

His thumbs were stroking my cheeks, and they paused for his eyes to dive again. This time, he pulled back, and they fell past my face and chest. My thighs began to burn when his gaze reached them. With no rush whatsoever, he climbed back up until his stare was on my mouth.

I swallowed, silently clearing my throat. "Oliver, I told you this so ... you would know to be gentle."

He sighed, and his air smelled so good. "My sweet girl."

His hands tightened on my cheeks, and so slowly, he leaned down and pressed his lips against mine. With my eyes closed, I instantly felt the roughness of his beard, a sensation I'd never had before on my skin and one I was seriously loving.

My mouth parted, taking more of him in, and I was filled with the warmth of his tongue. As the pads of his fingers bore down even harder, mine found his waist, holding his belt buckle, squeezing the thick leather strap. I inched up and felt the softness of his sweater, the heat from his body coming through the material.

His thumbs moved to the corner of my lips, and he was pushing against them like he was molding me just the way he wanted me. And I was taking all of it—the lesson, the attention, these feelings he was creating that were pulsing through me.

And just when I started to gain more of his tongue, when my hands flattened against his stomach, his muscles contracting under my grip, he pulled away.

My eyes opened and caught his.

And I felt myself gasp.

I hadn't heard it; neither had he. But once I sucked in that breath, it didn't move from my lungs.

It couldn't.

Not with the way he was staring at me.

My God.

It wasn't just his eyes or his touch. It was a feeling created by both that was burrowing into me.

I gasped again, but it was because his hands were on my shoulders, and he was turning me around in the same position I'd been in before.

His chest pressed into my back, and my exhale heated the glass, my hands rubbing against the window to cool them.

A stunning city was before me, but my entire world at this moment was behind me, and he was all I could focus on, especially once he said, "You taste more delicious than I imagined."

I didn't recognize this hunger, this neediness that was owning me, but I certainly wasn't the same girl who had walked into this pod.

"Tell me what you want, Chloe." His fingertips were underneath my sweater, running up and down my stomach, each dip sending another wave of tingles through me. "Do you want me to tell you about London?" His lips were closer, pressing along the edge of my ear. "Or do you want something from me instead?"

I couldn't breathe even though I was positive my chest was rising and falling.

London was twinkling in front of us, but I couldn't process anything I was looking at. All I could concentrate on was his heat.

The feel of him pressed against me.

How every nerve ending in my body was humming.

"You."

His lips moved once again to the side of my face, just below my ear. And when he exhaled, half of the air trickled down my neck, causing goose bumps everywhere, and the other half went across my face. "You're not getting all of me in here."

His thumb brushed my ribs, and I shivered, giving him the same reaction when he did it on the other side.

"But you can have a part of me." His teeth grazed the bottom of my ear. "Any part, Chloe." He moved my hair out of the way, his lips now on the back of my neck where I felt just the faintest swipe of his tongue. "Which do you want?"

I had never felt consumed—until now.

All I could think, feel, taste ... was Oliver Bennett.

He was asking me to make a decision that was far outside my scope of knowledge. I didn't know what any of the parts felt like; choosing one felt impossible.

I lifted one of my hands off the glass and closed my eyes, navigating toward the feel until I found the back of his palm. For being in a pod made entirely of glass, it felt like the safest option. And for my body, it felt like a good place to start. "This."

He growled—a sound I'd heard from him, but not this deep or drawn out. "We'll save my mouth for next time."

"Oh God." I shivered again.

I couldn't even imagine what it would feel like to have his lips on that private, sensitive spot. And then, suddenly, I got the tiniest hint of it when he began to pull at the button at the top of my jeans, the thick metal knob popping through the hole. He held my long locks a little tighter with his other hand, his lips still on the same spot on my neck.

I no longer knew I was in the capsule, on a ride, moving higher and higher in the sky.

I no longer knew anything aside from the fact that my palms were pressing on the freezing glass, and they were holding on with everything I had.

Because he had opened my zipper, and there was tickling and throbbing and an urge to tilt my hips back and forth, the lower he got.

I quivered, whispering, "Oliver," into the window as he dipped into my panties, grazing a whole different area of skin.

"That's my sweet girl." His breath warmed my neck. "Fucking perfect."

My lips opened the same time my eyes did, and just as I was connecting with the lights, his fingers slid down the front of me, curved around, and circled my wetness.

"*Ohhh,*" I moaned at this incredible feeling.

I only knew my hand, the expected movements, the boundaries I didn't push past because I just didn't know better.

This ... was nothing like that.

His fingers didn't stay still. He pulled back to the front, a place he had passed so quickly before, and he rubbed the top. Back and forth. Slow and fast, a different amount of pressure applied each time his hand shifted.

"Oh my God," was all I could groan.

He went deeper again, and his finger was sinking into me. Just the tip.

"It's so fucking sexy to know I'm the first guy to touch your pussy." He released my hair, and he was on my nipple, rolling it, giving me a pressure that was the most overwhelming combination.

But it didn't stop there.

He had put his palm on my clit, and now, he was going in as far as his middle knuckle.

"So tight ..." I heard him echo over my skin.

This was a whole different level of being consumed.

This was ownership.

"Oliver ..." My forehead pressed against the glass. "Oh my God."

He was all the way in, holding steady, his palm pulsing against my clit.

My legs were spread wide, hands still flat on the window, my eyes on the blinking white below.

But I was lost in a bubble of passion that I couldn't find my way out of.

And it only got more intense as his hand began to move— his fingers and his palm.

"This"—I tried to breathe—"feels so good."

He went back as far as his nail and then drove in again—a pattern he repeated over and over. His palm was moving just as fast, both of them twisting in a circle.

"That's it, sweet girl." He pinched my nipple, and I moaned so loud. "Relax into my hand, and I'm going to make you come."

Everything inside me started to move. My head tilted back against his shoulder and my mouth opened and, "*Yesss* ..." was what poured out.

I knew we were climbing. I knew we were getting closer to the top.

But I couldn't open my eyes because so was I.

His teeth surrounded my earlobe, and he said, "You just got even wetter."

Everything inside me was closing in. Tightening. The part of him that circled, the part of him that plunged were both moving faster.

It was taking over me.

In every way.

And then a ripple moved through the bottom of my stomach and went straight up my chest, causing my back to arch. "Oliver!" Another quiver shot through me, and I realized I was there—at that edge.

I knew what it felt like when my fingers took me there, but

having him do it was so much more intense that I couldn't let go. I just held on, stalling in this spot where my entire body was shaking.

"Tell me, Chloe." His lips were now in the center of my cheek, teeth grazing my skin. "Tell me how good it feels."

He did something inside me, circling me in a way where he hit a certain spot, and I lost it.

"Oh fuck," I howled. Shuddering, churning—it was movement in so many directions. Then, he upped his speed and pressure, and I screamed all over again. "Oh my God ... this feels ... amazing."

He kept his mouth on the side of my face, watching each wave pass through me as his hand ground out my orgasm. And I could do nothing but experience the ride he took me on, the way it grabbed ahold of me and wouldn't let go, even after my body stopped convulsing.

He sensed when it was time to slow and gradually slid out of me, his lips now kissing my cheek. "That was fucking beautiful."

My eyes closed again, and all I could do was moan in response.

EIGHT

"YOU'D BETTER HAVE SO much to tell me that you don't even know where to start," Molly said when she answered my call, the background filled with music, making it hard for me to hear her.

"Where are you?"

"Julia's. Give me one sec." It sounded like a door closed, and then, "There's a few of us hanging out, but I just went into her room for privacy. Spill it, woman. I've been dying for you to call."

Home.

My friends.

Things I hadn't thought about since the moment Oliver picked me up at my dorm.

As I paced my small room, I told her about my evening with Oliver and how it had ended a few minutes ago outside my building once he walked me home from the Eye.

"A finger fucking master," she said when I finished my story. "I'm obsessed with him already. Marry him."

I laughed, tossing two textbooks into my bag, and zipped the compartment shut. "I knew you would be."

"Too bad you guys didn't have more time together."

Because I had agreed to our date without checking my schedule, I hadn't realized I had a study group that I couldn't miss, so I was only able to give Oliver a few hours. That was why we hadn't gone for dinner or to a pub after.

"Trust me, I feel the same."

"Doesn't matter. You had one hell of a night ... and I absolutely love what he's doing to you."

I was grabbing my keys off the desk when I stopped and smiled. My cheeks started to warm as though his hands were on them again. "We were in a glass bubble for the entire world to see, and I gave no fucks. The real question is, what is this guy doing to me?"

She groaned in a way that told me she approved, and then several seconds of silence passed before she said, "Are you ready for this, Chloe?"

I knew she wasn't trying to make me second-guess myself. As my best friend, she was just making sure I was all right. And right now, I appreciated that more than ever.

I left the keys on my desk and sat on the end of my bed, taking a few deep breaths before I answered, "Yes, I'm ready." I paused, and it all came flooding back to me. "Molly, he never made me feel like my lack of experience was a weakness. He just took control and knew exactly what I needed and wouldn't stop until he got what he wanted from me."

"Jesus ... I think I just came."

I laughed, shaking my head before my voice turned soft. "He's made it easy for me to be ready for this."

"As your best friend, who's way too far away to kick his ass, you have no idea how happy that makes me." Before I could comment, she asked, "When's the next date with him?"

"Not sure, but I'll see him tomorrow in class." I pushed myself off the bed and went back over to the desk, grabbing the keys. Then, I checked the time on my phone. I was almost twenty minutes late to the study group. Fortunately, it was being held just one floor above me. "I have to go. Call me when you wake up since it'll be too early there for me to call you with the details."

"Ugh, time zones can suck it." I heard the noise in the background, telling me she'd rejoined the girls. "I'm proud of you, you little exhibitionist. Now, go study so you can have round two tomorrow."

"God, I love you," I said, and we both hung up.

NINE

"GOOD MORNING, GORGEOUS."

My skin tickled, and a smile spread over my face as his voice and those words wrapped around the back of my neck, similar to how they had last night, but now, we were in class, and he didn't sound as growly.

I glanced over my shoulder, meeting the handsome face that I had kissed last night. An evening that had been replaying on repeat in my head, only stopping for the three hours that I'd slept. Then, it'd started right back up the second I woke up.

"Morning," I replied.

While he searched my face, I took in his beard, recalling the way it had felt on my face when he kissed me. I glanced at the collar of his light-blue shirt that was almost the same color as his eyes, imagining how sensual the scent would be this early. His hands were on top of his desk, and the second I connected with them, I felt my entire body blush.

"You look tired. Up all night, studying?"

I slowly found his eyes again and nodded. "It was a very late one. How did you sleep?"

"I went to bed, smelling you." His eyelids narrowed, and a shudder erupted in my stomach. "It was the perfect evening."

I'd kept my scarf on since it was chilly in the classroom, but I began to loosen it, my body heating to the point where I was sweating.

The thought of my wetness drying on his hand, of him smelling me—it was too much. But he wanted me to think about it—I could tell that by the smile on his face and the flirt on his lips and the desire that was pouring from his stare.

It was obvious he knew what he was doing to me, and he was enjoying it.

And I wanted more—more of his attention, time, and certainly more of his fingers.

"How many of you have read the assignment?" the professor said from the front of the class, signaling it was time for me to turn around.

I gave Oliver a smile, taking in the one he returned, and I faced the front. Now that I was straight ahead, I immediately felt his stare on my shoulders and back and on the center of my neck, the same spot he had licked last night.

The last time I'd been in this seat, before his hands even touched me, I hadn't taken a single note because my mind was on him. Now, my skin was on fire, and I knew there was no way I could concentrate on what the teacher was saying, especially when all I could think about was his fingers. How long they were and what they'd felt like when they were knuckle-deep inside of me.

I knew it was pointless to even take out my laptop.

"If you read," the professor continued, "you know that, today, we're going to discuss marketing strategy from a global perspective."

I was wrapping my arms around my waist, holding my stomach when I felt a change. It was the same shift that had occurred in the pod last night when Oliver walked over to me at the glass wall. When the air warmed and thickened. But this movement only sent me his face, which was close to the back of my ear, and I was captivated by his leathery, masculine scent.

"Tonight," he whispered, "it's my tongue's turn."

TEN

OLIVER MADE it impossible for me to get lost while walking to his apartment. That was his promise when he sent me directions for our seven o'clock date. Since his place wasn't far from my dorm, the instructions came as a series of texts that told me where to turn to get there. I found the gesture so much sweeter than a direct link that would just open my Maps app.

After Molly helped me get ready through a video chat and I knew there was nothing else I could possibly do to get myself prepared for tonight, I put on my jacket. Molly had suggested I take an oversize purse that could hold a few essentials in case I ended up spending the night—something I certainly wouldn't have thought of—so I lifted the bag over my shoulder and headed outside. I wasn't even down the front steps when I received a text from her.

Molly: Update me.
Me: It's been, like, 10 mins since I've talked to you.
Molly: Well, have you left?

Me: Yes.
Molly: Um, hello? That's a significant update, I'd say.
Me: LOL. I literally just walked out of my building. I haven't
even gotten through his first direction yet.
Molly: Move those buns, woman.
Me: I'll text you the second I can escape to the bathroom or die
from nerves and call you from a hospital bed. Whichever
happens first.
Molly: Just make it to his place in one piece and die after his
mouth is on you. Dying before would just be a tragedy on so
many levels.
Me: I needed that laugh.
Molly: Love you.

Still holding my phone, I continued following Oliver's instructions, and it wasn't long before I was outside a large three-story building. Flowerpots hung out the upper windows, and cute, round arches spanned the whole length of the first floor, making the entrance even more inviting.

I found his name in the call box, pressed the button, and "Come on in, Chloe," came out of the speaker.

That accent.

Boston would never sound good again, not after I'd heard Oliver say my name.

The door buzzed and unlocked, and by the time I entered the small lobby that the group of townhomes shared, Oliver was opening a door on the other side.

Our eyes locked, and it became so difficult for me to breathe.

My God. That man was sexy, dressed in a sweater and jeans and bare feet—an outfit that was so casual, unlike his stare.

"Gorgeous," he breathed as I approached, his eyes taking me all in, his lips eventually doing the same when they softly pressed against mine.

I could smell the shower he had recently taken, the cologne he had put on after, and the detergent from his clothes. I didn't know how scents could have such an effect on me, but everything I was taking in was only adding to the tingles that were pulsing through me.

When he pulled his lips away, I reached into my bag, took out the box, and handed it to him.

"What's this?"

I smiled, knowing my cheeks were as red as my mouth. "I had to bring something even though you told me not to. I saw these, and they looked delicious."

And because it hadn't felt right to show up empty-handed when he invited me over for dinner, I'd made a special trip to the bakery after class.

He took the box from my hand and leaned forward, his mouth going to my cheek. He kissed it as gently as he had my lips and said, "Thank you." Then, he signaled for me to walk in.

"Wow." I was stopped in the center of the entryway, looking around the large, beautiful space that opened into the kitchen. "This is so nice."

The apartment I'd shared with Molly wasn't anything like this. His kitchen alone was almost the size of our entire place.

His hand grazed my side as he passed me. "My best mate's father owns the flat," he told me as he walked to the counter while I was left shivering from his touch. "He lets the four of us stay here for free."

"He's a nice dad." I continued to look around, moving farther into the kitchen. "Are your roommates here?"

He hadn't told me much about the plans for tonight besides

how to get here, what time to arrive, and that he didn't want me to bring anything.

"They're at The O2 for a concert."

I knew that meant they wouldn't be back for a while, giving us the house to ourselves.

I tried not to let that stir in my brain for too long, but we were alone, and that was what I'd been hoping for.

"Cookies?" he said, smiling when he opened the box.

I moved over to the island where he was standing, staying on the opposite side. "I tried to find something super American and failed—for obvious reasons. They were the best I could do, and fortunately, chocolate chip is my favorite, so hopefully, you don't hate that kind."

He took out one of the oversize cookies, checking it out. "They'll be perfect with a cup of tea." He set it back in the box and came closer, his hands cupping my face, thumbs grazing just under my jaw. "This was sweet of you." His lips hovered above mine. "Except now, all I can think about is how that chocolate would taste on your body."

I sighed, and even my breath was unsteady.

He didn't blink.

His fingers didn't lower from my face.

He just held me until it felt like the tension in my body was going to make me scream, and then he whispered, "I hope you're hungry."

Hungry?

I couldn't nod, as he was holding me so tightly, so I breathed, "Starving," even though I couldn't imagine putting anything in my mouth right now. Not with the nerves that were eating through my stomach.

"Spaghetti Bolognese, the only dish I've mastered from my mum."

His fingers lightened when I smiled. "You cooked?"

I'd smelled it when I first came in and just assumed he had ordered out, which was what I would have done if I were back at home.

"Surprised?"

"Very." I laughed, and it felt strange with him holding me this way. "But pleasantly. What other talents do you have, Oliver?"

His lips moved to the shell of my ear. "You're going to find out later tonight."

His eyes took me in again, and then his hands were gone. He headed to the other side of the kitchen where two bowls were waiting on the counter. He scooped pasta into them from a pot on the stove and carried them over to the table.

"Take a pew," he instructed as he passed me on the way to the counter where he grabbed a bottle of wine.

I took that as he wanted me to take a seat, and when he joined me, he poured some into the glasses.

I couldn't help but look at the table with excitement, at the meal this incredibly handsome guy had cooked for me.

There was no question in my mind.

I was ready.

His hand wrapped around the thick stem, and he held his wine up in the air. "To ..."

"London," I added before he could say any more. It fit on every level.

He must have agreed because he smiled and clinked his glass against mine. "To London ... and to you, sweet girl."

"Me?"

He nodded, leaning forward just a little. "Because I'm going to fucking devour you tonight."

The heat that was becoming so familiar returned, although I wasn't sure it had ever left. And then he chuckled as though, in his mind, he was confirming everything he had just said, and I sat there, melting under his gaze.

"Eat, Chloe."

I hadn't even lifted my fork, so I clearly needed the reminder.

I dipped it into the bowl, twirling the wide noodles around the metal before putting them in my mouth. I covered my lips with the back of my hand. "Oliver"—I chewed, taking in more of the flavor—"this is excellent."

"My mum's a great cook. I've tried to learn as much as I can from her."

I couldn't believe how good this was, and I went right back in for another bite. "It shows," I said. "It's really delicious."

I saw how the compliment affected him, the smile that was different than all the others he'd given me.

"Thank you." He stuck his fork back in the pasta but continued to look at me, his teeth grazing his bottom lip. "Some crazy shit happened today. I filled out my graduation paperwork. Nuts that it's so close."

"I can't believe it's only four months away." I shook my head. "At the end of the semester ... when I'm due to go home."

"You're going back right away?"

I'd been thinking about this a lot, and even though the study abroad program was over in May, I didn't have to return to Boston until the end of August.

"I don't have to," I admitted, wiping my mouth. "I could stay here through the summer."

His hand left his fork, and his arms crossed over the table. "One term and maybe the summer ... that's all you're giving me, Chloe Kennedy?"

I nodded.

Because that was easier.

Because something in my chest already hurt so badly.

And that was a feeling I'd never felt before.

"Then, we'd better make the most of our time together."

He was the one who had spoken the words, but I had said the same ones in my head.

ELEVEN

"YOU FEEL FUCKING AMAZING," Oliver growled across my neck as he stood behind me.

His room faced the garden in the back, and the lights that shone over the fence gave a hint of a glow, allowing me to see the outline of our wineglasses on his nightstand. We'd had a few over the course of the evening, drinking just enough to give a warm, quiet buzz, and a calm was now humming through me rather than being overwhelmed with nerves.

That was why I hadn't felt any anxiety when he walked me to his bedroom or positioned me near his bed where we were standing now. It was also why I could relax into his chest as he reached for the bottom of my shirt, pulling it over my head. His lips were on my neck before the chill hit my skin, and he was unclasping my bra, my breasts falling from the cups.

As I heard the lace hit the floor, he began kissing down my shoulders. "So fucking beautiful, sweet girl." His thumbs rubbed back and forth across my hardened nipples.

"*Ahhh*," I moaned, my back pushing into him where he was taking all of my weight.

His hands didn't stay in one place for long, rubbing across my stomach and over my breasts, down to my waist and back up. I felt every inch of movement—and not all were the softest of touches, like when he tugged my nipples, pinching just the ends.

I quivered from the sensation and then again when he said, "I thought you would like that," in my ear. With his face in my neck, he could feel each ripple through my body, and there were several. And just when I quieted, I heard, "Wait until you feel this."

It was a warning.

His hands dropped from my body, and he moved around to the front of me. His lips were now on my breast, and the loudest sound I'd ever made came out. He wasn't just licking; he was using his teeth on my nipple, his fingers roaming my whole body, and the combination was almost too much. My back arched, and I panted through my lips. Before I could cry out again, he was unbuttoning my jeans, peeling them off along with my panties. And suddenly, I was completely naked before him.

His hand went to my waist, keeping just the tips of his fingers on me, and then he took a step back. His eyes slowly dipped down my body, every shift of his gaze sending me more of his heat. More of his desire. Gradually, he lifted his stare to meet mine and said, "How did I get so lucky to be the first man to have you?"

He was barely touching me, but his eyes felt like they were inside me, stroking every part that would make me moan. And I was positive there had never been a moment in my life when I felt more beautiful.

"Oliver ..." I said softly, trying to find a way to respond to him, to describe how lost I was, but his hands cupped my face, and his mouth lowered to mine.

As we kissed, he started taking off his clothes, and the reality of what was happening set in.

I wanted this, and I wanted Oliver—more than anything.

Once everything was stripped from his body, he pulled me against him, all of my bare skin now touching his for the first time. He felt so coarse with hair and muscles and broadness.

With a hard-on that was grinding into me.

My God.

This was what a man felt like, and I was about to experience all of him.

His hands surrounded mine, and he placed them on his chest, holding them there, fingers flat like they'd been on the glass in the London Eye. "Learn me," he breathed, and he slowly lowered my palms.

He was guiding me. Teaching me. And I was absorbing every second, wanting to make him feel just as incredible. So, I explored, tracing his shoulders and back and arms, trying to really get a sense of what he felt like. The more of him that I touched, a whole new kind of heat began to throb inside me. Maybe it was the sounds he made or the way he felt under my fingertips.

But I couldn't get enough.

And then, "Fuck, Chloe," vibrated through me.

My fingers had landed on the lower part of his stomach, stalled at the section where the hair was the roughest.

His hand moved on top of mine. It wasn't to push me. It was as though he wanted to feel the moment from both sides of my palm.

"Go slow," he growled across my face. My thumb grazed the tip of him, and he exhaled, "Fuck yes."

While his mouth was pressed against mine, I began to learn the curves and thickness of his shaft, the texture of his skin, the way he moaned when I slid to the top and lowered to the base.

Each time I stroked him, his hips pumped forward, his breathing got heavier.

"Are you ready for me?" His hands had been still since I touched him, but he was on my clit. Then, he dropped lower, and my ass bucked from the feeling. "So fucking wet."

The urge for him to touch me there had been almost unbearable.

Now, he was giving me exactly what I wanted, and I couldn't stop shaking. "Oh God."

He rubbed my clit back and forth, the pleasure so intense that I couldn't kiss him. I could only breathe against his lips and feel this build immediately take hold.

"Oliver ... *ahhh*."

My fingers circled around him, lifting and dropping, and we were moving together, but it didn't last because he lifted me into the air and wrapped my legs around him. I clung to his shoulders, staring at his incredibly sexy face, smiling as he carried me onto the bed. He placed me in the center, my head on a pillow, and his lips were around my nipple. He bounced between breasts—sometimes just flicking, other times using his teeth. And all I did was moan as he went down my stomach and stopped at the top of my clit. He pushed my thighs apart and positioned his body between them, his face inches away from me. Anticipating what this was going to feel like, I pushed my head into the pillow, and I stabbed the comforter with my nails.

And then I felt him.

A breath of air across the most sensitive part of me, just enough to know his placement before the next thing I felt caused a gasp to shoot from my mouth.

I couldn't hold it in.

Because his tongue was there, on that personal place, and he was licking it.

Tasting it.

Swallowing me.

And the wetness and heat from his mouth were beyond anything I had expected. I was doing everything I could to keep my legs apart, but as his tongue flattened and spread across me, swiping in every direction, his finger drove inside me, and I completely lost it again.

"*Fuuuck*," I sighed.

The combination took control. There was so much pleasure running through me; I couldn't follow it all. Oliver was still working my nipple, his other hand between my legs, where he was dipping and circling, his tongue was relentlessly licking.

He didn't tell me he wanted me to come, but everything he was doing to my body was screaming that demand. And I was trying to hold it off, to keep the build at the peak because it felt so good.

But I couldn't stop it.

My back arched off the bed, my hands clutching the blanket like it was squeezing me back. "Oliver," I moaned, his strength only increasing. "*Yesss!*"

He went even faster, and my eyes shot open. I glanced between my legs, our stares connecting, and a ripple shot through me. Instead of caressing my nipple like he had been, he tugged it, and a tremor erupted in my stomach, my moan so loud that I surprised myself.

This feeling had taken complete control, my head dropped back, and my lids shut as shudders began to move through me. Each time he swiped his tongue, another wave of the orgasm exploded, especially with his finger grinding into me at the same time.

When I finally calmed, he slowly worked his way up my body, pressing his mouth against mine. But this time, he kissed me with a passion that was entirely different than before. This

wasn't just hunger. I felt something else behind his kiss, something much more emotional. And while he was devouring me, I
heard the sound of metal foil tearing open. His hands put on
the condom, and then he positioned himself between my legs
again.

So many firsts, and I was tingling from each one.

His lips hovered above mine when he said, "This is going to
hurt, but I'm going to do everything I can to make it better." He
was brushing his thumb across my cheek as he spoke, his tip
directly where it needed to be; he just wasn't applying any
pressure.

"Okay."

I didn't know what else to say; my nerves were already
perking up at the thought of what was coming. The wine had
been holding them steady, and it still helped, but the anxiety
was there. And I was hyperaware of even the smallest shift, so
when he started to push in, I sucked in all my breath.

His hand tightened on my cheek when he said, "If you
tense up like that, you're never going to let me in." He kissed
the end of my nose. "I'll go slow. If it's too much, I'll stop."

He halted while he waited for me to respond.

I released the air I was holding in and tried to relax each of
my muscles. And as I did, he kissed me, and it was the distrac-
tion I needed because what was happening between my legs
was completely overwhelming.

Stretching was what it felt like at first, and then the burning
set in.

"Oh, that hurts," I breathed, trying to find that happy place
because I wasn't there right now.

"I'm so fucking sorry, Chloe." His eyes were on me,
watching me while I widened to take him in, and his nose
pressed into mine as his fingers squeezed my cheek.

Another small slide, the friction even stronger, and I was

doing everything I could not to tighten up again, breathing through what felt like tearing. "Damn it."

"I'll stop."

"No." My nails stabbed his shoulder even though I wasn't trying to cause him pain. "I'll get through this."

With each lift of his hips came more of that fierce ripping, a heat unlike he'd given to me before, and it only got more intense as he inched in. But he still continued, and so did his strong fingers, linking between mine. He lifted our hands over my head and held them there as he went in the rest of the way and paused.

"You're fucking incredible," he breathed against my mouth. "Beautiful." He kissed my cheek, going to the same spot on the other side. "Perfect." He returned to my lips. "And so goddamn wet."

I was focused on his words and continued to breathe through the pain, feeling the rawness and the ache. Even though my body was no longer stretching and widening, I was still pulsing from the invasion. And while I got used to him, he stayed frozen.

His mouth went to my nipple, the graze of his teeth crossing the tip before he shifted to the other one. He went back and forth, and during one of the passes, his mouth found mine, and he started to move.

I held my breath, expecting it to hurt worse. And at first, it did, the burn increasing from all the friction, and I was on the verge of telling him to stop. But then the intensity of it, the fullness that caused the pain to come out in my voice, gradually left. And in there, somewhere deeper than where I was now, I knew pleasure existed. Molly had promised—not right away, but she had said it would happen, and that was what I searched for as he went out to his tip and buried himself again.

"You okay?" He had pulled away from my mouth to look at my eyes, stilling while he read them.

I waited a few seconds to answer, "Yes." And because he didn't look entirely convinced, I added, "I'll be okay, Oliver."

His exhale was so incredibly hot. "My sweet girl."

When he started up again, it was a pace that wasn't much stronger than the one he'd used before. But his lips were quite the opposite, attacking my mouth in a way that told me he couldn't get enough of me.

And not only did I still feel so beautiful, but I also felt wanted.

Desired.

Fulfilled.

An entirely new sensation entered my body when his hand brushed over my clit. While he rubbed it back and forth, I hissed, "Holy fuck." Now, I could understand where the pleasure came from, and I moaned for the first time since he'd entered me.

His fingers went faster, easily reading me. "You just got so fucking tight again."

After so many firsts, having an orgasm during sex wasn't one I'd predicted. But Oliver had said he was going to make this feel better, and he certainly did. There was still pain, a rawness that felt like it would be there for days, but then there was the rubbing of his fingers, and those tingles went straight to my stomach.

"Oliver ..." I exhaled, feeling his veins pop through the skin on his arms as he held his weight. "*Ahhh.*"

The build was back, and I couldn't believe how fast it had returned. Like the time before, all I could do was hold on. Because, with him, I had no control over my body, and I was totally fine with that.

"So fucking tight," he moaned against my lips. I could tell

he was holding back, not wanting to hurt me, but his speed was still increasing. "Chloe ... fuck." His teeth took ahold of my bottom lip, his sounds telling me he was just as close as me. "Let me feel you come."

His demand in that accent was all I needed to hear before I released what I'd been holding in. As I shot through the peak, there was nonstop pulsing, and shudders followed like I was being licked by his tongue. I felt a second round of spasms when he lost himself inside me, moaning my name.

"You feel ..." he roared while he leaned his hips back and bucked forward. "So. Fucking. Good."

And so did he. Wave after wave of pleasure spread through me, his lips staying on me, even after he stilled.

His hands pressed against my cheeks. "I got to watch you come twice." He glanced at my lips and slowly to my eyes. "Hottest sight of my life."

A smile warmed across my face.

Despite it being extremely painful, I'd survived. I'd even enjoyed it. And next time, I knew it would be easier.

He eventually leaned back, carefully pulling out, and my eyes drifted down his body until I saw the red on the condom. It took me a minute to realize it was blood.

And that it was mine.

"Oliver—"

His hand was on my cheek before I even finished saying his name. "I expected this to happen. Don't worry, and don't be embarrassed." His thumb brushed my skin several times, easing the embarrassment I was feeling. "I'm going to go clean up. I'll be right back."

By the time I got comfortable, tucking myself in the comforter, Oliver returned. And once his arms were wrapped around me, I found his lips and kissed them.

"Thank you," I whispered.

I wasn't sure he had even heard me until he said, "For what, sweet girl?"

"For being the most amazing man in the world."

TWELVE

THE SOUND of an alarm was what woke me. My eyes stayed closed as I reached for the blanket, feeling a chill move across my bare chest. I pulled the comforter up to my chin, loving how softer than usual it was, how the pillow was extra firm—the way I liked it but hadn't had in a while.

I searched for my phone, where I kept it on the desk behind my head, and my fingers slammed into the headboard.

That was the moment it hit me—I wasn't in my dorm where my blanket was scratchy, and my pillows were super fluffy. I was at Oliver's, in his bed, where I'd stayed the night.

After I'd lost my virginity.

An excitement burst through me as the mattress shifted, the alarm turned off, the room becoming silent. Oliver's arms circled around me, pulling until my back was resting into his chest—a position I was learning he liked more than most.

"*Mmm*," he growled, his face in my neck where I felt him breathe me in. "How did you sleep?"

The feel of his body overtook me as did the memories from last night.

And as I lay in his bed, feeling the weight of his arms, I didn't even feel like the same girl who had come over to his place yesterday. Not with the ache that was between my legs and the scent that was on my skin.

I found his hand in the center of my stomach and clasped our fingers together, pushing through the morning in my voice. "Amazingly well." Having never spent the night at a guy's place, I was surprised I'd slept so soundly. Of course, by the time he'd eventually let me pass out, I had been so exhausted that I couldn't keep my eyes open. "How about you?"

"Perfect. Didn't wake until this morning." He kissed the top of my shoulder. "What time do you have class?"

"Ten."

"You'll stay for breakfast?"

There was a feeling in my chest that ached so strongly, and then a smile slowly grew across my cheeks as I said, "I would love to."

"I cook them pretty traditional ..." His beard brushed against the center of my back as he kissed it. "Fried eggs, bacon, sausages, tomatoes, mushrooms, and buttered toast."

"Yummy."

He chuckled and turned me around, laying me on his chest while his arms circled my back. "I like cooking for you."

"Feel free to anytime." I laughed back. "I'll eat anything you make; you're an excellent chef."

While he kissed the top of my head, I traced my fingers across his pecs, soaking in all of his warmth and attention. And we stayed just like that, tangled in a web of legs, blanket, and heat until I heard, "How about we take a shower before I go into the kitchen?"

I glanced up; his light-blue eyes were so bright in the morning sun.

"You can wash yourself out of my beard ..." His teeth gnawed his bottom lip while he stared at my mouth. "But I'm going to lick you again first."

THIRTEEN

"I WANT your details to have sub-details, and don't you dare leave a single one out," Molly said as she answered my call in a deeply hoarse morning voice.

I owed her a lifetime of mimosas for the way she was handling the time difference and the fact that she wasn't getting any sleep because of me.

But now that I had a minute alone, I had to call regardless if my best friend was awake.

"I don't know where to start," I sighed, dropping yesterday's clothes in my laundry bag. I wrapped myself in a robe and climbed into my bed.

"Find a place, sister, because it's the ass-crack of dawn, and patience doesn't exist at this hour."

I pulled the scratchy blanket up to my neck and stared at the bumpy ceiling, wishing so badly I could crawl into her bed, tuck myself under her lime-colored comforter, and purge the whole night to her.

"You know this already, but ..." I started, my eyes closing while I processed what I was about to say. "It happened."

"*Yasss*, and about fucking time."

My eyes shot open, and I burst out laughing. "This is why I love you."

She waited until we both quieted before she asked, "Was he good to you?"

Each time I moved, the soreness between my legs brought back another memory from last night. And every ache made my heart pound faster. "He cuddled me this morning, showered with me, and then cooked me breakfast before he walked me home." I took a breath, feeling the warmth spread through me. "He was perfect, Molly. In every way."

"I just died."

I rolled onto my side, holding a pillow against my chest. "I know." I rubbed my chin over the top of the pillow. "I felt him everywhere. I mean, there wasn't a part of me he wasn't paying attention to."

"More details, girl. Way more."

My eyes were closed again, and I squeezed my lids together, seeing the moments play out. "Once I got past the beginning part—which wasn't pretty, at all. My God, that hurt —he touched this spot and ..." I took a breath as I recalled the intensity of that sensation. "I completely lost myself."

"He made you come after he took your virginity. The man is a fucking unicorn."

"Well"—I laughed—"he technically made me come twice." I filled her in on what his tongue had done first.

"Oh, honey, I have all kinds of wildly inappropriate reactions, but the most important thing I can say right now is, I'm so ridiculously happy for you." She paused, and I could see her expression even though she was thousands of miles away. "You picked a good one, babe."

He wasn't a man I'd dated for a long time or someone I could say I'd fallen in love with. But my gut told me he was someone special, and these were the strongest feelings I'd ever had.

My voice was extra soft when I replied, "I'm so thankful."

"Me too." She was quiet for several seconds. "Now that you've survived sexy times, is the plan to just spend the semester together? Thank God you met him at the beginning and not the end ... can you imagine?"

I could. Because I'd thought about that.

And while he had brought me home this morning, my mind fast-forwarded to the end of the semester, and it was a thought I didn't like at all.

"We haven't discussed it," I admitted.

"Should you?"

Things between us were moving fast. It was what I wanted, and I could handle it all so far. But bringing up the next steps, when I had no idea what those steps even looked like, was a heavy conversation.

"Probably," I responded. "And it should happen sooner than later, I'm sure."

"Take it from someone who's been hurt in the past; setting expectations is never a bad thing. It could help a lot, given you're a newbie to all of this and you're dealing with a situation that isn't exactly traditional."

Molly was watching out for my heart, and I was so grateful for that. She knew much more about men than me, so I looked to her for guidance. But it didn't take someone with experience to know she was right.

In a handful of months, I was going back to the States, and that was something Oliver and I needed to discuss.

"Okay, that's on tomorrow's agenda," I said, refocusing my thoughts so a replay of this morning's good-bye kiss was now in my head.

Followed by his hands.

And then the tingling that took over when his beard grazed my cheek.

"Today," I continued, "I'm just going to live in the memories of last night."

She groaned in a way that made me grin. "I love that idea so much, babe."

FOURTEEN

I STOOD FROM THE DESK, where I'd been sitting for the last hour, and once I hung my bag across my body, I walked out of the classroom and down the long hallway toward the front of the building. This was my last class of the day; I'd had two with an hour break in between, where I'd gone to the library to write a paper. But it didn't matter how much I'd tried to focus on what I was writing or the notes I was taking during class because the only thing on my mind was Oliver, especially after reliving my conversation with Molly this morning.

And it was the impending talk I needed to have with him that I was focused on when I stepped out of the building. I was only a few paces from the door when I felt a hand on my stomach and heard, "Chloe," in Oliver's perfect voice in my ear.

As though it were completely natural in this cold weather, a wave of warmth passed through my chest and went straight to my toes.

I felt him.

Everywhere.

And I had all day, like each time I'd shifted in my seat or

rubbed my thighs together. And as he turned me toward him, it happened again, our eyes instantly connecting. He looked so handsome in the cold with his dark wool hat and puffy coat, each of his breaths hitting the air as steam.

"I was hoping to catch you." Through my jacket, I could even feel the power of his fingers, and they became stronger with every second that passed. "After last night," he continued, "I didn't want to tell you over the phone that I have to go away for a few days; I wanted to say it in person." He leaned forward, briefly pressing his lips against mine.

He was more than just heat.

He was sex and passion and thoughtfulness and patience, wrapped together with the most delicious beard and accent.

I shook my head as I realized what he had just said. "You're leaving?"

"Me and my mates are going skiing in Switzerland. We've been doing it since our first year. I meant to tell you last night." His eyes went to my lips the same time his hand caressed my chin, both making the heat in my body start to boil. "But you distracted me ... like you're doing right now."

We were in the middle of the sidewalk, not far from class, but we could have been in the center of the road, and it wouldn't have mattered. I couldn't move, not with the way he was making me feel.

"How long will you be gone?"

His thumb brushed against the bottom of my cheek, back and forth. "Five days." His gaze dropped again, the hunger in his expression growing, the more he stared at my mouth. "Another reason I didn't call"—he looked up—"I wanted to kiss you before I left."

I couldn't respond.

Because now, both of his hands were on my face, and I was completely melting, taking in every bit of air he exhaled.

As he pulled me against him, his lips crashing to mine, I felt his pulse in my chest, his taste on my tongue, and I didn't think I could feel more complete.

"Fuck," he growled as he separated us. "It's impossible to keep my mouth off you." I smiled, and he gave me one more brief kiss. "I have to go, but I'll text you in a little while."

I had no idea what to say. I wasn't even sure I was breathing. So, I nodded, just so he knew I heard him, and felt him squeeze me one last time before he walked away.

How will I give this up?

That was the thought that clutched me and wouldn't let go as I watched him move down the sidewalk and turn a corner, disappearing from my sight.

Oliver: I just ran my hand across my face and smelled you.

I stared at the screen, reading his text over and over. They were just letters, but they had the power to create these feelings in my body that were explosive. And they were doing just that, his touch so fresh in my mind.

Me: That must mean you miss me.
Oliver: So fucking much. Are you out?
Me: With my roommate at a pub.
Oliver: I wish I could hear you say that in your American accent.
Me: I feel the same about yours.
Oliver: Be careful tonight. Don't leave her side.
Me: Yes, sir. ;)
Oliver: Baby, that's a whole different kind of trouble you don't want to get yourself involved in ... yet.

I glanced up from my phone and immediately caught eyes with my roommate.

"Oliver?" she asked.

My relationship with her was much different than what I had with Molly, but she was a wonderful person to experience this with. "Yes. He's so naughty."

She lifted her beer and took a drink from it. "Is he asking for something?"

"No."

"What would he do if you sent him a selfie?"

I shook my head. "I have no idea ... nor do I even know where to start with any of that."

She stuck out her hand. "I do. Give me your phone."

I lifted my cell off the table and handed it to her.

"Turn your face toward the door," she instructed, holding my phone into the air.

I prepared myself for the shot, running my fingers through my hair, tilting my body in a better direction, aiming my face at a good angle.

"Got it." She tapped the screen several times as though she was checking to be sure, and then she returned the phone to me. "What do you think?"

I couldn't stop staring at the picture because it looked nothing like me—not the smile or the glimmer in my eyes. It was a happiness I'd never seen before, never felt, and I knew it was from him.

Oliver Bennett.

"Don't cover it with a filter or have me retake it. Send it just the way it is." I glanced up as she added, "Trust me."

Before I could overthink it or question myself, I attached the photo to his text and hit Send. "Done."

She clinked her glass against mine. "Now, we wait."

Oliver: Fuck me ... you're gorgeous.

I smiled as I glanced up from my cell, lifting my beer off the table. "He approves of the picture," I said.

"Of course he does." My roommate returned the grin. "It's his turn, and you'd better tell him that too."

She was good at this, and I was certainly going to take her advice.

Me: Show me something.

Bubbles appeared on his side of the screen, staying there for several seconds before an audio message came through, followed by another text.

Oliver: Listen to that when you're alone in your bed.
Me: That could be hours from now.
Oliver: It'll be worth the wait.
Me: Tease.
Oliver: Remember how I was rubbing your clit? That's what I want you to do while you're listening to it.

I glanced at my roommate, feeling the blush on my cheeks, and I saw that she was talking to a guy at the next table. Feeling a little less guilty, I returned my attention to the screen.

Me: You're relentless. But I like it.
Oliver: Now, you have an idea of what you're doing to me. Text me after.
Me: It could be late.
Oliver: I'm not going to bed anytime soon.

"I need another drink," I said as I put down my phone, my voice loud enough that my roommate stopped talking to the man next to her, and she glanced at me. "And I think I need something a little stronger than this." I was on my second beer, and it was less than half full.

"I like where this is going." She adjusted herself over the small barstool, called over our waiter, and said, "We'll have four shots, all tequila, and please make them extra cold," once he arrived at our table.

When we were alone again, I put my hand on top of hers. "I have to remember tonight. That's vital." I showed her Oliver's texts just to give her an idea of what we were dealing with.

When she read enough, she smiled and said, "We're just warming you up; we're not losing you. Don't you worry."

"Hello?" I said into my phone after I saw Oliver's name come across the screen.

It was past three in the morning. My roommate had gone home with the guy she'd been talking to at the bar, so I was alone. I had taken full advantage of the privacy, and while I'd listened to Oliver's forty-four second message that gave me instructions on how to touch myself, I had done exactly what he'd told me to. The picture I'd taken *After*—the caption I'd also added under the photo—I'd just sent to him a few minutes ago. I couldn't believe how fast he responded.

"I've never wanted to be in London so badly in my fucking life," he responded, sounding so different than what I was used to. Rough and more growly, like he'd been laughing for hours and he was giving me the little bit of voice he had left.

My eyes briefly closed as the heat began to spark in my body, spreading through me with fierce speed.

To take the shot, I'd turned off all the lights and posed in front of our full-length mirror, wearing only a tank top and panties. Relying on just streetlamps, which was hardly much at all, it made the picture extremely shadowy and too dark to show any details.

Still, it was a taste of me.

One he obviously liked.

"Come back to me, then," I replied, rolling onto my side, bringing the blanket with me.

"Can't happen, sweet girl."

I tucked the scratchy wool under my chin and adjusted my pillow. "Then, how many more days until you come back to me?"

Tequila was in my blood, and it hadn't died down even a little since I returned from the pub.

"Too many." He exhaled a long, deep breath. "My God, Chloe. Your fucking body is perfect. If I didn't want all my mates drooling over this photo, you'd be the background on my phone." He sighed again, reminding me of when he had done that across my body, his air so delicately hitting my skin. "When I get home, I'm going to kiss every inch of your skin."

I smiled and rolled onto my back, bending my knees and grinding my toes into the bed.

"Are you still sore?"

I didn't know why, but I couldn't sit still as his words vibrated through me, every move causing the tenderness between my legs to ache. But it was the softness in his question, his sensitiveness that was the reason I was melting.

"A little, but I'm okay."

I heard him take a breath. "I'll be gentler next time."

I put my hand under my head, kicking the blanket down, hoping that would cool me off. "Oliver, that's not what I want at all."

He chuckled, and it was the sexiest sound. "I'm fucking crazy about you."

I smiled as I looked up at the ceiling, thinking of him all the way in Switzerland and how many days until I saw him again. There were far too many.

"You have no idea ..." I whispered.

"Sleep well, sweet girl."

FIFTEEN

"HI," I said, answering Oliver's call as I passed the pub a block from my dorm. "Are you about to pop out from an alley and scare the shit out of me?" I glanced behind me just to be sure.

He laughed. "Not this morning, but I'll be back tomorrow night."

I continued to walk toward my building, shoving my free hand into my pocket to keep warm. "I can't wait."

Every time he called, every time we exchanged texts—both happening several times a day—it made me miss him more.

"It's going to be late," he said. "How about I text you the code to the back door, and you can wait for me at my place? I'll order you some food, and if you get tired, go to sleep, and I'll wake you."

I was a little blown away by his offer.

I tried to imagine what it would feel like to be there by myself, eating food he had delivered and then getting into his bed. I'd spread out over his big, comfy mattress with his extra-fluffy blanket, all of it smelling of leather and lust, and wait for him to return.

There was a feeling in my chest, almost like my lungs had frozen and the air was jump-starting them. And once they were filled, a burning sensation began to spread through me.

"That sounds perfect," I replied, and I walked up the steps of my building. My hand was now slick inside my jacket, and I pulled it out to grab the handle of the door. "I'll see you tomorrow night."

"Yes, you will."

As I climbed out of the taxi, I repeated Oliver's code in my head so I wouldn't forget it as I rushed up to his door. I slipped off my glove to enter the five-digit code, and once the lights above the lock turned green, it unlocked.

Since I'd been here before, I knew the basic layout of the home and where the most important things were located. I just didn't know small details, like where the light switches were. My hand banged around the wall, searching the dark entryway until I found the cold metal knob.

The inside looked exactly as it had the last time I was here. It was a bachelor pad, which meant most things didn't have a home and it was semi-clean. None of the guys had Molly's level of organization; that was for sure.

At the thought of her, I took out my phone and pressed the button to call her.

"Are you at his house?" she asked as she answered.

I took a seat on one of the barstools in the kitchen, resting my arm on the counter. "Yep."

"When's he due back?"

"They're just waiting for their flight. It's a short one, I believe."

"Girl, what the hell are you going to do in the meantime?"

I shrugged even though she couldn't see me, and I wandered over to the fridge. "He's sending me dinner, so I guess I'll eat and watch TV. I have no idea." I took a beer off the shelf, found an opener in one of the drawers, and sipped it while I walked to his room. My heart pounded as I turned his doorknob. "Oh my God," I moaned as I swung open his door.

"What, woman?"

I closed my eyes, taking a long, deep breath. "His room smells amazing." I inhaled again, not wanting the scent to ever go away. "Whatever he sprays on his body is seriously magical."

"I think that's just part of being a unicorn; smelling magical is a requirement." She giggled. "What's his room like?"

"A king-size bed." My eyes fell over the white comforter, remembering how it had felt when I stabbed it with my nails. "There's a giant flat screen on the wall with books and clothes are kinda everywhere and a massive bag of soccer balls takes up an entire corner."

"Sounds like a typical boy's room."

He had several framed pictures on the wall, and I went over to them. They showed him and his roommates skiing and at the beach and in pubs. There were also numerous shots of Oliver with his parents and three sisters, and more of whom I assumed were grandparents and extended family.

I headed over to the bed and took a seat on the end. "What are you doing tonight?" I could hear noise in the background.

"I'm meeting the girls for drinks, so you're about to get in the shower with me."

I pulled the phone away from my face to check the time, quickly doing the math. "Are you going to Sissy K's?"

"Of course."

A heaviness moved into my chest. When I had been able to squeeze in time to go out, that was the bar we always went to. "I really miss you."

"Babe, you have no idea."

Before the nostalgia really set in, there was a buzz from the front door, and I knew that meant Oliver's food had arrived. "Gotta go. Call me when you wake up."

"Love you."

I slid the phone into my back pocket and hurried to the main door where the delivery driver was waiting outside. "What do I owe you?"

He handed me the bag. "All taken care of. Enjoy."

"Thank you," I responded and shut the door, bringing the food into the kitchen.

It smelled delicious as I set it on the counter, reaching inside the bag to remove the three containers. I pulled off the first lid and found fish and chips. The second was a meat pie. The third was a pile of warm, gooey chocolate chip cookies.

My mouth wouldn't stop watering as I looked at all the favorites he had sent.

Me: You are so sweet. Thank you so much for dinner. I will never be able to eat all of this, but it looks amazing.
Oliver: Enjoy, gorgeous.

Oliver: Our flight is delayed. No idea what time we'll be home. Get some sleep.
Me: Safe travels. xo

I woke to the feeling of cold. It was on my face and across my chest and lying on top of me.

"Oliver"—I shivered—"you're an icicle." My eyes slowly

opened, and I pulled my arms out of the comforter and wrapped them around his neck.

"The heater broke in Jake's car, so we drove back from Heathrow in a fucking freezer." As I held him tighter, his beard grazed my cheek. "You're so warm."

The scent of his room had been so strong when I first got here, but it was nothing compared to smelling it fresh from his skin, the leather and lust notes I now only associated with him.

"Fuck, I missed you."

A smile spread across my lips, and I kissed his cheek, the coldness almost sweetening his flavor. "I'm happy you're back."

When I'd eventually gotten into his bed, I'd taken off all my clothes, except for my panties, and put on one of his T-shirts. Each time he exhaled, it breezed down the thin cotton of his shirt, causing goose bumps to rise over my skin.

He lowered his mouth to the collar, growling as he traced all the way around my neck. "It's so sexy that you're wearing this."

My head tilted back, my mouth opening as he kissed down the center of my chest. "*Ahhh.*"

Because his shirt was so loose, I'd tied it at the side, forcing the fabric to cling to me. I could tell Oliver had noticed, especially when his lips surrounded my nipple over the material and he sucked it into his mouth.

"Oh God." I quivered. The texture, heat, and coolness from his mouth felt like an explosion.

"You like that." He looked at me as he spoke, the glow from the TV lighting up his face in the dark room, a hunger tearing through his eyes.

The sight was so sexy; all I could do was moan, "Yes."

His mouth lowered down my stomach, his hands framing my sides until he reached the only other fabric that was covering me. I felt his lips press against the center of my panties, and then a blast of warm air ricocheted through me.

"I've wanted to taste this for days."

"Oh God." My head ground into the back of the pillow, my heels doing the same to the mattress while I tried to find air.

He spread my thighs even more, continuing to breathe against me, each burst causing me to wriggle beneath him. The anticipation of his tongue was almost too much to bear, and with his face still so cold, it only added to the intensity I was already feeling.

"Oliver," I hissed when he slid my panties to the side, his tongue instantly swiping me.

He licked to the top and dropped all the way down. Then, his fingers moved through the wetness, and I was experiencing a whole different kind of full.

Enough days had passed that I was no longer sore, so each dip of his finger began to feel better and better, and combined with his mouth, he was bringing my body to a place I couldn't return from.

He must have sensed it because he started to move faster, adding even more pressure when he gave me a second finger. The tingling was taking over, a fierce build in my lower stomach that was stretching across me, tensing my body before it erupted.

I shook.

Everywhere.

Tremors racked my body as waves of pleasure shot through me. After each one, I expected Oliver to stop licking, for his hand to still. But he kept on, giving me what I needed until he knew I couldn't handle any more.

That was when I glanced at him, seeing that he had pulled back his mouth a few inches but hadn't moved any farther.

"You are"—I tried to find more words and was struggling —"incredible at that."

Before I had the last syllable out, he was reaching for my panties, wiggling them down my legs, and as he moved back up, I saw he wasn't wearing any clothes.

He'd already placed a condom on the bed, so he lifted it in his hand, ripped off the top of the metal foil, and rolled the latex on.

It was a shaft I remembered so intimately, my body tingling again as I stared at it, and then it was out of my sight as he positioned himself over me. I hugged his neck and felt the coolness of his skin and the roughness of his hair as he rubbed his chest against me. And I loved the way both of them felt.

His palms surrounded my face. "It's not going to hurt as bad this time, all right?"

He kissed me, and he wasn't gentle, sucking out what little air I had left, but he was taking my mind off the burning as his tip slid in. He was right about the pain; it wasn't nearly as intense, and I knew what to expect, my body remembering him as though he'd been here only moments ago.

"You feel so good," he said with his lips on mine.

He moved them to my throat, and I tried to fill my lungs, calming myself through this initial part.

He didn't rush his movements. He knew I couldn't handle that yet. But he also didn't go as slow as he had last time because I could take more, and I was sure he could sense that. So, he continued to bury himself, and once he was all the way in, he didn't move.

He kissed both cheeks and across my nose and finally paused in front of my mouth. "It's so fucking hot that your pussy is molded just to fit me."

If I wasn't already pulsing, I would have started. And if I wasn't already melting, his eyes would have made me.

His hips reared back, and he drove into me.

My nails found their way into his skin, and I moaned, "Oliver ..."

"*Mmm*," he growled, gliding all the way in and back. "Is that starting to feel good?"

He must have felt the moment my body accepted him; that was when he picked up with a harder, faster pace. And each pump allowed me to learn the fullness and friction of this position. The way he was bending over me, how his short, coarse hairs were rubbing my clit. Suddenly, I was getting closer to the place where his tongue had just brought me.

Before that could happen, he slowed to a crawl and drew lines across my breasts with his tongue. He grazed his teeth over the peak of my nipple and breathed, "So fucking wet," on my mouth, and after a short kiss, he added, "I want you to feel this." His hands were on my hips, and he was no longer inside me, but he was moving us. "Trust me," he added when our eyes caught.

We hadn't tried any positions aside from him on top.

This was another first, but with all the others in the past, Oliver had proven I could trust him with my body, so I did again, and I followed where he took me, which was straddling his lap. My hands clung to his shoulders, and I watched him aim his dick.

All I had to do was drop down.

"Take as much of me as you can."

I stared at him, absorbing his accent and growly voice.

"It's going to feel better than you think."

I was lost.

Again.

And as though he knew I needed to be guided, his hand was on my waist, and he was holding me over his crown. I was a bundle of throbbing tingles, and that was what drove me lower.

The air in my body left as the pressure began to fill me with a heaviness I hadn't experienced so far.

"Wow," I sighed, stopping halfway.

His tongue was back to flicking my nipple, his hand circling my clit, and I was dropping down even further. Even though the fullness was overwhelming, I still wanted more.

And I gasped when I got it.

From up here, with his entire cock now inside me, it was a completely different sensation than the previous position. While I got used to it, fighting through the discomfort at first, I stayed still, and Oliver continued to move his attention to other parts of my body.

And eventually, he put his hand on my hip, rocked me forward, and said, "You're going to come so fucking hard."

I slowly let out the breath I'd been holding in and felt my body loosen, and I moved my hips on my own. "Oh my God," I groaned.

The build was there immediately, increasing with every arch of my back, every rise and fall over his dick. And within a few bounces, his hand was gone, and I was on my own. I kept up the same rhythm, my arms now circling Oliver's neck to bring him in even closer. I took in everything that was passing between us—the sensations, the sounds, the weight of our emotions—and I let it build inside me.

"You're getting tighter," he grunted against my mouth, rubbing my clit in every direction.

I knew I was riding him, but I was in a different world. One where passion was driving me, giving me this burst of confidence. And the feelings in my body, the sensations I'd been able to hold off, were now completely taking over.

My hips bucked, going faster than they had so far. "Yesss."

"Make me come, baby."

Knowing the peak was just seconds away, I couldn't stop. I

couldn't slow. The pulsing, the clenching, the bursting—it was all owning me.

And I lost myself.

Just when I thought I couldn't possibly feel any better, when the spasms couldn't dominate another part of my body, he jerked his hips upward and took the control from me.

Within a few pumps, I watched the orgasm pass through him. "Chloe," he grunted, his hands tightening on my face, his movements sharp and powerful. "Fuck yes."

I held on to the sound of my name while both of us trembled, our breaths matching as his movements stopped.

I was wrapped around his shoulders, mouth pressed to his when he said, "You're incredible."

I smiled at his compliment and buried my face in his neck, so I could have a moment to just take this all in. He wouldn't let me do it alone, keeping our bodies intertwined, his warmth surrounding me. He kept me squeezed against him, and several minutes passed before he said anything.

"Are you hungry?"

He was still inside me, sweat covering our skin, this intense feeling still lightly throbbing through me. Food just seemed like a faraway thing.

"I have no idea," I answered honestly.

"How about we take a shower, and then I warm up some of those cookies and make us a cup of tea?"

I knew that was something I would probably never hear back at home, especially not at my age, and that made me love it even more.

I unfolded from his neck and stared at his sexy face. "I'd say yes to just about anything right now."

He kissed me, and I was surprised by how gentle it was. He tightened his grip on my face, and his eyes narrowed. "No more trips." His stare dipped, gradually returning to mine. "I don't like missing you, Chloe."

Something tore through my chest. I wasn't sure if it was because we both knew my time here was really just an extended trip or because my feelings for him were growing, and that was scaring the shit out of me.

As I gazed into his eyes, I was positive it was both.

SIXTEEN

"GOOD MORNING," I whispered as I cuddled into Oliver's back, wrapping my arm over his side and tucking my face into the crook of his neck.

Only a few hours had passed since he returned home, his alarm having gone off seconds ago, signaling it was time to get up for class.

His fingers landed on mine, clasping them together. "*Mmm*." He rolled over and pulled me onto his chest, his other hand rubbing across my back. "Do you need to go to your dorm before class?" His movements paused while he waited for my answer.

"No." My fingers were lost in his chest, rotating between the small patch of hair between his pecs and running across his collarbone. "I brought everything I need with me."

He kissed the top of my head. "I like having you stay here."

"Me too."

The last time I'd spent the night, he'd just walked me home in the morning, but soon, I'd be getting ready in the bathroom he shared with Jake, and we'd ride to our class together—things I'd never done with a guy ... before today.

"I think I'll have time to cook us some breakfast."

The thought of Oliver standing at the stove—a sight I would never grow tired of—should have filled me with the most intense warmth. And it did, but that was what made this even harder. "I have to talk to you about something." My voice was so soft, not sounding like I'd just woken up.

That was because I hadn't. In fact, I hadn't even gone to bed, unable to get my mind off the conversation I'd had with Molly. I didn't know if this was the right time to bring it up, but I had to say something.

He leaned up on his elbow to get a better look at me and searched my eyes before he said, "What's wrong, gorgeous?"

I took a deep breath, unsure of where to start or how to say this. "Oliver, I'm fucking crazy about you." I'd used his own words, but they were so perfect; there was no reason to change them. "But ..." I shook my head, an ache moving through my chest that was threatening to strangle me. "I'm only here for the semester, and then I'm going back to Boston. And ..." I didn't know how the feeling could strengthen, but it was gripping me like the lock I tied around my bike in the city. "I know what that's going to mean for us."

I wasn't experienced when it came to men. But I wasn't stupid enough to believe a relationship could last when we lived thousands of miles apart and when we weren't in a financial situation where we could afford to fly back and forth.

His hand was now on my cheek, his thumb rubbing across my skin, each pass making this even harder. We stayed like that for a while until he finally broke the silence. "Have you booked your return flight?"

A heavy pressure slid to the back of my throat. "No."

When he went to my other cheek, he sent me a whiff of his

cologne, and it felt like the lock twisted and narrowed around my throat.

"Stay for the summer," he said. "You'll have to leave the dorm, so move in here and fly back to the States when school starts."

My mouth opened, eyes widening as I processed what he'd just said. "You want me to ... move in with you?"

That wasn't something I'd considered or thought was even an option. I'd planned on leaving when school ended even though I had no reason to rush back.

His stare intensified, shifting between mine. "I would like that a lot. Chloe ..." His teeth ground across his bottom lip, his light-blue eyes turning more emotional. "I can't change what's going to happen between us or fix where we live, but I can buy us a little more time."

In the softest voice, I said, "It still won't be enough."

"You're right." He kissed my cheek, leaving his mouth there. "But I have you through the summer, and you can bet your arse I'm not going to waste a single second of that."

One thought plagued my mind as I stared at this handsome, wonderful guy.

How will I ever say good-bye to you?

SEVENTEEN

"IS THIS WHAT MAINE LOOKS LIKE?" Oliver asked from the driver's seat of Jake's car.

I wrapped my other hand around his, sandwiching his fingers, as I glanced through the window at the countryside. "Almost identical." I grinned, thinking of the magnificent hills we had in my hometown and the cabins that lined the road similar to here. "Both places are just beautiful."

He hadn't given me many details on where he was taking me for the weekend, aside from wanting to leave after his class this morning and that I needed to pack warm clothes for two nights. We'd spent the last six weekends together, and we hadn't traveled more than ten miles outside the city. Now, we'd been in the car for over three hours, and I wasn't even close to guessing where we were.

He pulled my fingers up to his mouth, kissing the tops of my knuckles just as he began to slow down the car. He turned off the main road and onto a gravel path, weaving us through a thick section of woods. It wasn't dense like the forest of Maine but enough that I couldn't see where it ended. We stayed on the narrow trail for several minutes before it opened into a clearing, a house sitting at the end.

"Oh, it's adorable," I said, looking at the stone cottage that was pretty enough for a fairy tale. "Is this where we're staying?"

He shifted into park and nodded, the warmest smile growing over his face. "I'm happy you like it."

He gave my hand a final kiss before he released me, and then he climbed out of the car. I followed, meeting him by the trunk, where he grabbed our bags and carried them up the front steps. The key was already in his hand, and he had the door unlocked and was holding it open for me.

The inside of the home reminded me of the camps back in Maine that my friends' parents owned, where everything was an outdated shade and trimmed in a doily. But what I loved about places like this was their coziness, how the scent of the wood fireplace and the dusty books on the shelves made me want to snuggle and listen to all the stories.

I'd barely made it through the kitchen when Oliver came up behind me, wrapping his arms around my waist, turning me to face him.

"You've been working really hard ..." His hands hung halfway between my ribs and hips, thumbs swiping whatever they could reach on my body. "I wanted to take you to a place where I could get uni off your mind." He brushed his lips across mine. "My flat isn't far enough away, but this one certainly is."

I shook my head, emotion burning the back of my throat. "You're always so incredibly thoughtful."

Balancing school and this wonderful man hadn't been easy, and I was constantly struggling, trying to make it all fit in every day. Oliver was getting much more of my time than school was, and my grades weren't nearly as strong this semester as a result.

"Thank you," I said so softly, feeling the warmth of his skin seep through his sweater. "You are really all I need ..." I swallowed, breathing through it. "But this, this is really special." My body tingled as I gazed up at him, something that still happened every time he touched me.

"My pleasure." His eyes seemed to lighten as he stared at me, his tongue licking across the inside of his bottom lip. "I know it's cold, but there's a creek that's a good twenty-minute walk from here, and I'd really like to show it to you."

I circled my arms around him, clasping my hands behind his back. "I want to see everything with you."

It was the truth even if it wasn't possible, and that was more painful than I could process right now.

His fingers moved into my hair, holding the back of my head as he pulled me against him so not even air was separating us now. And that was how we stayed, locked together until he eventually backed away.

"Wait," I said, and he stopped. "Will you hold me for just a little bit longer?"

"Of course." His arms returned, his embrace even tighter, his lips now hovering over mine.

"I know, one day soon, we won't be able to do this." Each inhale hurt worse, making it so hard to speak. "And I ..." My voice trailed off when he positioned me in a way where my face rested against his chest, his mouth pressing into the top of my head.

"I'm not going to let go."

And he didn't, even keeping our hands clasped when he took me out the door and into the woods. Since I'd hiked mountains my whole life, this wasn't a hard trail to follow, and when we got to a section where we neared the water, we stopped on the bank and looked down.

I saw why Oliver had wanted to bring me here. It was the

perfect combination of nature with the trees, fresh scent, and the sound the water made as it trickled over the rocks.

I was taking it all in, my eyes closing when I said, "I never want to leave."

He was standing behind me now, his face in my neck, his arm wrapped across my chest. "I was hoping you'd love it here."

I glanced over my shoulder, waiting for him to pull his face out so I could catch his eyes. "Are you going to tell me the story behind this place?"

He still hadn't said whom it belonged to or why he had chosen it for the weekend.

"I used to spend every summer here as a kid." He released his grip, and I faced him. "That's my family's cottage. Started with my grandparents, and now that they've passed, it's my mum and dad's." I watched his chest rise as he filled his lungs with the biggest breath and gradually let it out, still saying nothing for several seconds. "I don't get to come here as much as I used to—I'm just too busy now—but when I do ... it always grounds me."

My hands slid under his jacket, palms flat against his stomach so I could feel him even more. "I love it here, and I love that it's your place."

I would never forget this—the creek, the charming little cottage.

Oliver.

Oh God.

Then, he made the moment even more perfect when he said, "There's a shop just up the road. You go take a bath and warm up while I grab us something to make for dinner."

"Yes. Yes. And more yes."

His smile was huge, and I could feel it on my lips. "I love you, Chloe."

My heart clenched and shook inside my chest, causing

waves to tingle through my body. "Oliver ..." The emotion moved to my eyes, hands tightening around him. They were words that had been pulsing through me, and I could finally say them. "I love you too."

When I tasted his lips, I knew getting on that plane would be the hardest thing I'd ever have to do.

EIGHTEEN

MY HEART POUNDED into my throat as I gripped my laptop with both hands, reading the email that had just come through. It was from the human resources department at Back Bay Digital, one of the largest marketing agencies in Boston and the most coveted internship program at my school. The email said they'd made their final decision on next semester and they would like to offer one of the positions to me.

This was one of the many internships Professor Naples, the head of the marketing department—and my advisor for the last three years—had had me interview for before I left for England. All the programs in the city were so competitive, and I'd prepared myself to be turned down by all of them.

I never expected a dream position at a company that could employ me after I graduated.

I clicked the attachment to read the details of their offer, which gave more specific responsibilities I would have and their compensation package along with the dates I would be contracted to work.

My eyes fell across the month they had listed, and all the air left my body.

The position started in June and went through the end of the year with an opportunity to extend it. But that meant I'd have to be back in Boston two months before I was planning to leave.

And it also meant I wouldn't be spending the summer with Oliver.

Normally, I would have forwarded the email to Professor Naples and waited for him to call so we could discuss the offer, and I would then phone Molly and my parents to celebrate the news.

But right now, I didn't feel like doing any of that.

I shut my laptop, setting it on the desk behind my bed, and I dragged the blanket up to my neck, tucking myself into a ball. My heart was aching, and it only got worse when I pulled up the Calendar app on my phone and figured out when I'd have to fly back if I took the internship.

Twenty-seven days.

And then I would have to say good-bye to the man I loved.

I sat across from Oliver at the pub, the one the guys went to so often that they knew everyone. I was starting to as well since I spent almost every night at their house. And even though I had an exam in the morning and should have been home studying, when Oliver had asked if I wanted to go out, I'd shut my textbook and grabbed my jacket. I hadn't read a single word of the chapter anyway. I hadn't been able to focus on anything since the email came in earlier today. I was hoping after a few beers and some noise, my head would clear.

But I was two drinks deep and not any closer.

"You want to talk about it?" Oliver asked.

I hadn't realized I'd been staring at my hands while they were circled around my beer. Slowly, I looked up, knowing my feelings were showing all over my face.

Before I could say anything, he reached into his pocket, took out some pounds, handed them to Jake, and said, "Grab the three of us a round."

"Happy to, mate," Jake replied, and he left us alone.

That was when Oliver reached for my seat and slid my chair closer to his. "What's going on, Chloe?"

I gripped the sweat-stained glass and said, "I got offered an internship today." His eyes were already filled with excitement, his hand squeezing my thigh. "At a pretty incredible marketing agency in Boston."

"Hell yeah! That's my fucking girl."

He leaned in for a kiss, and I tasted the beer on his mouth and smelled the leathery scent of his cologne. It was too much.

"Oliver ..." I pulled my lips away, searching deep in my chest for some air. "It starts in four weeks." The pain in my body began to get stronger. "I would have to leave the day after finals."

He cupped my cheek, thumb brushing back and forth like always. For the briefest of seconds, I saw the pain in his eyes, I saw the hurt, and then it was gone, in its place a calm gentleness.

"This is what you've been working for, gorgeous."

"But four weeks? That feels like nothing."

"I know." I heard the pain again in his voice, and it hit me —everywhere. "This isn't what either of us wanted or what we planned for." The light blue in his eyes was holding me in a way I wouldn't ever forget. "But you've got to take this internship and kick its arse and make me fucking proud. These opportunities come around once in a lifetime, and you're not going to let go of this one because of me. You hear me?"

I shook my head, staring at this wonderful man, the ache in my chest becoming unbearable.

Still not feeling close enough, I slid off the stool and fell into his arms, where they wrapped tightly around me. He was telling me to give this up two months sooner.

To give us up.

And he was so selfless when he had said that, but it was still hard to hear.

"I'm going to go to the loo," he said, pulling back from our hug. "Then, Jake is going to get up on the table and have everyone in the bar sing our girl a congratulations."

"What are we celebrating?" Jake asked, setting the three beers down, pushing two across the table toward us.

I laughed at the thought of Jake on a high-top and lifted the mug into my hands.

Oliver put his arm over my shoulders. "Chloe got a big internship in Boston, and she's leaving us in a few weeks."

"Is that right?" Jake asked, and I nodded. "I'd say that's a reason to celebrate. Of course, we don't want to see you go either."

Oliver's arm left my shoulders, and he kissed me on the cheek and said, "Be right back."

Since I was still standing, I sat in the same seat as before and drank the rest of my beer before I could move on to the cold one Jake had just brought.

"When do you leave?"

I swallowed, and I knew it wasn't the carbonation that was burning my throat. "Twenty-seven days. If I accept the position."

"Jesus." He rubbed his bare forearm. It didn't matter how cold it was outside, Jake only wore T-shirts, his arms covered in colorful cartoon tattoos. "He's going to miss you." He adjusted his thick black-framed glasses. "We all are, but, man, is he going to hurt over you ..."

It felt like my entire body was trembling, and I was doing everything I could not to let a single tear into my eyes, especially when I said, "You have no idea."

"I remember the way he was when we were in Switzerland, texting you all the time, calling. It's going to be hard when you're so far away." His hand went to my shoulder, patting the top of it. "You're going to come back and visit us, won't you?"

I didn't answer for two reasons. I was too afraid I wouldn't be able to hold off the tears and because another trip to London wasn't in my future. I certainly couldn't afford the ticket; I just didn't have that kind of money. My parents had already bought me this set of flights, and they didn't have the extra funds for another flight. Going back and forth to see him wasn't an option.

Fortunately, Oliver returned, and I didn't have to respond. Standing behind me, he wrapped his arms around my neck and said to Jake, "I think you have some singing to do."

The boys laughed as Jake got on top of our table.

"Excuse me," he shouted through the pub, using his hands as a megaphone. "I need everyone's attention, please."

Even the band in the corner quieted.

"Our friend Chloe fucking Kennedy"—he pointed at me, and the attention in the room shifted in my direction. Even the beer was unable to hold off my embarrassment—"will be flying home soon for an internship. There's a lot of people in this pub who are going to miss her, so let's give her a congratulations that she'll be able to take all the way back to America."

I felt the red move into my face while the entire bar began to sing to me.

At the end of the song, Jake held his beer in the air and shouted, "Chloe, have yourself one hell of a fucking time!"

I grabbed my glass off the table, and said, "Thank you," to everyone in the bar and to Jake before I took a drink.

Oliver's face went into my neck the second the mug left my lips. His hands tightened on my stomach, and he kissed my cheek. He was silent for a few moments, and then, "I bet you're never going to forget us."

"Oliver ..." I whispered, the pain making it too hard to speak any louder. "That would be impossible."

NINETEEN

ONCE I SIGNED the contract with Back Bay Digital, I knew my time with Oliver would go by fast, yet each day, we would grow closer. That was exactly what happened. I was learning so much about him, falling for every detail. But in the back of my mind was a countdown, a number that flashed before my eyes when I looked at him.

And it ticked away faster than I could breathe.

Especially once I started receiving emails from Professor Naples, discussing the class he was having me TA for next semester and the list of philanthropy he wanted me to participate in and the marketing events the school was putting on that I should attend.

I was back ... and I hadn't even left.

And my departure date continued to hang between Oliver and me, a topic we had avoided discussing since there wasn't anything either of us could do to change what was going to happen. But I felt it every day, this ache growing in the pit of my stomach whenever I thought about leaving.

And on my last night in London, it felt like it had eaten a hole straight through me.

Prior to going to Oliver's, I'd spent several hours with my roommate, helping her pack and load her things into a taxi, hugging her before she flew back to South Africa. Then, I'd spent the rest of the afternoon with Oliver and his roommates. That night, we all cooked dinner together, and I got a chance to spend some time with them before they went out for the evening.

Once we cleaned up, Oliver brought our wine into the living room, and we got comfortable on the couch. The doors to the garden were open, and I could smell spring in the breeze. He lifted my legs and placed them across his lap, cupping the bottom of my bare foot, rubbing over my arch.

"Whatever you do," I groaned, "do not stop."

I watched him laugh, and it was the most beautiful sight.

He'd asked me several times how I wanted to spend my last night in London, if I wanted to sleep at his family's cottage —a place we'd now visited a bunch of times—go out with the guys, or if I wanted to go back on the London Eye to see the city one last time. I'd weighed each option, and only one felt right.

London had gotten plenty of my time.

Now, I just wanted my Oliver.

He circled around my heel and through the middle of it. "Are your parents going to be able to make it to the airport?"

"No, they're coming to visit this weekend instead." I shook my head, my arms wrapping over my stomach. "I can't believe I'm going to be home tomorrow."

He ground his knuckles into the center of my foot, massaging up to my toes. "Molly's going to be happy to have you back."

He smiled, and it hit me right in the chest.

God, I would miss that grin. How it was cold on the edges and scorching in the middle. But mostly ... it was just wild.

Like my Oliver.

I sighed and heard the hitch in my voice each time my throat tremored. "She's been counting down the hours."

I thought of the sign she had threatened to make and bring with her to Logan Airport tomorrow, and when all of this didn't feel heavy, I would probably laugh.

As he moved to my other foot, I added, "Maybe you'll get to meet her in August."

A few weeks ago, the guys had begun talking about their annual trip, and I suggested they come to Boston.

His expression told me what I already feared.

"Ibiza won?"

When he nodded, I saw the disappointment on his face.

"I was hoping for it too, sweet girl."

I had known it was a stretch, but having him come to America was still my only shot at seeing him.

And now, that was gone.

His expression continued to deepen, his grip tightening, more emotion spreading over his face until he said, "Come here."

I didn't hesitate. I maneuvered my body around to throw myself in his arms, and once I was there, I squeezed him with every bit of love I had in me.

And I hugged him for so long that when we were standing outside Heathrow the next morning, it felt like I'd never let him go.

We'd taken a taxi, and it was double-parked in front of the terminal while we were standing by the trunk, my two suitcases by our feet. Police officers were directing traffic, whistles loudly blown when drivers were parked for too long.

We were running out of time.

But Oliver's arms didn't release me; he held them at my sides like locks, keeping me pressed to his body. "Fuck, gorgeous," he whispered in my ear.

My face was buried in his chest, hands clinging to his sweatshirt, as I breathed him in.

I'd thought about this moment, and I'd tried to prepare myself for it, so when the emotions came, I would be able to handle them. Except they were here, bursting through my chest, dripping from my eyes.

And I was falling apart, and I couldn't stop it.

As my hands readjusted, a fear came through me, reminding me that, in just a few minutes, I wouldn't be able to touch him. It was consuming that when I went to take a breath, I couldn't get the air in. "This can't be the last time I see you."

His lips pressed into the top of my head. "I hope it won't be."

There was another whistle and shouting, and from this angle, I wasn't able to tell if it was directed at our taxi or a different one.

But when Oliver sighed, "Damn it," I took that as my answer.

But I couldn't go. Not yet. I needed just a few more seconds with him. "I'm going to m-miss you."

One of his arms released me, and another shot of terror burst through my chest, thinking he was letting me go until I realized he was only bringing me closer. And now, with his lips pressed into my hair, I felt each of his exhales, each grunt of emotion.

And something inside me released.

It hadn't happened in the days building up to this moment when I shed so many tears. It was a sensation I'd never felt before, a raw gnawing that was like an animal tearing through me. "Oh God."

The pain was too much. I had to make it stop. I had to make this right somehow because I couldn't think past not being able to see him again.

"Oliver," I cried, pulling my face away, so I could look at his. "I ..." There were so many thoughts; they were moving in all different directions. I couldn't pull them together, and I couldn't get them straight. "Tell me not to go," I cried out, and I couldn't even see him through the tears. "Tell me not to get on the plane, and I'll give up the internship. I'll give up everything, and I'll stay here with you." I swallowed, and air shot through my lips because there were so many tears and no breath. "Just tell me, Oliver ..."

I felt movement, and I was wrapped in him again, filled with a warmth that didn't make it beyond my skin.

"Fuck ..." There was so much pain in his voice. "Chloe, do you know how badly I want to say those words to you?" His hand was on the back of my head, tilting my chin so I could meet his lips. "But I can't. I want you to have this internship more than anything, and I'm not going to be the one to take it away from you."

"B-but I'd do it ... for y-you."

His mouth was on mine, kissing me with a fierceness. "And I fucking love you for that, but I'd never let you."

My tears were making our lips wet, the truth of his statement causing them to drip faster. "H-how do I"—my chest felt like it was going to cave—"s-say good-bye to you?"

"Sweet girl ..." He pressed his nose to mine, breathing so heavy, not saying anything for a few seconds. "I know how you're going to be when you get back, so I want you to listen to me." He made sure I could see his eyes, and that was when the emotion started to fill them. "I want you to get your arse out there with Molly and party like hell and have the time of your fucking life." He tightened his hands as he spoke, emphasizing each word, his eyes now getting so watery that it was causing me to cry harder. "Make me and my mates proud, okay?" He paused, and my throat trembled as the first tear fell over his lid. "If you need anything, I'm here."

One of my hands released his shirt, and I lifted it to his beard, knowing the tear was in there somewhere. "Oliver ..." I sniffled.

And he just stared at me, not saying a word, holding me with such firmness.

I was already shaking, but I felt it get worse.

Because we were here.

At our last second.

Oh God.

He finally whispered, "My beautiful, sweet girl," and there was so much pain in his voice that it sent a rawness through me that made my stomach ache. "Promise me something ..."

I couldn't answer; I just stared at him and continued to hold his face.

"Promise you won't ever forget me."

With the streams falling from my lids, my vision was now completely gone. But I didn't need it because his lips were on mine. I sucked in his breath, and I circled my arms around his neck. I felt him give me everything he had left.

"Chloe," he said so softly.

And I knew it was over.

The kiss.

The moment.

Us.

My eyes opened, and I stared into his face. "You were so perfect to me, Oliver. I will"—sobs racked my chest—"never forget that."

"I love you." His mouth was on mine again, but it was a

gentle kiss, and I knew his tears were touching mine. And the whole moment was like a breath, over far too quickly.

As impossible as this felt, I had to be the one to leave.

I forced my fingers to release their grip on his sweatshirt, my arms dropping to my sides. "I love you ... too." I gasped, my hand going to my chest to help the air move through it.

I couldn't say any more; it would be too final, and I just couldn't handle that right now.

So, I stood there, taking in the feel of him, doing a final sweep.

And then his hands were off me, and he took a step back and said, "I'm going to watch you walk away."

I didn't think I could cry harder.

I didn't think the tears could drip faster.

But both were happening, and I couldn't control them.

As I took one final look at the man I loved, I clung to the two suitcase handles, squeezing the plastic into my palms.

Good-bye, Oliver.

I turned around and heard him choke, "Bye, Chloe," as I walked through the glass doors of the terminal.

I waited until I was around the corner, away from the entrance and his line of sight before I rolled my bags to a corner.

And I completely fucking lost it.

TWENTY

"DON'T LET GO," I cried the second Molly's arms were around me.

I knew there were people everywhere in baggage claim, several probably staring at us, but I didn't care. The tears had been flowing since I left Oliver at the airport, and there was no stopping them.

"Hug me tighter."

"Oh, babe." Her hands were in the center of my back, squeezing me with half the strength Oliver had used, her scent flowery and wrong but so right. "That flight had to be hell."

I waited for my chest to calm a little before I said, "The poor man next to me felt so bad that he hugged me at one point."

"A cocktail would have been much better."

"I left snot on his shirt."

"Good girl."

My arms tightened around her. "I can't laugh, Molly. Maybe one day. But not today."

She leaned back and looked at me. "Let's get you home and get you sloshed. Sound good?"

I shook my head, but it wasn't for the reason she thought. "Molly ..." The words burned in my throat. "He let me go."

She stared at me for several seconds, reaching into her pocket for a tissue that she held to my face. "Honey, that's because he's a good man. If he had told you to stay, you would have."

"I know."

"And, babe, that would have been a huge mistake." She took out another tissue since the first one was soaked and dabbed it over my cheeks. "I know it's hard to see this right now, but you're in your senior year with an opportunity of a lifetime. This is where you're supposed to be."

She was always so tough, but I needed to hear it.

Still, I couldn't get past one thing. "He watched me walk away." I could tell she'd heard me even though I'd whispered.

"And I bet that was the hardest thing Oliver has ever done." She looped her arm through mine. "I've got the vodka already waiting for us in the freezer and every dessert imaginable in our kitchen. We'll get through this."

"I don't know."

"Trust me."

Me: Home safe and sound. xo
Oliver: I miss you.
Me: More than you could ever know.

Oliver: Good luck on your first day. You're going to kill it.

Me: Aww. The perfect message to wake up to. Thank you.

Oliver: How was it? Did you survive day one?
Me: It was amazing. Really, really amazing, and I'm one lucky girl.
Oliver: That makes me so fucking happy. Go have fun with Molly and remember, celebrate your arse off.
Me: Promise. xo

Me: I know I commented on your post, but I'm just so excited you got the job you wanted. Now, I'm the one who's proud of you. You looked great in that suit, by the way. Missing you.

Oliver: I think I just got over my hangover. My mates made sure I did plenty of celebrating last night. Everyone was asking for you at the pub. I promised them all I'd say hi.
Oliver: Miss you, sweet girl.

Oliver: You've got every man in England, including myself, drooling over the American flag. Nice bikini, gorgeous. Happy Independence Day.
Me: Maybe that was my plan all along. ;)

Me: Seeing Jake sing karaoke was one of the funniest things I've ever watched. Looks like your trip to Ibiza was incredible.

Oliver: We had a blast, but we all agreed America would have been great too. I know uni is starting soon if it hasn't already. Have a good start, and remember what I said ...
Me: I'm making you proud, Oliver. Every day.

I knew it would happen one day. I'd be scrolling through my feed, and I'd come across a picture of Oliver with another girl. And I knew it would be hard, but I hadn't expected to feel like this.

We weren't talking every day; we weren't even talking every few weeks.

But, God, I loved him.

Still.

And I was clinging to our memories, but I was the only one doing it because he had found someone else.

I didn't know who she was; she wasn't someone I'd met before.

It didn't matter. She was there ... and I wasn't.

I had known one of us would move on far sooner than the other, and there was no question who it would be.

I just hadn't expected it to change everything.

My finger hovered over his profile while I took several deep breaths. His account was private. If I unfollowed him, I would lose access to his pictures and to his life.

But it was a life that no longer included me.

I clicked Unfollow, and then I removed him from my account.

I pulled the blanket over my head, burying myself in my bed, and I let out the deepest, most gut-wrenching scream.

But it was silent.

PART TWO

I've found forever ... in you.

TWENTY-ONE

"CHLOE, do you see something wrong with this picture?" Molly asked, staring at me from the doorway of my closet with her hands on her hips.

"I'm getting up." I sighed, stretching my toes, feeling the ache from wearing heels all day. "I just need five more minutes, and then I'll get dressed."

I had been at the office until almost ten last night and back there again at six this morning.

Even my hair was tired.

But I'd promised Molly I would go out with her, and there was absolutely no way she was going to let me cancel.

"One more minute, and you're going to be out cold." She put her finger in the air and rolled it toward her. "Get over here, missy."

Reluctantly, I threw the blanket off and climbed out of bed. "Where did all your energy come from? Did you call in sick and sleep all day and not tell me?" I asked, making my way over to her.

"I've had three Red Bulls, and I'm getting laid tonight. That should explain everything."

I laughed. "God, I love you. Now, what do you want me to wear?"

She grinned as she reached for one of the hangers. "This."

She took a black dress off the rack that I'd bought a few weeks ago at a boutique by my office. It was tight in the areas it needed to be, accentuating every curve on my body. And because all I did was work, I had nowhere to wear it.

"Aren't we just going to meet your boyfriend and his colleagues? This dress isn't exactly office attire."

She stared at me, brows raised. "I feel like you just proved your own point."

As I looked down, I caught a glimpse of my hands, seeing how badly I needed a manicure. In fact, all of me needed to be polished. That was what happened when you were in your first year of employment for Back Bay Digital. To stand out among the other full-time employees, I worked long, grueling hours, I said yes to everything management asked, and I answered my phone no matter what time it rang.

But I was so tired; I couldn't even keep my eyes open.

Her hands went to my shoulders, and her face softened. "I haven't seen you in five days, and I miss my best friend." She released me and took a step toward the door. "I'm going to go pour you a Red Bull."

"Add some vodka to it," I shouted when she walked out, and I began stripping off the black pants and shirt I'd worn to work.

I covered myself in a robe and hurried into the shower, in there just long enough to wash my body. By the time I returned to my room, my skin slathered in lotion, there was a Red Bull on ice waiting for me on the dresser.

I stood in front of the mirror, sipping the energy drink, and

I started to put on my makeup, adding eyeliner and bronzer before curling each section of my hair. I waited until my skin was fully dry before I carefully slipped on the dress. I finished the outfit with a pair of heels and perfume that I sprayed under my ears.

It was a spot Oliver had taught me about.

I took a deep breath, feeling the chills run through my body —something that still happened every time I thought of him.

One thing I'd learned over the last twelve months, which was how long it had been since I spoke to him, was that time wasn't going to push Oliver Bennett out of my mind. He was going to live there forever, and I just had to accept it.

It was a good thing the memories I had of him were amazing.

"Stunning," Molly purred from behind me.

I was still holding the perfume bottle in my hand, still staring at it.

"Thank you." I set it down and took a final look at myself. "God, this dress was a good find."

She pulled a piece of hair off my cheek. "I knew it was going to look good on you. Ready?"

I nodded and grabbed my clutch. I followed her into the living room where she picked up my keys off the table and handed them to me along with my jacket.

As I put them in my bag, I said, "What am I going to do when you move in with your boyfriend? Who's going to remember to always pack my keys?"

She put her hand on top of mine and walked with me to the door. "We'll make sure to find you a building with a doorman, so there will always be someone there to rescue you. Now, let's go get a drink."

I laughed, shaking my head. "I know it's coming soon, and I'm not at all ready for it."

She had met him the last semester of our senior year when she was doing her internship. She was picking up the coffee for her team when Marshall was walking by and saw her struggling with opening the door. He got her number, and they had been dating for almost a year.

She took a step closer and wrapped her arms around my neck. "We need to get you dating."

"Find me someone who's worth it."

Her smile reached all the way to her eyes. "Now, I'm on a mission."

I giggled again and grabbed her hand, looping our arms as I led us to the door. We had a four-block walk ahead of us and six stops on the train, and we were already late.

"The Red Bull is making these heels feel like clouds. Let's hurry before that wears off."

She laughed just as hard and squeezed my arm on the way out.

TWENTY-TWO

"WHAT CAN I GET YOU?" the bartender asked, his hands hovering, waiting to reach for one of the bottles.

I gripped the edge of the bar top, holding the cold leather, and said, "Prosecco, please."

The speakeasy wasn't too packed tonight, just a steady business crowd filling the main space and the small seating nooks that were like little dens built into the perimeter.

My eyes were falling over the row of wine, studying the labels, when I felt a piece of fabric brush across the side of my arm. I turned just in time to see a dark suit jacket leaving my skin, and with it came a scent. One that was so sharp and demanding—the smell of power if it came in a bottle.

I couldn't believe how much I liked it.

My gaze traveled higher to the silk tie, the broad shoulders, and the full frame that was at least six-three and all suit. And I found myself holding in my breath as I took in this absolutely gorgeous man with thick black hair and a clean-shaven face, blue eyes so dark that they looked navy.

"Have you ordered?" he asked in a rich, deep voice.

"He's making mine now."

It was easy to see there was nothing raw about this man. He had a polished, educated demeanor with a richness that went well beyond the cost of his suit.

He smiled, and I found myself sucked into it, unable to look away. "What's your name?"

With a stare as invasive as his, one I felt move straight through me, it seemed my name was something he should certainly know at this point.

"Chloe Kennedy."

He turned his body so he was now facing me, showing me details I hadn't picked up before—a narrow, angular nose and tiny wrinkles at the sides of his eyes. His hand reached forward, and when it surrounded mine, he said, "Lance Hamilton."

"Here's your Prosecco," the bartender said, and from the corner of my eye, I saw him set down the glass.

"Add that to my tab, and I'll take a scotch," Lance said with his eyes on me.

I knew my cheeks were blushing, and it wasn't because he was paying for the drink. "You don't have to do that."

"I can't let a beautiful woman like yourself pay for her own drink." His eyes narrowed. "Unless there's someone else here who should be buying it?"

"No." I shook my head. "Only you."

My hand was still in his, gripped in a shake that I felt all the way up to my shoulder, across my chest, and down to my other hand that was clenching the cold glass of champagne.

My comment seemed to make his smile grow, and he held my hand for a second longer before releasing me.

"I was just coming to find you," Molly said, startling me, her arm then snaking around my waist. "Looks like Lance found you instead."

I glanced at my best friend, knowing Lance could hear us. "You know him?"

"I work with Marshall," Lance said before Molly could reply, and he leaned down and kissed her on the cheek. "Nice to see you, Molly."

She grinned at him. "You too."

He hadn't been part of the group Molly and Marshall introduced me to when we first arrived, nor had I seen him at any of the parties I attended with her. If I'd met Lance before, I wouldn't have forgotten.

"I'll see you back at the table," she said, her arm leaving my waist, and she gave me a look I knew well. It was one that told me she approved, and then she was gone just as the bartender handed Lance his drink.

"Thank you again," I said as he handed the bartender his credit card.

He held his glass in the air, near mine, smiling. "To the morning and everything that happens in between."

I laughed, clicking my Prosecco to his scotch, and it felt like a warmth had crept over me, even before I put my lips to the glass and swallowed.

"You're friends with Molly?" he asked, nodding in the direction in which she had walked, where our large group had a table and several couches.

"We were roommates in college. Still are."

He took the card back from the bartender, and in one swift movement, he had the billfold open, the pen in his hand, and his signature on the bottom of the receipt. When a copy of the bill was tucked into his pocket, his hand went to the small of my back, and he guided me through the crowd. Before we reached our table, he paused in front of one of the nooks. Inside the small space was a couch, dim lighting, and privacy.

And this one just happened to be vacant.

"Do you want to sit?" He was holding out his arm, giving me the option to go either way.

I chose the quieter one and ducked into the nook.

When he sat next to me, I got a whiff of his cologne again, and I smiled as I took it in. "If you work with Marshall, you must be an attorney."

Marshall had just passed the bar last year and was still fresh to the business. But I got the feeling Lance had more experience and was a few years older, putting him at around thirty.

"I am." He spread his arms across the back of the couch and nodded. "Tell me what you do."

"I work for a marketing agency."

Those navy eyes continued to stare at me, but something in them changed. In fact, they felt like they were looking right through me.

"There's more."

I laughed. He really was an attorney who had read me so easily.

Before I let my brain process that piece of information, I said, "I wish there were more."

"You don't like your job?"

I crossed my legs, leaning my shoulder into the back cushion as I aimed more of my body toward him. "I like it enough. I'm only in my first year, and aside from an internship at the same company, I don't have a lot of experience."

"Where would you go if you had a choice?"

I took a drink, savoring the bubbly flavor, trying not to lose myself in his stare. "I'd love to work for a start-up and help build their market from scratch or work for an established company to expand its international presence."

"You just described most of my clients."

I smiled, rubbing the base of the glass over my thigh.

"Maybe I'll come park myself in your lobby and beg one of your clients for an interview."

"I don't think you'd have to beg, Chloe."

It was the way he'd said it that had me reaching for words. Because the ones I was going to say were gone. Forgotten. And the only thing I could grasp at this moment was his gaze.

"Where are you from?" he asked.

I felt sparks of energy run through me, and I knew they weren't from the Red Bull.

"Camden," I said. "It's a small town on the coast of Maine. How about you? Did you go to school here?"

My eyes dropped to his tie and cuff links, the expensive-looking watch that kept peeking out of his shirt.

"I grew up in Connecticut, did my undergraduate at Tufts, and went to Yale for law school."

There was such smoothness in the way he spoke, like words came as easy to him as opening a billfold and signing his name.

I wanted to know more.

"Tell me something, Lance ..." I felt a tightness in my chest, especially when he swallowed a sip of his drink, his tongue slowly swiping across his lip to lick off the rest of the scotch. "What does fun look like to you?"

He definitely didn't seem to be the type who would stand on a table in the middle of a bar and sing congratulations or even someone who would tell his friend to do it. Lance was more the type to own the bar.

When he turned his glass, still staring at me, the one large square cube rattled against the sides. "I ski in the winter and go to the Cape in the summer. I like being on the water or on a mountain."

Or inside a woman.

I saw the words on his face; he just didn't say them.

While his unspoken thoughts passed through me, a heat moving with it, I said, "Maine has some of the best skiing."

"I go to either Sugarloaf or Sunday River almost every weekend in the winter."

He could have chosen to go to New Hampshire or Vermont, even the Berkshires—they all had amazing trails. But the two mountains he'd listed were both in Maine, and for some reason, I found that extremely attractive.

"What does Chloe do for fun?"

I looked away, needing a break from his piercing gaze to think about his question. But it didn't give me the pause I needed because his presence alone was consuming me.

"Does sleep count?"

He smiled, and it was painfully beautiful.

"I've been working so much; I haven't been out walking or even hanging with Molly as much as I want. I would say traveling is my real passion."

The lines in his forehead deepened when he asked, "Where's the best place you've been?"

"London." As I took a breath, memories began to flash in my head. "I studied there for a semester during my junior year. It was a magical time."

Lance's stare was so far inside me; it felt like he was watching the same memories of London play out in my head.

"Where's the next trip?"

I brought the Prosecco up to my lips. "Vail. I go next week. It's for work, but I hear the drive from Denver is magnificent."

He wiped his mouth with his fingers, drawing my attention to both. And both were seductive for entirely different reasons.

"It is," he said, "and so is their skiing."

"They won't have enough snow while I'm there, but I'm going to get some hiking in."

"*Mmm*," he responded like he was tasting something delicious, and then he reached into his suit jacket and pulled out his phone, staring at the screen. "Chloe, you will have to excuse me for a second. This is a client." He held the phone up to his ear and stepped out of the nook, moving several paces away.

I quickly opened my clutch and checked my phone, seeing a text from Molly on the screen.

Molly: OMG. Just OMG. Yes to Lance. So. Many. Yeses.

As I glanced up, he was turning around. Our eyes caught, and his followed me all the way back to his seat. The heat was certainly there, but I could tell something had changed and that he didn't like it.

"Unfortunately, Chloe, I have to go."

I felt my lips smile. "Lance ... this was fun."

He moved to the edge of the couch, and his knee briefly brushed mine. The feeling of the fabric against me sent a scorching wave of heat across my skin.

"Should I get your number from Marshall, or do you want to give it to me right now?"

My heart began to beat so fast; I was positive he could hear it. At the very least, my face was giving it away that my pulse was skyrocketing.

I put my hand on my chest to calm it. And as I said my number, he typed it into his phone, and slid it back into his pocket before he reached forward.

I sucked in a mouthful of Lance-scented air as our hands clasped. It wasn't a shake. This was a way for him to touch me without worrying a hug was too much.

"You'll hear from me."

"I hope so."

It was nothing more than a whisper, but I had a feeling he'd heard it.

Especially when a smile came across his face.

God, he is so sexy.

His fingers released mine, and he said, "Good-bye, Chloe," before he was gone.

My face tingled like I'd been out in the cold for too long, the sensation moving to my chest and arms. I breathed through it, trying to ground myself again, the last few minutes almost dreamlike.

Once I had my bearings, I got up from the couch, and as I got closer to the table, Molly saw me and rushed over.

"Holy shit," she said, looping her arm through mine. "That was chemistry like I've never seen." She was walking me back in the direction I'd come from. "You guys were literally so transfixed; I don't think either of you even realized I was standing there."

"It almost didn't feel real; it was so good."

She stopped at the first empty nook, and we sat inside.

And once we got settled, I said, "If the guys are colleagues, you must have all the details on him?"

"Colleagues?" She studied my face. "He didn't tell you?"

I turned my body toward her but kept my legs crossed. "Tell me what?"

"Lance's grandfather opened the practice a million years ago; his father now runs it, and he's grooming Lance to take over." She laughed. "Hamilton Law Group—the name ring a bell now?"

"Jesus." I felt my eyes widen. "He didn't mention a single word of that."

He was humble; it was such an attractive trait. But I could tell he had money; the signs had been everywhere.

"He doesn't usually go out with the guys. I mean, he's about to be their boss, so it's a careful line to balance. I was surprised to see him here, but clearly, I picked the right evening to drag you out."

My heart still hadn't calmed.

And to think, I had almost missed this for sleep.

I swallowed. "Tell me everything you know."

She used her fingers like a checklist. "He's twenty-eight, and I heard he has a place in the Back Bay. His parents have a penthouse in Beacon Hill. Marshall was there for a Christmas party and said it's insane. They also have a mansion in Connecticut and a corporate jet and probably vacation homes." She chewed the corner of her lip. "They're the real fucking deal, Chloe."

I waved my hand in the air. "You know I couldn't care less about any of that." When my arm dropped, I wrapped it around my stomach. "I gave him my number. Who knows if anything will even come of it?"

"Excuse me," I suddenly heard, and Molly and I turned our heads at the same time.

A waitress was standing in front of us with two glasses of Prosecco on her tray. "Mr. Hamilton wanted me to bring these over. He apologizes again for having to leave so early." She gave one of the drinks to me and the other to Molly, and she left.

A grin moved across Molly's lips. "You're not sure if anything will even come of it?" She clicked her glass against mine. "You want to retract that statement now?"

I took a long drink and finally breathed, "Fuck."

"Because you want to get fucked? Or because you're in over your head, and you haven't even dipped in your chipped toenail?"

"Well ... both."

We laughed, and a chill ran through my whole body when she said, "You're going to hear from him soon. Lance Hamilton isn't the kind of man who waits for anyone."

TWENTY-THREE

SINCE MOLLY WENT HOME with Marshall after the bar, I returned to our apartment alone, immediately climbing into bed, bringing my laptop with me. Once it was open, I typed Lance's name into Google, and the first thing that appeared was Hamilton Law Group. From their website, I was able to see the history of the business and how it had been passed through the family, the same way Molly had described.

Under Lance's bio, I learned he had also studied a semester in London, getting experience with international law. He had graduated the top of his class from Tufts and Yale and had been the captain of the lacrosse team.

Since his social media accounts were public, I took my time scrolling through his pictures and posts and all the ones he'd been tagged in. I just wanted to get a feel of him beyond what I had experienced tonight, and this was the biggest window into his life.

I became so lost in Lance, at the photographs of him around the world and the pictures of him with politicians and busi-nessmen and athletes, that the sound of the text coming through my phone made me jump. I giggled as I looked at the screen.

> *Molly: Googling the fuck out of him, aren't you?*
> *Me: I thought you'd be getting laid by now.*
> *Molly: You're peeing with me.*
> *Molly: But say it ... I'm right.*
> *Me: Of course you're right. ;) Brunch in the morning?*
> *Molly: I'll meet you at Stephanie's on Newbury at 12. LY.*
> *Me: xo*

"Hello, this is Chloe," I said as I held my phone to my ear. I had no idea what time it was, and the number hadn't shown up on caller ID, but I had to answer in case it was a client.

"It's Lance."

My eyes burst open, air swishing through my chest, and I pushed myself up in bed. "Hi."

"Did I wake you?"

How is it possible that he sounds even sexier in the morning?

I glanced at the nightstand to check the time; my room was far too bright to even guess. It showed a little past nine, and I'd gone to bed at two. I couldn't remember the last time I'd slept that many hours straight.

"No, no, I'm up," I said, not wanting him to feel bad. "It sounds like you're a morning person." I climbed out of bed and walked straight to the coffeemaker.

"You're not?"

"Only when I have to be."

He laughed, and the sound made me smile as I popped in the coffee pod.

"Are you saying I should rethink inviting you out for breakfast?"

This time, he made it hard for me to breathe. "Nope, I'm not saying that at all."

"Then, meet me in an hour."

My finger hovered over the brew button on the coffeemaker. The idea of seeing him again so soon was causing my body to pulse.

An hour?

And just then, I remembered the brunch I'd scheduled with Molly before I went to bed, and I quickly pulled up our texts, surprised to see one had come in from her before I woke up.

Molly: Don't hate me, but rain check. Love you hard.

"I think I can make that happen," I replied.

The excitement was far past building in my chest, and now, it was exploding.

"What's your address?"

I hit the button, hearing the coffee start to heat, and I gave him my address.

"A car will be there to pick you up."

My entire closet flashed in my head as I tried to think of something to wear.

"I'll see you soon, Chloe."

I had one hour to get ready, and something told me Lance was extremely punctual.

TWENTY-FOUR

WHEN THE DRIVER dropped me off at the restaurant, I gave Lance's name to the hostess. She informed me he had already arrived and escorted me to the main dining room. I'd heard of this restaurant, but I'd never been, so I didn't know the layout or where to look for him.

But that didn't matter because the second I stepped into the open space, I immediately felt Lance's eyes on me, only taking me a second to spot him. It didn't matter that I was wearing skinny jeans, knee-high boots, and an off-the-shoulder sweater because while Lance's stare followed me the entire way to the table, it felt like he saw right through me.

And my body was totally on fire from it.

He stood as I got closer, taking a few steps to greet me.

I could smell him in the air, the scent getting stronger as his hand rested on the outside of my arm, his face moving in until his lips were brushing my cheek.

And once I felt the feel of his mouth on me, my eyes closed, the air completely leaving my lungs.

I was enveloped in Lance Hamilton, and it felt like the most perfect moment.

"Thanks for meeting me," he said, his lips no longer on my skin as he pulled away.

Even though I was moving to the other side of the table, I could still feel his mouth on me. And I could still smell that rich, powerful scent as I took a seat.

"Thank you for inviting me," I said, putting my napkin in my lap. "And for sending us the drinks after you left. That was sweet of you."

"Did you have a fun evening?" He adjusted the sleeves of his crisp button-down before his hands disappeared under the table.

I was still trying to catch my breath and get acclimated to the intensity of his gaze. "One of the best I've had in a while."

"Good," he said, just as a waitress approached our table.

"What can I get you to drink?" she asked me. "A mimosa perhaps?"

"Sounds delicious, but let's make it a poinsettia, thank you."

She wrote down my order and looked at Lance as he said, "Blood Mary. Extra spicy," and then she was gone.

Once we were alone again, I felt a wave move from the tip of my toes all the way to my neck. It was heat, unthawing my body, each nerve ending tingling, like he had lit a match under every single one.

"How did you sleep?"

Such a simple question, yet it felt like the most intimate one he'd asked since we met.

I tucked a chunk of hair behind my ear and took a breath. "Usually, I'm up no later than six. Not this morning. I don't know what happened, but it was amazing. How about you?"

"I don't require much. Three or four hours, max."

Just as I was about to respond, the waitress dropped off our cocktails and said, "Enjoy these. I'll be back in a few minutes to get your order."

My fingers circled the thin stem of the glass, and I held it in the air. "To the evening and everything that happens in between." As he smiled, I added, "It was too good not to steal from you."

"You can have anything you want from me, Chloe." He clinked his glass against mine and brought it up to his lips.

I was several seconds behind, processing his statement, when the bubbly finally hit my tongue.

I swallowed several mouthfuls and was setting down the glass when I heard, "Have you been here before?"

My fingers continued to hold the stem. "Never; however, I've heard great things." There was a leather-bound menu in front of each of us, and I opened mine, quickly scanning the main courses. "What's good?"

"Are you a fussy eater? Or have any allergies?"

I glanced up at him and shook my head, wondering how he'd found a button-down that was the exact color of his eyes.

"Then, how about you let me order, and I'll surprise you?"

My hand released the top of the menu, and the book closed. "Sounds like more fun." I took another sip. "Lance, tell me stuff. I want to know more about you."

Even though he wasn't smiling, there was a lightness in his expression. "I hate tomatoes more than anything, but I love ketchup. I iron every morning; I do a better job than any dry cleaner I've ever tried. And I'm not patient. I like getting my way, and that's what makes me one hell of an attorney." He didn't lean his elbows on the table. He clasped his hands together on top of his menu instead. "Why don't you tell me who I'm looking at right now—or better yet, maybe I should tell you?"

I could feel my pulse in my throat. "Please," I said. "I'm dying to hear this."

His stare turned even more intense, something I hadn't thought was possible, and he was silent for a few seconds. And once again, I felt that pull like he was inside me.

"I get the feeling you're a fighter, and that tells me things don't come easy. You've probably had to make sacrifices to get to where you are." His eyes narrowed. "You're adventurous but not free-spirited. You would go to Cinque Terre for the color of the water, not to go cliff diving." He dragged his bottom lip into his mouth, returning it slick. "And you're extremely selective with who you spend your time with. If you give them an hour, it's because they've earned it." He twisted the long celery stalk in the glass before he took a drink, and I watched his Adam's apple bob as he swallowed. "How'd I do?"

I had known things with Lance were going to be different. I had known that the moment he caused a spark to pass through my whole body and stop me from breathing. But while I sat in that restaurant with his eyes fixed on mine, his smile growing, that was when I really knew this man was about to change my entire life.

And I was ready for him.

"Lance," I began, preparing to answer his question, but I was cut off as the waitress appeared at our table.

"Have you made any decisions?" she asked.

With his menu still closed, Lance looked at her and said, "We'll start with an order of the French toast bites." His eyes shifted to me, and he continued, "She'll have the truffle eggs benedict, hollandaise on the side." His gaze returned to her when he finished, "Spanish omelet with dry toast for me."

She took our menus and left, and my hands circled the edge of the table, squeezing it between my fingers, as I searched everywhere for air, slowly glancing up.

"You just ordered my favorite breakfast."

He glanced to the side, showing me a perfectly shaved jaw, his dark hair in place, a starched collar I now knew he'd ironed this morning. "Does that win me a second date?"

I laughed, feeling the redness move through my chest and up to my face. "Between that and your description of me, I'd say you've earned it."

TWENTY-FIVE

"YOU'VE MET ANTHONY," Lance said to me, referring to his driver as we approached his SUV a block from the restaurant.

Anthony was holding the backseat door open for us, and I took his hand just as he voiced, "It's nice to see you again, Miss Kennedy."

"You too." I tightened my grip and used his help to step into the back. "Thank you," I added as I got into my seat.

When Anthony had picked me up earlier, I hadn't realized he was Lance's personal driver; I just thought he'd sent a car service. But knowing he'd taken that extra step was protective in a way I'd never felt before.

"Anthony, we'll be taking Chloe home," Lance said as he sat next to me.

I waited for Lance's eyes before I said, "Thank you for the ride."

Before I'd even put my coat on at the restaurant, he'd told me he was taking me home. I hadn't argued. It would give us more time together, and that was what I wanted.

He reached across the small space between us and clasped our fingers together. His skin was so warm even though it was chilly outside. "My pleasure."

His stare was too much with his hand on me, especially when thoughts were beginning to build in my head, ones that involved the way he would wrap around my body. So, I turned my face and glanced out the window, watching the Back Bay pass by the glass.

But I wasn't there for more than a few seconds when his fingers tightened around mine, and he asked, "When are you free?"

"I leave for Colorado in two days, and I'm going to live at the office until my flight. How about when I get back next week?"

"I'd like that."

He lifted our hands and set them on his thigh just above his knee. My palm went flat against his jeans, his running over the back of mine.

He was sending shivers through me.

"Just so you know ..." I took a deep breath, realizing how hard that was getting. "I really wish I could see you sooner."

He lifted the same hand up to his mouth where he softly kissed across my knuckles and then placed us back in his lap, and we stayed like that for the rest of the drive.

When we arrived at my building, Anthony parked out front and opened my door.

"I'll walk you out," Lance said from behind me.

I climbed outside, thanking his driver again, and I heard Lance behind me as I unlocked the front entrance. Once I had the door open, he reached above my head and held it for me, and I walked into the small lobby.

"Thanks for being my fun today."

His hand slid higher on the doorframe, the heat in his stare growing. "I want more than a second date, Chloe."

The tingles had fully taken over my body. "What do you want?"

"A kiss."

I smiled as his words simmered down my throat. "That you can certainly have."

His hand moved through the air, landing on my waist, and he pulled me over to him. I loved the feeling of his fingers, the sensation of being so close, how his chest felt under my hands when they pressed against him.

His mouth didn't immediately take mine. Instead, his gaze deepened, reminding me of the intensity between us. His hands slipped under my jacket, and I could feel the heat from his fingers through my shirt.

"I've thought about this since you walked into the restaurant." His lips were almost on mine. "What you were going to feel like." He dipped in a little closer, his nose grazing my cheek, and I felt a wave of goose bumps rise across my body. "What you were going to taste like."

His words were like foreplay, and I was bending from each one, arching, anticipating what his breath would feel like when he whispered across another part of my face.

It happened when he said, "If kissing you once would be enough."

Those words lingered right above my mouth because that was where his was.

"Lance ..." My voice was so soft, and I was unable to say any more.

But I didn't need to because, within seconds, he was kissing me, his mouth moving in a way that showed me his hunger and desire, and the way his hands gripped me only emphasized it.

All I could do was take—the slow, deliberate slides of his

tongue, the grinding of his fingers into my muscles that were making me so wet. And just as I was swallowing his warm exhale, he pulled away.

My lips instantly prickled.

"I should have known," he said, his beautiful navy gaze holding mine so steadily, "kissing you once would never be enough."

TWENTY-SIX

ONCE LANCE SHUT the lobby door behind him, I took out my phone and hurried up the stairs to my apartment, calling Molly before I was even inside.

"Tell me everything," she said as she answered.

After making plans with Lance, I'd replied to her text and told her about his call. She'd made me promise I'd phone her the second I got back from our date.

"Oh. My. God."

"Chloe, why are you whispering?"

I locked our door and took off my purse, hanging it on the back of the chair. "Because I feel like he's so far inside me that he can hear what I'm about to say."

"I hope you're talking about his dick, and we're about to have a whole different conversation than the one I thought we were going to have."

I laughed as I took off my jacket. "I think we both know that didn't happen this morning."

"Then, what did? I'm mimosa'd and ready to hear it all."

My voice returned to normal as I groaned, "Molly ... that

142

man." But it didn't matter how loud I made myself; the words just weren't there. I could come up with as many adjectives as I wanted, and those wouldn't even dent him.

"Is he all kinds of wonderful?"

I took a deep breath. "In every way." I walked over to the window, pushing my shoulder into the glass, looking between the street and the tiny living room we'd shared for the last four years. "He's perfect." I glanced down at my hand, feeling the way it tingled, wondering if the feeling would ever return or if Lance would permanently cause my body to feel this way. "He kissed me, Molly ... and ... I couldn't breathe."

She sucked in her own air that I heard so clearly through the phone. "Once I saw the way he was looking at you at the bar, I knew, done-zo for you both. When are you seeing him again?"

"Ugh, not until I get back." I pushed myself away from the window and headed into my room. "Don't get me wrong; I'm excited about the trip, but the timing is just awful."

"Like, the worst ever." She laughed. "By the way, you're welcome for canceling brunch."

I made a noise that almost sounded like a snort. "Bring home pizza for dinner. Love you, bye," I said, still laughing when I disconnected the call.

In my room, I stripped out of my clothes and covered myself in a robe. I went into the bathroom to fill the tub. I dropped in some salts and oils Molly and I always kept on hand and lit the few candles we had in the room. And then I turned on some music and stepped into the water, stretching my body across the tub. My eyes closed, and I relaxed into the lavender-scented warmth.

I hadn't been soaking for more than a few minutes when I heard a text come across my phone.

I leaned out of the water and looked at the floor where I'd

placed my cell on a towel. I saw Lance's name on the screen, and a whole different kind of warmth began to fill me.

Lance: Still thinking about you.

It was as though he'd read my mind.

TWENTY-SEVEN

Me: Same. And that kiss ...

Lance: What fun is planned for tonight?
Me: Pizza with Molly. You?
Lance: Not much, I'm afraid. I'm meeting with a client this evening. You girls have a good time.

Me: I just walked by where we had brunch. It made me smile.
Lance: I like starting my day with a text from you.
Me: Just a text?
Lance: You won that round.

Lance: What time is your flight tomorrow?
Me: 8 a.m.
Lance: Looking forward to it?
Me: I'm anxious to see Vail, but I'm just as excited about our
second date.
Lance: Get there safe, so you can get home to me.
Me: ;)

Me: The drive from Denver to Vail was heaven.
Lance: I'm jealous you're breathing in all that mountain air.
Me: It's delicious.
Lance: So were you in the picture you posted from the airport
this morning.
Me: <3

Lance: Tell me there's fun and not just meetings?
Me: It's on its way—one more day, and then I can explore. But
what I've seen so far is dreamy. Almost like a fairy tale.
Lance: I bet you're smiling again.
Me: Lance, it's not because of Colorado.
Lance: I like that answer.

Me: My evening meeting was canceled. Looks like freedom is
even closer than I thought.
Lance: Cold and thirsty?
Me: Yes, and YES.

Lance: In the village, right on the corner by Checkpoint Charlie, is a candy store. They have the best hot chocolate I've ever had in my life.

Me: I'm going to walk there in a little bit. I'll let you know how yummy it is.

TWENTY-EIGHT

BACK BAY DIGITAL had booked me a hotel that was only a short walk to downtown Vail, so when Lance told me about the hot chocolate, I knew I had to go. As I approached the quaint village, there were rows of shops, small boutiques, and restaurants on both sides of the road, all built in this cute, rustic-chic design. And at the very start of it all was a security point that closely resembled the one in Berlin—at least from what I'd seen in pictures of Germany. I held my scarf tightly about the bottom of my face and hurried the rest of the way to the candy store.

"Can I help you?" an older woman asked as I walked in, a set of bells declaring my entrance. Her voice was deep from years of smoking, and she carefully moved to the edge of the counter, away from the fudge she'd been packing into a box.

"I hear you have the best hot chocolate."

She laughed, and I could tell it was out of confidence. "That's what we've been told for the last forty years. Just one?"

I nodded.

"Can I get you anything else?"

"Maybe." I walked to the counter closest to me and began scanning all the baked goods. "Let me look around."

While she went over to the coffee station in the corner, I scanned the shelves of chocolate-covered fruit and the assortment of cookies and all the decedent candies and other baked goods. By the time I reached her, she'd already set the to-go mug on the counter.

"I'll also take a piece of the white bark." It wasn't my usual dessert of choice, but the Oreo cookies that were melted into the top looked incredible.

She chose a large piece and placed it in a bag, and while she rang up my credit card, I sipped the warm drink.

"My God," I groaned against the top of the mug. Lance wasn't kidding; this was the best hot chocolate I'd had in my life. "What do you put in here?"

She set the receipt on the counter with a pen. "That's a secret I'll take to the grave."

"Whatever it is, it's magic."

She smiled, the wrinkles on her cheeks telling me that was her favorite expression. "Oh, honey, there's magic all over this town. You'll see."

"If it's anything like this, then I'm looking forward to it." I put my card into my purse and prepared myself for the cold that was about to hit me the second I stepped outside. "Thanks again."

Holding my treats, I made my way to the door. The bells chimed as I stepped onto the sidewalk, and the snow crunched under my boots, the purest, freshest air filling my lungs as I made my way past the shops.

I was taking in the details of this mountain town, comparing it to ones in Maine, when I heard, "Do you know where I can get a good hot chocolate?"

It felt like the wind had been taken out of my body, and in its place were the strongest, most consuming tingles.

My God ... *that man.*

Stopped in front of a bookstore, my entire body shaking in excitement, I turned around. An SUV was pulled up along the curb, the backseat window rolled down, and the most gorgeous face was staring at me from the center of it.

"Colorado looks beautiful on you, Chloe."

I shook my head, trying to process it all. "What are you doing here?"

I didn't wait for him to answer before I walked toward the car, and he got out at the same time, meeting me on the sidewalk.

His arms opened, and I moved into them, his body folding over mine in a hug. I instantly felt his warmth, his scent surrounding me. Each time I inhaled, I swallowed and savored more of it.

"I couldn't wait until next week to see you."

My face was buried in his chest, so I pulled it out and glanced up at him. "I can't believe you came all the way here ... for me."

His hands went to the sides of my face, his mouth moving closer to mine. "I'd go anywhere to have a second date with you."

When he locked my lips in a kiss, I knew what the woman in the candy store was talking about.

This town was filled with magic.

TWENTY-NINE

"I STILL CAN'T BELIEVE you're here," I whispered, squeezing Lance's hand as I held it in my lap in the backseat of the SUV. I'd probably said that a few times since I got in the car. I'd also stared at him the entire drive, needing the reminder that this wasn't a dream. Because it felt almost impossibly sweet that he would come all this way just for me.

"I told you I wasn't patient, and I didn't want to go another day without seeing you."

My teeth drove into my bottom lip before I said, "I really, really love that you have that trait."

He took my glove off to kiss the center of my hand, only adding to how special this moment already was.

"Thank you for being my fun today ..."

He kissed my forehead, and then he wrapped his arm around my shoulders, pulling me against his side. We stayed like that for a few minutes before the car began to slow. We turned up a narrow driveway off the main road, following the windy path up the side of the mountain until we reached a house that sat at the very end of the driveway. It was three stories of all glass that was built directly into the rock, and it was absolutely stunning.

"The fun is just starting," he said as we came to a stop.

Lance slid out first as the driver opened the door, and I followed closely behind him. With our hands entwined, we walked together to the front door.

"Wow," was what fell through my lips as I took in the view from the entrance. We were so high up; I could see for miles. Lance opened the door, and I walked inside and groaned, "Holy shit," because the scenery in here was just as spectacular.

Where the whole interior was made of glass, I could see the mountains from every angle, towering as high as the clouds. And the way the inside had been decorated, it all complemented the view rather than competing with it.

With my hand already in his, he led me toward the back of the house, and we passed through the kitchen and living room.

When we stepped outside, I gasped, "My God," my free hand covering my mouth.

Out here was a whole additional living space with couches and a firepit, TVs, a mini kitchen, and bar—all overlooking the same view. And in the center, cut into the mountain, was a swimming pool and Jacuzzi, both butted up to the edge of the cliff.

"Is this where you're staying?"

He stood behind me, his hands on my waist.

His lips weren't far from my ear when he growled, "It's where we're both staying." His grip tightened, and it felt so good. "I don't care if you stay in the guest room. I just want you here. With me."

My fingers searched for his skin, and the first piece I came across, which was his wrist, I clung to. "I don't want to go anywhere."

"Dinner in front of the fire tonight?"

Since he couldn't see my face, I turned my neck just enough that he had a view of my smile. "That sounds magical."

I held the stem of the wineglass and stretched my body over the thick wool blanket Lance had set up for us on the floor. This was where we had been since dinner, just feet away from the crackling fire, the windows surrounding us on all sides, the mountains as the backdrop.

It was paradise.

I leaned in closer where he lay inches away to get a better smell of his skin. The wood-burning scent had mixed with his cologne, creating this spicy combination. I kept my lips at the base of his throat and inhaled, savoring the smell while his hand flattened on my back, running down to the top of my ass.

"*Mmm*," he groaned. "You feel good."

His hand rose to my shoulder and slid to my waist, massaging, learning, taking his time with each spot.

I propped my head up on my elbow and said, "For date three, we can just watch a movie on the couch and eat leftover pizza and drink mediocre beer." I smiled, feeling the fire on my cheeks. "I just mean, I don't expect you to top this. You, just you, Lance Hamilton, are more than enough."

The flames reflected off his eyes, dancing inside the navy. "I'm really going to enjoy spoiling you."

I sighed, putting my palms on his cheeks, and used the pads of my fingers to trace his eyes and nose. I didn't want to just memorize his face; I wanted to know it by touch as well. When I reached his lips, I felt the fullness of the bottom one, the arch across the top, and I said so quietly, "More magic."

His hand lifted to the bottom of my ribs, a seriousness

moving into his stare. "People disappear when there's magic involved." He paused, his gaze reaching into my chest. "But I'm not going anywhere." His hand slid up my stomach, his thumb brushing just under the wire of my bra.

I let his words sink in.

They were heavy.

But in the way I wanted.

In the way I was looking for.

"Then, kiss me, Lance," I begged.

He immediately closed the gap between us, and my tongue slid over his. With each breath, my body bent into his, and with each bow, he took more of me. My hands combed his hair, tugging the dark strands, as he went to my waist, lifting my shirt, giving himself access to my bare skin.

His palms rubbed across my stomach, stalling on each hip. "Chloe," he hissed. There was desire in every syllable; both were vibrating through me. His eyes hungrily dipped down my body, and when he returned, my thighs clenched together, the tingling almost unbearable. "I fucking need you."

Four simple words, but quite possibly the sexiest sequence I'd ever heard.

"I'm yours," I breathed against his lips.

That was all he needed to hear. Suddenly, my clothes were peeled off my body, his falling on the blanket next to mine. Once we were naked, he tore his mouth away, grabbing a condom from his wallet before his attention turned back to me.

He took a second to pause, and in that moment, I felt him take all of me in.

"Chloe, you are so beautiful." Lance treated my body as though it were a contract he was reading.

With one confident, continuous movement, his fingers dipped between my legs while he tore off the top of the foil. My thighs widened, my breath panting through my lips as he circled my clit, spreading the wetness with one hand, putting the condom on with the other.

From where he'd placed me, while his two fingers were knuckle deep inside me, I watched him roll the rubber down his long, thick shaft. And all I could do was moan, "My God, you're so sexy."

Lance's body was incredible, muscles etched into tight skin, dark patches of hair across the top and bottom of his torso.

This was what a man looked like.

Before air even hit my parted lips, he took my nipple into his mouth. His fingers picked up the pace, but he didn't just move them in and out. He turned his wrist, giving me pressure from all angles before sliding to my other breast. His teeth framed that peak, his tongue flicking the end.

"Yes," I moaned, holding the tops of his shoulders, feeling the hardness under my nails while his cock positioned between my legs.

He was teasing me, bouncing against my entrance, each bump making me louder. And when I couldn't take another second, he inched his way in.

"Chloe ..." he breathed, and I knew our exhales sounded the exact same. "Damn it, you feel good."

It was an overwhelming fullness at first, so satisfying that I pulled back from his kiss and ground my head into the heavy blanket and released the longest moan. "My God."

His lips were on my throat, kissing up to my chin and down to my breasts while he drove into me. Each stroke was like one of the dips of his signature, a sweep he was an expert at making, and the most intense pleasure was spreading through me.

"Jesus, you're wet," he murmured right before he lifted me off the blanket and put me on my knees.

Once I was on all fours, he moved in behind me, and I

barely had time to take a breath before his dick was sliding back in.

"And so fucking tight." He was gripping my ass, and then he traveled up my side to my breast. He pinched my nipple, rolling it between his fingers.

I was stabbing the blanket, shouting, "*Ahhh*," as I lost control of everything that was happening inside me.

"I need you closer," he roared, his hands flattening against my stomach, and while he stayed behind me, he pulled me up to a kneeling position. His arm stayed wrapped around me, his face now in the back of my neck, and he thrust back in.

Because we were both upright, I was able to use my legs to balance my weight, and I moved with him at the same time. With each pump of my hips, that familiar spark began to flicker in my lower stomach. I reached above my head, circling my arms around his neck, eliminating all the air between us.

His hands were instantly roaming. Each spot he touched came with a new sound, a deeper, more intense rumble. I all but screamed when he grazed across my clit, my ass bucking in response.

"*Mmm*," he groaned.

I was almost there, building slowly each time he ground into me, the tingles causing my body to light on fire. "Lance ..."

He was tugging my nipple and rubbing my clit, all of the sensations working together, the peak of the build within my grasp.

"Yes," he hummed, "I can feel you coming." His fingers spread across my stomach as the first ripple tore through me. "Give it to me, Chloe."

A few more thrusts, and I was clutching him from the inside, shuddering from each wave. This wasn't just an orgasm; this was ownership of my body. And from the sounds I heard coming from him and his sharp, powerful movements, I could tell he was only seconds behind.

"You are," he moaned in my ear while his grip tightened, and as his hips reared, I felt the moment his orgasm came through in his thrust, "incredible."

I was pulsing, sensitive waves now filling me, every caress of his fingertips, causing more tremors to move over my skin. I grasped him with my hands, holding on to whatever I could reach, and I helped pump the release out of him.

"Chloe," he roared, holding me so tightly until our bodies eventually came to a standstill.

When he pulled out and removed the condom, he turned me around and hugged me against his chest. We didn't move. We stayed just like that, finding our breath again.

Several minutes passed of panting and touching and gentle kissing before he said, "How about we bring our wine into the hot tub?"

Even though I'd calmed, I was still so consumed by him; I'd forgotten we were on a blanket in front of the fire, in Colorado, surrounded by mountains.

"I didn't bring a bathing suit."

"You're cute ..." His laugh was richer than normal.

Then, I was in the air, my legs wrapped around his waist, and he was carrying me outside.

THIRTY

"I'M TAKING you to one of the most beautiful spots in Vail,"
Lance said the next morning as we started our hike.

Since I only had a day left and he wanted me to see as
much as I could, we'd gotten up early, showered, and stopped at
my hotel so I could change into warmer clothes and boots. He
took me through the village, and as we made our way toward
the trails, I found myself staring at him. I'd done the same thing
this morning when he was shaving at the sink. He'd stood there
with a thick lather on his cheeks, a white towel hanging low on
his waist. The muscles in his back shifted and tightened each
time he moved his arms.

And I'd just taken in how beautiful he was.

At one point in my life, I'd craved the feel of a rough, thick
beard scratching my cheeks. That sensation would mean Oliver
was present, and that was something I'd wanted so desperately
and couldn't have.

Those days were gone.

Now, I longed for skin that was clean and polished and
—*my God*, Colorado looked just as good on him.

His grip on my hand strengthened, and I felt it so clearly through our thick layers of gloves. Then, his pace slowed. The trees in this area were slightly denser, and we had come across a creek with a covered bridge.

"Wow," I breathed, watching the coldness stream over the rocks, shallow enough in some areas that I could see large boulders breaking through the surface. "This is positively stunning."

Orange, red, and yellow leaves were everywhere, a kaleidoscope of shapes and hues, making a canopy that blocked out most of the sky. And as the water danced down the narrow river, it almost sounded like a song.

I pulled out my phone, attempting to take a picture, and Lance said, "Not yet, trust me," and he led me onto the bridge. When we were halfway across, he added, "This is the view I want you to see."

We were inside a bridge that had a cover. There was absolutely nothing to look at in here.

Before I could ask, he brought me to the side, and he positioned me in a way where it all made sense. From this spot, through the thin, small slats of wood, I could see the windy creek until it disappeared into the trees, the bumpy mountains and the massive pines that lined them, the snow that covered it all, twinkling like diamonds from the sun.

But it was this angle, this tiny little viewing hole, that made it all even better.

"Lance, this is breathtaking."

Magic.

That word kept resurfacing, the more time I spent here.

The more time I spent with Lance.

"I have to make my way back here one day." My voice was soft even though we were the only ones on the bridge. "This can't be the only time I see this."

He stood just to the side of me, his hand on my waist, tightening when he said, "I'll bring you whenever you want."

Slowly, I put my back to one of the most amazing sights I'd ever seen to take in another that was even more magnificent. My hands went to his shoulders, a smile warming my face. "Will it always feel this way?"

It was a question I'd wanted to ask before, in a different place and a much different time. But I had known always wasn't possible for Oliver and me.

That wasn't the case now.

An intense, fierce tingle moved through me just as his mouth touched mine. "I don't know ..." He went in for another kiss and said, "I've never felt this way before."

THIRTY-ONE

IT WASN'T until after seven when I was finally able to drag myself out of the office for the night. I went to the train station, taking the T for four stops and then walking just a few blocks to Lance's building. It was a commute I now knew extremely well; since I'd returned from Colorado six months ago, I had been staying at his place almost every night.

"Good evening, Miss Kennedy," the doorman said as I approached Lance's high-rise in the Back Bay.

"It's a cold one out there." I shivered, hurrying the remainder of the distance and stepping through the door he'd opened and into the lobby. "Thank you."

"You're most welcome." He shut it behind me and followed me to the elevator, pressing the button for Lance's floor. I was more than capable; it was just the process here. "Have a good night," he replied as the door closed.

I watched the numbers on the screen light up, rising the eighteen stories until it stopped at the very top.

Each time I came here, my heart thumped in my chest, the anticipation increasing as fast as the elevator. And when the door slid open, with the thought of seeing him the only thing on my mind, a smile would move across my face.

I rushed through the door and into the entryway, where I began to take off my coat, leaving it with my purse on a chair not far from the entrance. Once I rounded the corner, the space opening into a giant living room, I saw him. He was lying on one of the leather couches, watching the news, wearing jeans and a starched, untucked button-down and bare feet—his relaxed look.

And I found it so sexy.

"My beautiful baby ..." he groaned when he spotted me.

I would never get used to the way this man looked at me, like we were still at the bar, meeting for the first time, and he wanted to devour me as though he'd never tasted me.

I left my heels on the floor and climbed on top of him. "I missed you today."

His hands went to my back, warming it before lowering to my ass. "Kiss me."

I pressed my mouth to his, loving how the flavor of Lance had become so familiar; I craved it during our moments apart. How the touch of his lips usually made the stress of work vanish entirely.

But as I pulled away, Lance studied my eyes and said, "Talk to me about it."

He knew. He saw it.

I sighed, giving him a few gentle kisses on his cheeks until I knew he wouldn't let me avoid his question any longer, and I pushed myself up and sat next to him on the edge of the couch. "Molly is moving in with Marshall." I looked at my hands, seeing the bracelet she had given me for my birthday last year. "I knew it was coming, and we've been preparing for it, but it's a lot of change." I swallowed, and it hurt so badly; I tried to stop myself from tearing up. "I'm just really going to miss living with her."

He was leaning up now, spreading his arms. "Come here."

I fell into them, feeling the closeness as he tightened around me. "I know this probably sounds silly," I admitted. "I mean, I spend most nights here, and she's at Marshall's. It's certainly not the end of a friendship or anything like that, but we've been roommates since the day I moved to Boston, and Molly is the only family I have here."

He tucked a chunk of my hair behind my ear. "She's your best friend; I understand why this is hard on you." He kept his hand on my neck, holding it while he rubbed the bottom of my cheek. "But I want you to know something, Chloe." His navy stare narrowed, and that was when I saw all the emotion. "Molly isn't the only family you have in this city." His words simmered in my chest, flowing around my heart in a circle. "You have me."

I hadn't even considered how my statement could affect him. Over the past several months, he had become one of the biggest parts of my life.

I put my hand on top of his, linking our fingers. "I know. You make me feel that every single day."

He kept his hand on my face, holding it tighter than before, and I released his fingers when he said, "When's your lease up?"

"Not for another two months."

"What are you thinking?"

I'd been weighing the options in my head since Molly and I chatted about it over lunch, and I'd come to a conclusion.

"I'm going to give our landlord his sixty-day notice next week, and I'll start searching for a studio apartment."

His hand dropped to my thigh, fingers spreading across the

width of it. "Don't rush. You can move in here until you find a place or stay permanently, which is what I'd prefer."

I felt my eyes widen.

His hand returned to my face like he knew I needed it there.

Because this conversation didn't feel real.

It felt like a fairy tale.

One I wanted to live in forever.

I found his hand again, needing the hills of his knuckles and the heat from his skin. "You want to wake up next to me every morning?" I had so many questions; it just felt important to start here.

His stare didn't waver, and I felt it all the way in my toes.

"More than anything."

My eyes welled, the first drip only making it a hair past my eye before he caught it.

"So would I," I whispered. Another tear fell; I was unable to stop them at this point. I threw my arms around his neck, hugging him to me.

While I squeezed, I glanced over his shoulder at the condo that was soon going to become my home. I had no idea what that would be like, but I knew Lance would find a way to make my life fit in seamlessly here.

"Tell me what night of the week you want to see Molly, and I'll make it happen."

I unraveled my arms, needing to see his face. "How are you going to schedule girls' night?"

He smiled, and it was more devious than I'd ever seen from him. "I'm Marshall's boss, Chloe. That won't be difficult."

My head tilted back, and I laughed so hard. "My God, that was hot."

He was just as loud as me, and when we finally quieted, I stared at him, a smile still covering our faces.

"I'm so ridiculously nuts over you."

"Baby ..." He held me in his arms again, and I could feel his heart, how fast it was beating, how it was matching my own. "Remember something, Chloe"—his lips pressed into the top of my head—"I will fix anything for you; you just have to come to me."

I squeezed his shirt into my fist, inhaling the scent of power that came off his skin. "I believe that." I took another breath, feeling the stress leave my body. "And I promise you, I will."

THIRTY-TWO

MOST NIGHTS, Lance and I kept the shades open when we went to bed so we could wake to the light of the city. Tonight was no exception; it was just still dark out when my eyes flicked open. But the moon and adjacent buildings gave enough of a glow to show me the ripples in the white comforter as Lance moved beneath it, his hands locking on the sides of my body.

"Oh God." I quivered.

The T-shirt I was wearing was his, and he moved it aside to kiss across my breasts and down my stomach, continuing to go lower until I felt him breathing against my entrance. The first swipe of his tongue was over my panties. It was just a tease but enough pressure to make me moan.

My head pushed into the fluffiness of the pillow, my knees bent, and I hissed, "Lance," as he moved an inch lower and teased me again. I loved that when it came to my body, he was never in a hurry.

He kissed the outside of my thighs, biting, tasting my skin before he gradually moved the material and kissed each bit of skin he revealed until I was fully exposed. "My queen," he

166

groaned as he licked my clit, pausing at the top, breathing against me. He was still for just a moment before his tongue began to flick back and forth, his two fingers plunging inside of me.

"*Yesss*," I breathed, and I clung to the pillow under my head, concentrating on the way he was devouring me.

His fingers combined with the friction from his mouth, and the build was there almost instantly. And that was what he wanted; I could tell by the ferocity he used to lick me.

"Lance ..." My body was on fire, holding on to this sensation for as long as I could. "Fuck."

He was moving even faster, and breath was panting through my lips, my thighs becoming so numb that I couldn't hold them apart. His tongue began moving from side to side, his fingers grinding into me deeply, and I couldn't fight the build any longer.

With each thrust of his hand, each swipe from his mouth, a new wave of pleasure burst through me. And my hips rode out every one, bucking against his face, earning myself longer, fatter licks. Before he pulled away, he softly kissed my clit, and then he worked his way up my body, pausing to give each nipple a kiss. Resting next to me on the bed, he pulled me onto his chest.

"Good morning." I giggled, wrapping my leg over his.

"I had a dream about you." He kissed the top of my head. "And when I opened my eyes, there was only one thing on my mind."

I turned my face, kissing the spot where my cheek had been. "Feel free to start every morning that way."

He laughed. "You're forgetting, you usually get up before me."

"Damn it." I smiled, tracing my fingers around the hair on his chest. "How much of you do I get today? Or are you spending most of it at the office?"

"All of me ..." The little light showed me the curve of his lip, how it was growing across his face. "All day." His hand moved lower until he was gripping my ass. "And all night."

I locked our gazes. "You can have *anything* you want right now. What is it?"

He didn't hesitate when he said, "I just had it."

Eight months, this man had been mine, and he still continued to blow my mind.

"What's your next pick?"

His fingers went to my neck, holding it there for a few seconds. "To have you all day."

I lifted his hand higher so I could kiss it, planning the blow job I was going to give him in the shower after I fed him. "Done," I said. "Now, how about some breakfast?"

"I'd like that."

I kissed his cheek, climbed off the bed, and said, "Meet me downstairs in a few minutes," on my way to our bathroom.

Once I finished washing up, I stuck my hair in a messy bun and slid on a pair of yoga pants and a tank top and slippers before I headed for the kitchen. There was a loaf of French bread on the counter that I'd picked up from the market yesterday. I cut it into thick slices, dipping it in an egg bath and setting it on the buttered griddle.

I was just placing the last piece on the stove when Lance came up behind me, circling his hands around my stomach, holding me just like that.

"Smells delicious." He kissed the back of my neck. "Do you want coffee?"

"I would love some."

While he went over to the brewing station, I flipped the bread. And while I waited for that side to brown, I grabbed some fresh strawberries, blueberries, and blackberries from the fridge and added the fruit to the plate, eventually putting a few pieces of French toast on each one. I sprinkled cinnamon over the bread, and I set the plates on the table along with some heated syrup. Then, I took a seat next to Lance at the bar.

He lifted his fork and broke off a bite full. "This smells incredible."

I took a drink of my coffee, my eyes briefly closing while I swallowed. No matter how hard I tried, I couldn't get mine to taste like his. "*Mmm.*"

My lids opened just as he was smiling, popping a few strawberries into his mouth before he said, "You surprised me today."

"Yeah?"

"With the pitch you have coming up next week, I assumed you'd be at the office all weekend."

I shrugged, taking my first bite of fruit. "I should be there. I just don't have it in me."

"Anything you want to talk about?"

I took in a forkful of the French toast. "I'm not happy there anymore." I paused, gathering my thoughts. "You know traveling was a part of my job that I loved, but since I've gotten promoted and this position is grounded, I just feel extremely stuck."

"I had a feeling." His hand was on my back, rubbing across my shoulder blades.

I took a deep breath, setting my fork down. "It's the only job I know; it's going to take me a second before I'm ready to leave it."

He turned my chair to face him more, and our knees touched. "Take all the time you want; there's no reason to rush this."

"Promise me something?" I wasn't looking forward to this part of the conversation. When he nodded, I added, "Promise you won't pull any strings, and you'll let me do this on my own?"

It was an offer he made all the time and one of the sweetest things he could ever do, but I couldn't accept his help. My career was my own, and I wanted it to remain that way.

He nodded. "I'll only step in if you ask me to."

I reached across the small space, my hand going to his cheek. He hadn't shaved yet, and the stubble felt so foreign on him, but his gaze was one I wanted to live in.

Forever.

"I love you," I breathed.

We didn't say it constantly; he wasn't that kind of man.

We said it during the important times.

Like this one.

"I love you, baby." He brought my fingers up to his mouth and kissed them.

I got off the stool, and I hugged him.

And neither of us said another word.

We didn't have to.

THIRTY-THREE

"WHAT DO YOU THINK?" Lance asked as he wrapped his arm over my shoulders, pulling me closer to him.

We were in the backseat of an SUV that had just picked us up from the Sarasota-Bradenton Airport. And as we drove with the windows down, the sun warming my face, I got the faintest hint of coconut.

"I think we should stay forever."

It had been a colder fall than normal, and Boston had left my body completely chapped, but I could already feel the humidity moisturizing my skin.

"You know I can make that happen."

I heard the smile in his words and snuggled into him harder but kept my eyes on the window. From what I had seen so far, Sarasota was beautiful, a city that hugged the gulf with a skyline full of buildings that shimmered from the ocean. "I'm in palm tree heaven."

His lips went to my cheek, and he left them there. "Florida smells so good on you."

I turned to give him a quick kiss, staying nuzzled in his

chest until the driver slowed, pulling into a narrow, almost hidden path. There was so much greenery; it was hard to see where we were headed, but after a very short drive, the road opened into a large courtyard, and in the back was the house. The two-story contemporary home was made of the most stunning white stucco and blue glass.

The only thing Lance had told me about this trip was the town we were coming to and that we were staying a week. The rest was a surprise, which was my favorite way to travel with him. But what I knew about this wonderful man was that there was something special to him about Sarasota, or he never would have brought me here, and I couldn't wait to see what it was.

Once the driver opened my door, I climbed out, and Lance's hand immediately clasped mine before he brought me to the entrance, pressing several buttons that unlocked the door. It was only open a few inches, just enough to peek inside, when my eyes widened, air quickly filling my lungs.

"Oh my God, Lance."

He continued to open the door even more, revealing a sight that couldn't be more breathtaking than the one I was staring at.

"Welcome to Siesta Key," he said, his hands now on my waist.

I couldn't look at him. I was too fixated on the scenery. "This is ..." I started, but then my voice faded as my feet took me deeper inside while I searched for a way to put this all into words.

The massively high ceiling and all the glass created a giant, open space that was centered around the view of the most spectacular beach I'd ever seen in my life. And this home showed that view from every angle—the sky, the horizon, the ocean, and sand. From every place I stood, whether it was in the kitchen, living room, or the incredible pool deck, I could see every detail of it. Some places were indescribable. Vail was close, and so was their ranch in Montana, but Sarasota was the top.

"Paradise," I finally whispered when I felt his hands again. "This is the best one."

I tangled my fingers in his. "We definitely agree on that."

And while he held me, we stayed silent, listening to the sound of the waves, staring at the water and sky and the way the two almost clashed because they were such vibrant but different shades of blue.

He kissed the top of my head, and he left his lips there, breathing me in. "Happy two-year anniversary, baby."

It was the third night of our stay, the evening of our actual anniversary, and Lance had hired a private chef to prepare dinner. Once we got dressed, he took me onto the pool deck, where a table had been set up with candles and flowers and all white linens.

The sun was just starting to lower in the sky, the blue changing to different shades of pink and purple, the water really beginning to darken to black.

"Is this real?" I paused in front of my chair, unable to take a seat yet. The sky couldn't be more breathtaking, but seeing the beach and ocean underneath it and the spread he had put together for us was an unforgettable combination.

"I knew you would love it here."

He gave me the softest kiss, and helped me into my chair, pushing me closer to the table. He took the seat across from me, smiling as he placed his napkin on his lap. We'd been in the sun nonstop since we arrived, and he looked so delicious with a tan.

"I'll never get tired of seeing the amazement on your face when you witness something for the first time."

I felt my eyes glimmer as his words passed through me.

So many more firsts.

And these were because of him.

"I'm so curious ... why has it taken you so long to bring me here?" I took a quick glance at the horizon, the pink turning to magenta. "We've traveled all over." I grinned as I thought of all the trips, the weekends skiing in Maine and the ones in Utah and Colorado, weeks spent in Europe and the Caribbean during the holidays. "We've even been to South Beach." I then gazed at the house, taking in all the glass and white and beauty. "Seems like, aside from Vail, it would have been one of the first places we visited, especially if it's one you love the most."

With an expression on his face I wasn't able to read, he rose from his chair, lifting his champagne glass before he walked over to me. I grabbed my drink as well and then clasped my hand in his. And silently, he walked me onto the sand. The way the property was nestled on the corner, this section of beach had more privacy than the others, so it felt like we were all alone.

We were halfway to the water, the sky filling with bright orange tiger stripes, the sun getting closer to the edge of the ocean, when Lance began to slow. And when our eyes connected, I knew I was finally going to get my answer.

"When I was in elementary school, my parents bought a house on this beach," he started, his voice so gentle and smooth. "Whenever we came here, my father changed. He relaxed and turned into this calm version of himself that we rarely ever saw. I was too young to understand, but as I got older, I felt it—the pressure to get good grades, to pass the bar, to take over the responsibility of my family's legacy. And I found, every time I came here, I was doing the same thing as my father."

When he paused, I squeezed his hand, and there was the tiniest hint of a smile on his lips right before he kissed me. It was tender, no deeper than a breath, but his scent and presence and mouth took ahold of me. He pulled back just a few inches, and his navy stare was just as powerful.

"The reason I never brought you here is because it's taken almost a year to build this house, and now, it's finally ours."

I scanned his eyes, my chest filling with an immense number of tingles. "Ours?"

He reached for my cheek, holding it so steady. "Our place ... our home." He brought my fingers up to his lips, kissing every knuckle.

I couldn't breathe. His gaze was so intense, how it was locked on mine, holding it in a way that felt completely different. It deepened, something I hadn't thought was possible, and he slowly brought my hand down to the small bit of space between our bodies. Once he held it there for a few seconds, he took a step back and gradually got on his knee.

"Oh my God," I breathed, my free hand going over my mouth.

"Chloe ..." He looked up at me from the sand and reached into his pocket, pulling out a small black velvet box. "Even after I dropped every one of my faults on you, you never tried to change who I was. You've always accepted the impatient, demanding man that I am, and you haven't fought this lifestyle that I dragged you into when I know you would still probably prefer a much less lavish one."

Tears stung my eyes, and they dripped, nothing I could do to stop them.

"Baby, you haven't left my mind since the moment I met you."

I felt his emotion in every inhale, I saw it, and it was grasping my heart, melting it.

"Everything in my life has led me to this moment, and now, I'm asking you to make me the happiest man in the world." He

175

opened the box, showing the most exquisite diamond wedged inside. "Chloe, please be my wife."

I swallowed, squeezing his hand so tightly, tears dripping over my lips as I said, "Yes." I sucked in a breath of air. "Oh my God, yes."

There were too many tears filling my eyes to see the details of the ring as he slid it on my finger, but I felt its heaviness and the foreign sensation of the metal. And once it was all the way on, he rose and pulled me into his arms, lifting me in the air.

"I love you so much," he hummed in my ear, circling us over the sand.

"I love you." A whole different wave passed through me, like the ones I heard just behind us, but these were slamming inside my chest as I processed what this moment really meant. "Lance"—my fingers raked through the back of his hair —"you're going to be my husband."

His lips hovered in front of mine as he growled, "For the rest of my life, you'll be my queen."

We came to a standstill, and he kissed me.

"Molly!" I shouted as she answered my call while I was rushing to the bathroom. "He asked me to marry him. We're engaged."

"GAH!" Her scream was even louder than mine. "I'm crying. I can't even—I just can't. Babe, you're getting married."

My feet were wet and sandy, and I was trying not to slip on the pavers around the pool.

Our pool.

"Molly"—the emotion was back in my voice—"it was so perfect. In every single way."

"Where is the ring, woman? And why aren't you blowing up my phone with a picture of it?"

"Because I'm peeing, and I only have a second before I rejoin Lance for dinner. Later tonight, I'll send you everything. I just didn't want you to hear the news through text."

"Oh, Chloe ..." There was a seriousness in her tone that made me pause, a sound that reminded me of a time so long ago. "He's the one."

"I know." I rushed straight into the pool bath. "Now, we have a wedding to plan, maid of honor."

"You'll have a subscription to every bridal blog in your inbox before you return from Florida," she shrieked. "And I literally just planned your bachelorette party while you were flushing the toilet."

I laughed so hard; I almost snorted. "God, I fucking love you."

THIRTY-FOUR

LANCE SMILED at me from across the table, his hand circled around a ginger old-fashioned, a drink he only ordered when we came to our favorite Peruvian restaurant in downtown Sarasota. There was a plate of wahoo and tuna ceviche in between us that we'd been picking at while we sipped our second round of cocktails.

Each time he shifted his fingers over the glass, his gold wedding band caught the light and shimmered. The ring was thicker than mine but identical, something I'd insisted, instead of the diamond band he'd wanted me to get. The four carats he'd proposed with in my engagement ring—that he'd designed himself—was more than enough bling for me.

He had been just as hands-on with our wedding.

With an extremely long list of attendees he had to invite, he was very specific on what he wanted to feed them, what they drank, and how they were entertained. A Hamilton wedding had to be memorable.

Exactly one year after he proposed, we exchanged vows in front of five hundred people at the iconic Boston Public

Library, followed by a party in the Bates Hall, a room on the same property, that not a single attendee would ever forget.

The wedding had been very much for Lance, but the two weeks we'd spent on the Amalfi Coast of Italy for our honeymoon couldn't have made me happier.

Now that we'd reached our six-month wedding anniversary, it wasn't the date that had brought us to Florida.

This time, it was because of me.

As my husband looked at me, even his eyes were smiling back. "I'm so proud of you," he said. "You've worked so goddamn hard for this."

My cheeks reddened, my grin as large as his. "Thank you, my love."

After several promotions at Back Bay Digital, the company still hadn't felt like the right fit, so I'd started my search, and it had taken a while. But, as of three days ago, I'd accepted a job with an online travel booking company to work in their digital marketing division. The position was in management, where I'd have my own team with a higher title and salary than I'd had before. There was an opportunity for growth and travel. It was everything I wanted.

Once the paperwork had been signed, Lance had said he wanted to celebrate, and this was where I'd chosen for us to come.

Our place.

I lifted my Prosecco and took a drink. "Let's take the boat out tomorrow," I suggested. "Maybe dock in St. Pete and have lunch."

We'd only landed a few hours ago, and after getting settled at home, this was our first stop.

He smiled. "You just want to see the bridge."

The Sunshine Skyway Bridge, what we would have to pass under to get to St. Petersburg, was one of my favorite sites in the area. Flying over it on the way to Sarasota was just as pretty, but being close to it, the arches and grandness of its structure, was just amazing.

He reached across the table, putting his hand on mine, as I said, "I can't get enough of it."

"That's what makes me happy." His thumb rubbed over my knuckles. "But we were just here a few weeks ago. Now that you have a little time off before you start, I was hoping you would want to go to Europe, maybe London."

"London?" I said, laughing. "You've never mentioned that you want to go back there."

He took a bite of the fish. "I haven't been since I lived there. I'd like to see it with adult eyes."

Lance knew about Oliver, how I'd lost my virginity to him, that he was my first love, and that we'd dated throughout the semester, my heart torn in half when it was time for me to leave.

It wasn't that I was avoiding the city altogether or that I didn't want to make adult memories.

I just wanted to keep that part of my life separate from the one I was living now.

"I bet that would make an unbelievable guys' trip," I said, both of my hands now surrounding his. "In fact, I think you should take Marshall and the boys there before the end of the year because we know it's only a matter of seconds before Molly gets pregnant again. Then, Marshall will be on a strict no-drinking-until-Molly-can-again policy, and he won't be any fun at all."

"Jesus, he's a patient man."

We laughed.

"I'll bring Molly to Nashville, which she's been talking about visiting anyway now that little May is six months old."

"I'll text my assistant in the morning to have her start working on it."

I didn't know why, but I felt relief.

I reached for my drink, finishing the rest of the glass. When I set it down, Lance's eyes were on me, and I said, "You're about to make Molly the happiest girl; she's so desperate for a vacation."

He said nothing; he just smiled.

PART THREE

Even if it hurts.

THIRTY-FIVE

"HEY!" I said to my husband when he answered my call. "You wouldn't happen to have a few free seconds for me to pop in, would you?"

I knew it was a long shot, but I had to try. The news I wanted to share with him wasn't something I wanted to say over the phone, and I didn't know if I could wait until tonight to tell him.

I heard the sound of his keyboard, and he replied, "If you can come right now, I do."

I grabbed my jacket and purse and waved to my assistant on my way out my door. "I'll be there in five."

"I'll see you soon, baby," he said and disconnected the call.

Having left Back Bay Digital eight months ago, my new office was only two blocks from his, and several days a week, we would meet for lunch.

But food had nothing to do with why I was going there today.

I was greeted by the doorman the moment I arrived at his

building, and once I was inside, I immediately went over to the reception desk to check in.

"Good morning, Mrs. Hamilton," Chelsea said, entering my name into the computer. "Can I get you anything to drink?"

"I'm fine, thank you."

I waited to be buzzed through and continued to the elevator, joining several of the associates inside, seeing one of them had already pushed the button for Lance's floor.

"Nice to see you again, Mrs. Hamilton." One of the women grinned.

I didn't know if I would ever get used to being called that, and I really preferred just my first name, but Lance's family had set a precedent many years ago, and I wasn't going to be the one to change things.

"You too, Cindy," I replied.

"Great shot from the Bruins game," one of the men said to me from the corner, regarding the picture Lance had posted of us last weekend when Boston played in Tampa.

Now that we were spending so much time in Florida, he had purchased us season tickets.

"Who were you rooting for?" one of the paralegals asked.

The elevator came to a stop, the door sliding open.

Standing in a small space full of Bruins fans, I responded carefully, "I'll never tell," and I laughed.

"Don't blame you." One of them cackled back.

I waved good-bye and turned in the direction of Lance's office, his door open when I arrived.

His eyes instantly found me. "My beautiful wife."

I shut his door, and as I reached him, he turned in his chair. I stood between his legs, my hands resting on his shoulders. The scent of power filled my nose while I took in his solid-weave dark gray wool suit that looked so incredibly sexy on him.

His hands dropped to my ass, pulling me closer to kiss him. "Did you miss me?"

As I dragged my lips off his, heat moved across my face, and so did my grin. "Of course, but I'm here because I have news." I reached for the coffee on his desk. "*Mmm*," I moaned. "You always have the best."

"I'll have Chelsea bring you one."

I shook my head. "I don't want any more." I took another drink from it, and I heard him chuckle as I brought the mug to the front of his desk where I sat in one of the chairs. "Major stuff happened today at work."

"Sounds like it." His eyes dipped to my mouth. "Tell me."

I took a deep breath, using my free hand to grip the edge of his thick mahogany desk. "Management called me in for a meeting and offered me a promotion." His expression was a reward in itself, and I kept going, "Now that we've been purchased by International Bookings, they're looking to put together a small team that will merge the US and European markets into a global brand."

"And my baby was selected." He rubbed the side of his clean-shaven face, his smile never falling once. "Chloe, this is your dream." He licked across his bottom lip. "What you've wanted since the day I met you."

My chest heaved, goose bumps spreading over my skin. "But there's a catch, and it's a big one."

"I figured."

"The position would be a six-month contract, requiring me to stay at their headquarters in Amsterdam every two weeks." Before he could say anything, I added, "This is a ton of travel, and it would be a significant amount of time away from home. It's a decision I want us to make together."

He waited as though he wasn't sure if I was done speaking. Then, he said, "Get over here," and held out his arms.

The love I had for this man was flowing as fast as my blood when I pushed myself out of my seat and hurried over to where his arms circled around me.

"I'm so proud of you." He held me tighter, his face going into my neck, his hand palming the back of my head. "You took a big leap with this company. I know it terrified you and how hard it was. But, baby, look at how it's paid off."

I gripped the back of his neck, feeling the stiffness of his gel and how it glued his dark locks in place. "I got through it because of you."

He continued to hold me but leaned back so he could see my face. "I know you want this."

I swallowed, feeling the rush move through my chest. "I do, but I want us more."

He clutched my face, holding it tightly. "You can have both, Chloe." He gently pressed his lips to mine. "It's only for six months. I'll schedule my travel for the weeks you're gone, putting us home at the same time." One of his hands dropped to my red hair, a long curl circling around the back of his palm. "We'll make it work."

I took a deep breath, feeling the tightness take control of my excitement. "But what about our plan?"

I hadn't stopped taking my birth control, but we'd been discussing when I should, and we agreed the time was getting much closer, possibly even by the first of the year.

That was only two months away.

And I was ready to start a family with him.

When his eyes turned serious, I grasped the fingers he was still holding against my face. "As much as I want you to take this job, it's going to be hard, watching you leave every month." He slowly exhaled, his lips briefly touching mine. "But if our child was inside you and I had to go that long without touching you or kissing your belly, I don't know if I could handle you getting on that plane."

The rawness of his honesty stabbed right through me, and it was pulling at my throat. "Lance ..."

His grip caused my voice to fade out, and he said, "After your contract, we'll revisit the idea of having a baby."

With tears in my eyes, I threw my arms around his neck and whispered, "I already miss you."

THIRTY-SIX

AMSTERDAM WAS ART, and it was everywhere I looked. It was a city built around canals with the simplest yet most exquisite small bridges, buildings with dark brick facades, and charming houseboats parked right in the waterway.

I'd never been to another place like this, and I absolutely loved it.

Since I'd booked my own travel, I had given myself a two-day cushion. I wanted to get a feel of the city, get acclimated to the hotel I would be living in every month, and get over the jet lag so I had my bearings on my first day of work.

The alarm went off at six, and I grabbed my phone from the nightstand and called Lance.

"Good morning, baby," he said as he answered.

The six-hour time difference would make phone calls challenging, but he didn't usually go to bed before one.

"I was hoping you wouldn't be asleep yet."

"Are you going for a walk this morning?"

I turned on the light and climbed out of bed, stretching my body as I rose. "Getting ready to go right now." I yawned.

"Just be careful."

He could make me smile, even this early in the morning, at how protective he was. Part of the reason I had chosen this hotel was its proximity to the office and city center and because it was in one of the safest areas, which Lance had insisted on as well. Not that it mattered because he still would have worried.

"You know I am," I replied.

"Excited for your first day?"

I went to the dresser, taking out my warmest pair of yoga pants and a fleece. "Very, and I'm anxious to get started. I was reviewing some of their programs last night, and I'm loaded with ideas."

"You're going to blow them away."

The grin still hadn't left my face as I zipped the jacket up to my neck and slipped a headband on. "I'm certainly going to try."

He was quiet for a few seconds, and then I heard a short laugh. "You haven't checked your texts yet, have you?"

"No, hang on." I was standing in front of the sink, getting ready to brush my teeth, and I pulled the phone away from my ear. I clicked on my messages, seeing one had come in from Lance and several from Molly. I tapped on his first, and a picture popped up. "Oh my God."

This was the cutest photo I had ever seen of my husband. He was standing by the window in his office with the most beautiful smile on his face, holding May in his arms, pointing at the glass like he was showing her something in the distance. Her little hand was gripping his lapel, and she looked so tiny against him.

"Molly brought her in to see Marshall, and I got to steal her for a little bit."

He claimed he wasn't a patient man, but that was all I saw

when I looked at this shot and how he was going to make the most incredible father.

"I'm melting right now."

He chuckled even harder. "I knew you would be."

I glanced down at the sink, the water running, my hand gripping the edge of the porcelain while the other held the phone to my ear. "I miss you so much." My voice was soft, and it wasn't because I had just woken up.

Despite how exciting this was, it was hard, too, and it would only get harder, the longer I was here.

"Go have a great first day at work, baby. I'll call you when I wake up so I can hear how it's going. Now, go enjoy your walk."

I took a breath, sticking my toothbrush under the stream. "I love you," I said just as softly.

"I love you more."

I waited for him to hang up before I zipped my phone in my pocket and finished getting ready.

One thing I'd learned during my travels was that the wind felt the same in every city, and it hit my face the second I stepped onto the sidewalk. I pulled my scarf a little tighter, and I began to move, stretching my muscles, feeling the hardness of the pavement under my feet.

There wasn't a nook I hadn't explored around our condo in Boston and our house in Florida because every morning, I walked at least four miles. But here, everything was new, and I wanted to see every inch.

Weaving down the sides of the canals, I explored some bridges I hadn't been on yet and a pathway that led to a park. There was a market that butted up against the grass, and I went there next. Vendors were just starting to stock their booths with fresh cheeses and breads, produce and protein. But it was the tulips that captured me. They came in colors I'd never seen before, a tangerine that had the richness of a sunrise, an eggplant-colored one, even ones that were the darkest black.

When I neared the halfway mark, I headed back to the hotel where I showered and got dressed and met my coworkers in the lobby. Since they were staying at the same place, we walked to work together. By now, the sidewalks were packed with suits and tourists, giving Amsterdam a much busier and different feel than the rawness I'd felt early this morning.

Once our small group checked in at reception, we were brought up to a conference room on the top floor of the building where we were going to meet with the management team. And because we'd been given an itinerary ahead of time, I knew a tour of the building was going to follow where we would then be introduced to the rest of the staff.

After a few minutes of sitting at the long, oval table, I checked the time on my phone. It was still early with several minutes to spare, so I excused myself and went to the restroom.

As I came out of the narrow stall, I fixed my tight pencil skirt and adjusted the button-down I'd tucked into it. When I got to the sink, I washed my hands and checked my makeup to make sure it hadn't smudged or that my curls weren't too badly windblown. Satisfied with what I saw, I tossed the paper towel, and I left the restroom, walking toward the conference room.

There were offices on both sides of the hallway, and I peeked into the doorways as I passed them, trying to get a sense of the people who worked here and the environment we were coming into.

I was halfway to the door when I heard, "Sweet girl," spoken from somewhere behind me.

But it was ...

Those words.

That accent.

His voice.

Oh God.

My feet immediately stopped.

My breath hitched in the back of my throat.

I didn't know if being in Europe was triggering memories of London and it was causing my mind to play tricks on me or if I'd really heard him.

But I was in the Netherlands, not England.

I was—

"Chloe," the same voice said.

Now, there was no question in my mind.

If there were a wall, I would have gripped it with both hands, but I was in the center of a hallway that was made almost entirely of glass.

My mouth was watering, my hands clenching.

I tried to take a breath, and I slowly turned around.

My bones locked.

My muscles contracted.

And all the air left me when I said, "Oliver ..."

THIRTY-SEVEN

ONCE I SAID Oliver's name, my voice faded out, my throat so tight that I was unable to say any more. If there were words in my head, they were gone.

Because I couldn't even ...

Breathe.

The tightness in the back of my throat only got worse as I watched him walk down the hallway, and with each step, memories of our time together began to resurface.

Things I hadn't thought of in a long time.

And as I watched his face, it was like seeing a ghost.

Someone my heart had said good-bye to six years ago.

Someone I never intended on seeing again.

"My God." He laughed when he was only a few steps away, pushing the sleeves of his sweater up to his elbows. "Chloe fucking Kennedy, you haven't changed one bit." He held out his arms. "Get your arse over here."

And then it all came back to me—every reason I had fallen in love with this man. And each one tumbled faster, the momentum causing my heart to shake as he closed the distance between us.

"Oliver Bennett ..." I whispered right before his fingers landed on my shoulder, and he used it to pull me toward him.

His face bent to mine, his beard brushing my cheek as he kissed it.

The sensation of his whiskers on my skin was the strangest feeling, and I could recall it so easily. And with the closeness came a whiff of his scent, the leather that I remembered so well.

And the lust.

My lungs constricted as he pulled back and said, "How long has it been?" His brows rose as his eyes took their time looking around my face. "I was just graduating, so that was—"

"Six years ago," I said, finding my voice.

Age had suited him well. There were tiny wrinkles at the corners of his eyes and deeper ones in his forehead. His beard was trimmed shorter, more professional, but he still had that careless, thrown-together look.

"That's right," he said. "Six years ago. My God, you look stunning, Chloe."

I knew his compliment was showing on my face, so my stare lowered until it landed on his hand, searching for a shiny band on his finger.

I didn't see one.

"I can't believe you're here," I said as I gazed back up.

He laughed, and it was a sound I remembered so well.

His left hand went onto his head, where he tugged the longer strands, and I was positive there was no ring on it. But it was also when I noticed a woman walking by with several pads of paper in her arms, and it reminded me that the meeting was going to start any second.

"Oliver ..." I breathed, searching once again for words that just weren't coming to me. So, I pointed over my shoulder at the conference room door and said, "I have to go. I'll ..."

"We'll catch up." He smiled.

I didn't know what to say, so I put my hand in the air, trying to make it somewhat resemble a wave, and I turned around. And for the slightest of seconds, it felt like I was in the airport all over again. My heels felt like hundred-pound weights, my legs weren't stable, my breath released in short pants as I made my way down the hallway.

But I rushed because I was so desperate to get back in my chair, to have something to hold on to. When I got into the conference room, I dropped myself into the stiff leather chair and squeezed the armrests, trying to find my breath again.

"Did I miss anything?" I asked my coworker sitting next to me.

"A woman came in right before you and said they'd be just a few more minutes."

I nodded, and to keep my mind busy, I reached inside my purse and took out my phone. As I held it in my hands, I clicked on the first social media app my finger landed on, and I found myself typing Oliver's name into the search. Just as the results came on the screen, I heard the sound of shoes hitting the floor and voices, and I glanced up as several people were walking into the conference room.

I quickly put my phone back in my bag, and as I was looking toward the door again, the man coming through it caught eyes with me.

And it was Oliver.

Oh God.

"Good morning," the woman standing directly across from me said while a few other men and women spread out around her. After a quick count, I saw there were six in total while the four of us sat on the other side. "On behalf of the management team at International Bookings, I would like to welcome you."

My eyes gradually shifted over all six of their faces.

But only one of the managers was staring back.

And that was Oliver.

THIRTY-EIGHT

"CHLOE," I heard Oliver say, my body stiffening as I stepped into the hallway.

I searched until I found him a few paces away, leaning against the glass wall of an adjacent office. As our eyes locked, I reminded myself to fill my lungs.

I turned to my coworkers, who were all coming out of the conference room behind me, and said, "I'll meet you guys downstairs in a few minutes."

As the three of them headed to the first-floor cafeteria for lunch, I made my way over to Oliver. He had several notebooks in his hands, which he'd used during the meeting, the sleeves of his sweater pushed up again.

"I still can't believe you're here," I said, joining him by the wall.

He had spoken about his department during the three-hour meeting, answering questions, proving he was most definitely here in every sense of the way. His presentation was impressive, sounding just like the charismatic man I remembered well. The entire time I'd listened to him, I'd sat in my chair, gripping the edge of the table, my brain a jumbled storm that couldn't make sense of anything.

That hadn't changed one bit.

"I've been thinking the same thing since I saw you in the hallway," he replied.

I glanced to my side, watching my coworkers step into the elevator, and I moved my gaze back to him. "How long have you been in Amsterdam?"

His hand went to his beard, brushing the whiskers with his fingers. "Two years."

"I never thought you'd ever leave the guys." I smiled, surprised at how easy the memories were coming back, some so small and unimportant that I hadn't thought of them since I left England. "In my mind, the four of you would live together forever." I laughed. "I know that probably sounds silly."

He chuckled, and I recalled how often he used to do that.

How often we used to—together.

"I think a few of them would have preferred that," he said, his icy-blue eyes gleaming. There had always been a lightness to Oliver's face when he talked about his friends, and that hadn't changed. "But they're all back in London, some of them up to the same shit."

"And you're here."

He shrugged, and his exhale, even feet away, hit my face, full of leather and more lust than before. "Sometimes, you have to leave for a while to remember why you fell in love in the first place."

My heart lurched up to my throat, dangling there, waiting to fall back.

"I'll return to London one day when it feels right, and I'll probably never leave again." He smiled, and for some reason, it fit for the moment, but his eyes told me it wasn't a happy one for him. "Chloe, what the hell are you up to?"

I took a breath, shaking my head. "I'm here ... for the next six months." I didn't recognize my voice or the words coming out of my mouth.

"You're going to enjoy Amsterdam. It's one sexy fucking city." He took a step, but it didn't feel like he'd moved at all. "My office is on the third floor. Come by sometime. We'll have tea; no one drinks it around here."

I laughed at his joke and for so many other reasons.

"It was really good to see you, Chloe."

"You too."

His smile grew, his fingers finally leaving his face, and he turned around and walked toward the end of the hall.

I didn't know why, but I found myself watching him, my stare slowly moving down his body to the sweater that loosely hung on his torso, the khakis that were a little wrinkled—an outfit Oliver made oddly stylish.

And I forced myself to look away, knowing I needed to get in the elevator and meet my coworkers in the cafeteria, but there was something I had to do first.

Since I was holding my jacket and purse, I put both on and grabbed my phone out of my bag, heading outside the building. I was shaking too badly to do the math and figure out what time it was in Boston, but I knew it was early. I scrolled through my contacts, pressed the button, and held the phone to my ear.

"*Hiii,*" Molly whispered.

I began to walk down the sidewalk. "Did I wake you?"

"No. I just got May asleep. If she hears me and opens her eyes, I might lose my mind. I'm just warning you now."

I wrapped an arm around my stomach, desperate for the pressure but I couldn't feel it through my jacket. "Sounds like it's been a long night ... or morning."

"There's literally not a single part of my body that hasn't been vomited on in the last eight hours."

"I'm sorry I asked."

"Please, for the love of God, tell me something that doesn't involve bodily fluids so I can get my mind off the ones I'm still smelling."

I tucked myself in an alley between two buildings, pushing my back against the wall, my free hand flattening on the brick. I took a long, deep breath. "I just saw Oliver ... Oliver from London."

"Shut. The. Fuck. Up."

"Molly, I was coming out of the restroom before our meeting this morning, and he called out my name."

"What? How? Did you die?"

My heart was racing again, the beating moving into my throat where a tightness started. "I'm still dead, I think." I glanced at the mouth of the alley as a large group walked by. "We only talked for a few minutes. I guess he's been here for two years."

"Wait ... he works there?"

I laughed even though I found none of this funny. "Yeah, he manages the customer service sector, which is a huge division of the company but not one I'm going to work with. Unless it's in passing, I won't see him here at all."

And with the three hundred employees in this building and my office several floors above his, the chances of us running into each other were even less.

"Girl, what does he look like now?"

I paused as the image came back into my head, seeing his smile first and his eyes, and I tried to take another breath. "The same but with the tiniest wrinkles and a little more mature look, and ... it looks perfect on him."

"Of course it does. They just keep getting better, and we go to complete shit."

I could hear how sleep-deprived and puked on she felt.

"Molly ..." My throat felt even tighter. "What the hell do I tell Lance? I don't even know how to address this or what to say or ..." I stopped when it became too much, when I tried to picture my husband's reaction when I told him the news.

"Do you plan on seeing Oliver while you're there? Or spend any time with him?"

"No," I answered immediately.

"Since you've already said you're not going to work together, then I suggest you say nothing to Lance." As she hesitated, I reached inside my jacket and placed my hand on my chest. "All it would do is start an uncomfortable and unneeded shitstorm, and every time you got on the plane to return there, Lance would stress for nothing. Your relationship doesn't need those kinds of insecurities when things are so great between you two."

I didn't disagree with her at all. I just didn't know what to think about any of it. "God, this is nuts."

"Right?" I heard a noise in the background. "Oh fuck. *Ahhh*, May, *nooo!*"

"Give her a kiss for me. I'll text you later. Love you, bye," I said. I pulled the phone off my face and slid it into my pocket.

I knew I should go back inside to have lunch with my coworkers. I was running out of time before the next session, and I needed food to get me through it. I just couldn't imagine putting a single thing in my mouth right now.

I tilted my chin up, looking toward the top of the building, seeing how massive it was in size.

But knowing Oliver was somewhere in there made it feel teeny.

THIRTY-NINE

I WALKED out of the office at a few minutes before six and went straight to the market, the same place I'd grabbed lunch because it was only a block away and the food was good. I felt the evening chill move through my jacket, shivering as it reached my neck, and I went over to the section of soups on the hot bar. I filled a container with Spanish lentil and chorizo, grabbing a large chunk of crusty bread, and bagged them both before I walked up to the counter.

When it was my turn to check out, the cashier rang me up, and I headed for the door. Just as I was reaching for the handle, the glass swung open, and I caught eyes with the man in the doorway.

Once I saw that they were icy blue, I heard myself gasp, "Oliver ..."

"Chloe." He grinned, holding the door even wider as he stepped inside, now only a few feet away. "I see you've found the hidden gem of the neighborhood." He loosened the collar of his jacket. "Or what I like to call dinner."

In many ways, it was like Oliver Bennett had never left my

life. I could look at him and remember many of his details—
food he would order, expressions that would come across his
face, how bringing up his sisters would make him extremely
nostalgic. But as I looked at him now, I felt like he had experienced so much life since I last saw him, and those details felt
minuscule in comparison to what I'd missed.

"It's so weird to run into you here ..." I shook my head.
"But, yes, they have the best soup. Why do you get your food
here? You used to be an amazing cook."

His hand went to his hair, and he dragged it through the
longer light-brown strands. "It's not worth cooking for one."

There was the answer to the question I'd been curious
about since the moment I saw Oliver.

And now that I knew, I had no idea what to think.

But our eyes were locked, neither of us speaking, and I had
to say something.

Because this silence felt wrong.

Especially when the sensation in my chest began to move,
sliding to my throat and down to my stomach.

And I had to make it stop.

And ...

Lance: Just got out. I'll call you in 10.

My cell was in my hand, the screen tilted to give me a
better view, the letters that made up Lance's name almost
glowing.

I slowly glanced back up at Oliver, and it was like his eyes
had never left.

But mine had.

"I have to go," I said, my voice so soft.

He shifted in the doorway, giving me enough room to get
by. "Tomorrow night for dinner, you should stop by the shop

that's three doors down." He pointed to the left, but his eyes stayed on me. "Get an order of patat with mayonnaise. The fries look a bit strange covered in mayo, but it's really good."

"Thank you," I breathed.

He nodded. "Have a good evening, Chloe."

He was still holding the door for me, so while I clung to the phone in one hand and my food in the other, I moved past Oliver on my way outside. And when I passed him, the sleeve of my jacket brushed against his coat.

It wasn't any stronger than a breath.

But I felt it.

Just that single graze of fabric ... and I wished my arm had never moved in the first place because the tremors were ricocheting through my body.

I pushed forward, and when my feet hit the sidewalk, I rushed straight to my hotel. And even though I never turned around to check, I felt his eyes on me until I was out of sight.

Me: Just got back to the hotel, about to eat. Call me when you can.

Lance: Looks like you fell asleep. Sweet dreams, baby.

Me: I know we just got off the phone, but I miss you, and I wanted to tell you again.
Lance: You know I'll never get enough of hearing that, my beautiful wife.

Me: xoxo

Lance: Jesus, Chloe, that photo of you is stunning, baby.
Me: You're making me blush.
Lance: I wish I could kiss across that collarbone ...
Me: Hold that thought. I'm video-chatting you in 2 mins, and
you can say it again while you're looking at me.
Lance: My naughty girl.

Me: Six days.
Lance: I'm glad I'm not the only one counting.
Me: What's the first thing you're going to do?
Lance: Put my hands on you and not take them off.
Me: Love that and you.

"Do you know what time our flight is on Friday?" my coworker asked as we were walking through the hallway of the office. We'd just finished several presentations on the first stage of our new brand launch, and we were heading for lunch. "I swear, I don't know if I'm coming or going lately, and we're only on month one."

"God, can I relate." I laughed. "Our flight is at ten tomorrow morning, and we land in Boston at noon."

"Are you planning on stopping by the Boston office at all while you're home?"

"Hell no." I smiled. "There's nothing I can't do from my house."

She sighed. "Such a good perk about this job."

We were just rounding the corner, approaching the conference room, when I peeked through the glass wall to see who was leading the large meeting inside. My stare slowly drifted to the head of the table where I saw Oliver standing, his thrown-together look not at all distracting from the smile and charisma I saw as he spoke.

As I moved past the window, I waited for his face to turn, for his eyes to find me. And right before I took my last step, it happened. His mouth continued to talk to the group, but our gazes connected, and a blast of warmth shot through my body. I held his stare for one, two, three seconds, and then I continued around the corner where we could no longer see each other.

But I felt him.

Even after I walked out of the building for lunch.

Me: One more sleep until I'm in your arms.
Lance: Get home to me safely.

"Hi," I whispered the second Lance's hand touched the back of my head.

His fingers spread so he could hold more of my hair, his other arm going over the top of my shoulders. "Baby, welcome home."

Those words caused my throat to quiver, little waves passing over my tongue as tears threatened to fill my eyes.

Home.

Exactly where I wanted to be.

And it was as though he knew what I needed because he

squeezed me tighter, eliminating all the space between us. "Damn it, I missed you."

I felt it in his grip this raw urgency that was coming through his fingertips.

"I missed you more," I breathed.

Neither of us pulled away from each other while we stood on the curb outside the terminal, Anthony parked a few feet away in Lance's SUV.

And eventually, I heard, "Are you hungry?"

I swallowed, a heaviness moving through my stomach. "Take me anywhere as long as my hands and eyes don't have to leave you."

He laughed, and I hugged him tighter. "I know you didn't eat the food they served on the plane, and the empty bag of Doritos I see in your purse doesn't qualify as dinner. I'm getting you something to eat."

When he separated our bodies, our eyes connected, and his hands went to my face.

It felt so right.

Him.

This.

Us.

I swallowed again, waiting for his lips, and I closed my eyes when I felt them. My arms strengthened their grip around his neck, and I took in his scent, feeling the power of his hands at the same time I smelled it.

And then, suddenly, he was gone, his hands slowly leaving my face. "Let's get out of here."

I nodded, taking his fingers as he helped me into the backseat.

"Mrs. Hamilton," Anthony said once I got inside the SUV, "it's so nice to have you back. You've been missed by everyone."

"Thank you, Anthony." I sat in the middle of the backseat,

and once Lance climbed in, I looped my arm around his. "You all were terribly missed too." I smiled at him in the rearview mirror.

"Where am I taking you?" Anthony asked.

Lance turned toward me, his eyes roaming my face before he said, "I have a feeling my wife is craving sushi. Let's go to her favorite."

Anthony chuckled. "No problem. I'll take you there right now."

At one point in our relationship, Lance would have turned to me and asked if he had guessed right. He didn't need to do that anymore.

He knew.

And as Anthony pulled away from the arrival gate of Logan Airport, Lance's lips pressed against my forehead, and he held them there while he hummed, "It's so good to have you home."

My eyes closed, my chest aching. "You have no idea."

"One down, baby. Five to go."

Each exhale shuddered through me, and I thought of all the things I was going to do with my husband over the next two weeks. The restaurants we were going to visit in Boston and the weekend trip we would hopefully take to Florida and the cuddling we were going to do in bed.

Then ... I would return to Amsterdam.

And *this* would start all over again.

FORTY

"OH MY GOD," Molly squealed as her face came into view on my phone, "I miss you so much; I can't handle it. Come home already."

I stared at my best friend's face and smiled. "Just one more week, babe, and I'm going to hug the shit out of you." I leaned over to the nightstand and grabbed my glass of water. "By the way, I'm having the worst déjà vu right now."

"Right?" She frowned, and as she adjusted the phone, I saw she was in her living room. "At least now, you're only gone for two weeks at a time. I don't think I could handle more."

"Neither could I."

The phone shifted again, and she appeared to be lying down. "Are things good? Loving work?"

"My team had our final presentation today, where we pitched the first stage of the brand relaunch."

"And?"

I couldn't sit still on the bed; I was still so excited about it. "We killed it."

She was smiling as hard as me.

"It went better than all of us had hoped. The initial feed-back has been super positive, but we won't know for a few days."

"So insanely proud of my girl right now." She wiggled her shoulders, dancing. "You're sacrificing a lot to be there, and you're kicking ass."

"Thank you."

Her eyes narrowed, and a devious grin spread across her lips. "Any more run-ins with London?"

I laughed, shaking my head. She knew nothing beyond the first time I had seen him. "In passing," I replied. "Nothing crazy."

And that was all it had been when I saw him in the market and in the conference room.

Words, glances.

An increase of my heartbeat.

"I wonder what his story is now. For some reason, I'm dying to know."

"I—" The sound of the room phone cut me off, and I had never been more thankful. "Hang on a second, Molly." I reached for the landline on the nightstand. "Hello?"

"Mrs. Hamilton, this is Luuk from the front desk. I have a delivery for you. Would it be all right if I brought it up to your room now?"

"Yes, of course. Thank you." I hung up and turned back to Molly. "Hold on. I have a delivery, and I need to slip on a robe because I'm far too lazy to put on a bra."

She laughed as I climbed off the bed and went into the bathroom, wrapping the terrycloth around me before I headed for the door.

A gentleman was arriving just as I opened it, and he said, "Hello, Mrs. Hamilton."

He handed me a large paper bag, and I instantly smelled food inside.

Then, he added, "Have a good evening," before he left.

I thanked him and set the bag on the table.

"What is it?" Molly asked, watching me as I tried to open the top with one hand.

"Something yummy-smelling. I'm just not sure what."

Although I had a feeling it was from Lance. We'd spoken right before I called Molly, and I'd told him about our presentation and how I was going out later with my coworkers to celebrate.

After pulling apart several staples, I unfolded the paper and looked inside. There was a cold bottle of champagne, three different kinds of soups, and a loaf of French bread. In the far corner was a sleeve that I lifted into my hand, and my heart clenched when I saw what was inside.

Chocolate chip cookies.

And taped to the plastic window was a note.

SINCE I'M ON THE ROAD THIS WEEK AND I CAN'T BUY YOU
DINNER, ACCEPT THIS INSTEAD.
I HEARD YOU DID A HELL OF A JOB TODAY.
CONGRATS, SWEET GIRL.
—OLIVER XX

"Babe, what is it?" Molly asked. "And is it from Lance? You're smiling so hard right now."

A wave of emotion passed through me as I slowly glanced up to look at the screen, my best friend staring back, eagerly waiting for an answer.

I swallowed, hoping the emotion would follow and go down to my stomach and stay there, leaving my throat entirely.

But that didn't happen.

It only came on stronger.

"It's from ... the management team."

My response wasn't entirely a lie.

But it certainly wasn't what I should have told my best friend.

"*Awww*, aren't they the sweetest?" she purred, and an ache shot right into my gut. "Listen, lover, May is going to start screaming any second for food, and chaos will erupt around here. Text me tomorrow." She pouted her lips together and blew me a kiss.

With a smile still on my face, relief flooding through me, I caught it and blew one right back before disconnecting the call. Once I was sure she was off my screen, I immediately dropped the phone on the table and looked inside the bag again.

Oh God.

This reminded me of the night I had gone to his house in London, and he'd had some of my favorites delivered. Six years had passed, and he hadn't forgotten the champagne or cookies.

Warmth was moving through my chest as I began to put the food in the fridge, leaving Oliver's note on the counter before I brought my phone back to bed. And as I got nestled under the covers, I knew I had to thank him. It was the right thing to do.

I went into the company's app, searching for Oliver's profile, which would have his number listed. Once I had it entered into a text, I started typing, my fingers feeling unbelievably numb.

Me: It's Chloe. I just got your delivery. That was so nice and thoughtful of you. Thank you.
Oliver: I hope you're celebrating your arse off tonight?
Me: Meeting the team for some drinks soon—nothing crazy. We all have to be up very early tomorrow.

My phone began to ring, Oliver's number now on the screen, and my heart started to pound so hard that I couldn't swallow.

I pulled the blanket up to my chin and held the phone to my ear. "Hello?"

"Much better, I'd rather hear your voice."

I took a breath, the air barely making it past my tongue. "Hi."

"Good evening, gorgeous. Where are you guys going tonight?"

No one had called me that in a very long time, especially not in that accent. I pushed that thought out of my head and said, "Someone mentioned heading to De Pijp," referring to one of the more popular areas in Amsterdam.

"That's a good choice."

"You've been?"

"Chloe, I've been everywhere."

After he laughed, there was silence, and breathing was becoming even more difficult.

"Oliver ..." I hesitated, the curiosity getting the best of me. "Fill me in on your life. I know ... nothing anymore."

"Life," he sighed. He took a second before he continued, "Well, after you left England, me and my mates stayed in that house for another couple years, and then we all either moved in with girls or got our own places." He paused, but I didn't inquire; I didn't think it was my business. "Now, Jake and I are the only single ones, and the other two bastards are married with kids." He took a breath, and I heard something change. "My mum got sick about two and a half years ago and passed away within a few months. Not even a week later, one of my brothers-in-law got diagnosed with MS." He exhaled, and I felt it—every bit of pain that was in him. "I needed to get away. This job opened up, and I took it."

Knowing how close he was to his family, I imagined these had to have been dark and extremely difficult times.

"I'm broken to hear about your mom and brother-in-law," I said softly.

"Me too."

"Didn't you tell me once that your parents got married at sixteen? How's he holding up? He must be beside himself."

"I can't believe you remember that." He let that sink in and added, "He's doing okay. My sisters have been on him to date, but he won't. That man will be loyal to the grave."

I put my hand on my chest, massaging across it. "You said you're single, but I'm assuming there were plenty of girls over the years. Maybe you've got some kids by now?"

"There have been relationships but no kids as a result—thank God. And no one who has made me want to stick around for too long ... like you."

When he paused, a sweat broke out over my entire body.

"Tell me what's been going on in Chloe Kennedy's life ... or it's Hamilton now, yeah?"

"Hamilton, yes." I sat up higher, tucking my knees to my chest. I didn't know why, but saying that name to Oliver felt so wrong. I waited for that feeling to clear before I said, "After I returned to Boston, I finished school and stayed with the same company I'd interned for until I took the job at International Bookings. I sorta met my husband through Molly. Anyway, we got married, and we don't have kids yet."

"Have you been back to London?"

I took a few seconds before I answered, "No. I've traveled a lot over the years, but I never made my way back."

"A few years ago, me and my mates went to America. Spent some time in New York and LA."

I could picture them in both of those places. I'd stopped following Oliver on social media long before that, so I never would have seen any of those pictures. "New York is so close to me."

"I thought about looking you up. Would you have wanted to be found, sweet girl?"

I sucked in as much air as my lungs would hold and opened my mouth. "Oliver ..."

He was silent for a few seconds before he said, "De Pijp starts to get busy around this time. If you want a good table at a decent place, you guys should go there now."

I had nothing.

No words.

No voice.

I groaned just so he would know I had heard him.

"Have fun tonight, Chloe."

He hung up, and I was staring at a screen that had a picture of Lance and me on it, skiing on top of Sunday River in Maine.

My throat stung as I clicked on his number, staring at it, mentally reciting each digit over and over. I typed *London* under the name, his information now saved in my phone.

FORTY-ONE

"OH MY GOD." I quivered as Lance's lips pressed against the base of my neck, his hands gradually moving up my chest.

The slickness of our wet skin caused his palms to slide so easily up my body until he reached my face.

"You feel so good," I groaned.

With my back pressed against the side of our pool, my arms spread wide over the brick pavers, he treaded water in front of me, his tongue licking up to my earlobe. He sucked it into his mouth before moving across my face, his lips eventually hovering above mine.

"I've missed the way Florida tastes on you, baby."

He was only touching my cheeks, but I felt him through my whole body, my limbs humming for his attention, thighs clenched, desperate to feel the pressure that I knew he could give.

"Kiss me."

Even though he'd had me twice yesterday after I flew in straight from Amsterdam, Lance wasn't gentle when he took my mouth, grasping my face as though it had been weeks since he tasted me.

"*Mmm,*" he said. "I need more."

"I'm yours."

Because there were so many boaters, I always wore a bathing suit in our pool during the day, like the one that covered me now. But Lance's hand was reaching behind my back, and with one sweep, he had the bow of my bikini untied and the small triangles pulled over my head. The bottoms were ripped off just as fast, both pieces of my suit now on the deck behind me.

Once his hand returned to the water, he growled, "Get over here," and wrapped my legs around his waist, keeping me hidden against his chest. Lance held me steady while he moved his shorts down and then positioned me at his tip.

Anticipating him, I held the softness of his cheeks with my fingers, and I pressed my mouth to his. As I felt his tongue, I arched my hips, rubbing myself back and forth over his head, teasing us so differently. And with each shift, I exhaled against his mouth, waiting for him to give me more.

Still, he wouldn't let me lower. So, I stayed frozen, my body pulsing around him, the need building, throbbing.

I took a breath, my lips diving back into his, and before my lungs were filled, I grunted, "*Ahhh,*" because, within one quick, hard thrust, he was inside me.

We were then moving toward the center of the pool, and my head was tilted back, my long locks dangling in the water while he was hitting the deepest part of me.

"Lance ... yes!" Each stroke caused my hair to get wetter until the water covered everything but my nose. With my ears in the pool, I could hear the movement of his body, the waves he was causing, the way his grunts rippled like bubbles over the top of me.

"So fucking tight," he hissed over my chest, his mouth pressed to the center of it while he breathed against me.

I wrapped my hands around his neck, and I held myself steady as the top of my clit began to grind into the base of his dick, creating friction that was utterly consuming me. "*Yesss*," I cried.

Before I was even finished moaning, he was lifting me, and we were moving through the water to the other edge of the pool where I placed my arms on the brick, facing the ocean, while Lance moved in behind me.

And as I took a breath, staring at the sight I loved more than anything, my husband filled me again.

Entirely.

His hands cupped my breasts as he squeezed my nipples while he pumped into me, and my body accepted every punch of his hips. And while he was working both parts of me, my orgasm started to build.

There was no skin in front of me to grab. No bed or pillow to stab my nails into. So, I gripped the bullnose as his pace began to quicken.

"Harder," I begged. "Please." I did everything but shout, "Oh God, yes!"

His fingers bit into me while he held on, using my body to rock back and forth, and from his movement, I could feel how close he was getting.

"Baby ..." His face was in my neck, teeth on my shoulder.

I turned my chin, so our mouths were closer. Each exhale shooting out of my lips until I moaned, "Lance ..." That was when a sharp, intense pleasure began to spread through me.

"I want to feel you come."

His hand slipped down the front of me, and after a few quick, hard passes across my clit, adding more pressure to what was already building, tingles shot through my stomach, and I lost it.

"Fuck," he grunted, and each of his thrusts was getting harder, telling me he was feeling the same. And then I heard, "Chloe," and I knew his body was reaching its peak.

A shudder took over, and I bucked my hips to meet him, riding out both of our orgasms.

"Jesus," he breathed when I stilled, sliding out to face me. He wrapped my legs around his waist and held my back against the pool, our mouths close as he lowered us into the water.

When I finally caught my breath, I asked, "Do you have to work today?" My arms circled a little tighter around his neck.

"Just a few hours' worth." He kissed my forehead. "I thought we would then take out the Jet Skis and drive them to the oyster bar for lunch."

"Yes, yes, yes." I laughed, putting my head back to get my hair wet again, and I pecked his lips on the way up. "And while you get all your stuff done, I'm going to work extremely hard on my tan."

He laughed, his hands now on my ass, gripping it hard.

"Go now so you can come back to me even sooner."

He growled as he kissed me, and I watched him pull on his shorts and lift himself out of the pool. I wasn't far behind, moving over to my bikini and tying it on before I stepped out.

When I'd first come outside earlier this morning, I'd placed my phone and sunscreen on one of the loungers, and that was where I headed. I took a seat, getting comfortable on the oversize cushion, and looked at my phone, scrolling through the messages that had come in.

I felt myself stop breathing when I saw one from Oliver.

London: Does America taste as good as when you left?

My husband had been inside me only minutes ago, and now, Oliver was on my screen.

And there was a sensation in my body that I'd never felt before.

Me: I'm in Florida right now, and I have to say, the view is pretty outstanding.
London: Let me see.

I aimed my camera at the beach that was only a pool deck away, the clear water lapping against the powdery-white sand. Satisfied with the picture, I sent it.

London: That's not the view I was hoping for, gorgeous.
Me: LOL. How's Amsterdam?
London: Certainly not hot and sunny like it is there.

London: You didn't hear this from me—the team approved the new branding. Major fucking congrats, sweet girl.
Me: WHAT?
London: Email coming in three ... two ... one ...
Me: OMG. I can't believe it. They loved all of it. I'm in shock right now.
London: So fucking proud of you.
Me: Thank you. :)

Me: Requesting to follow me, huh?
London: I don't remember unfollowing you ...
London: But I do remember when it happened.

Me: It was the only way I could move on.
London: Chloe, I was just trying to do the same thing.

London: Looks like someone wants to gain access to me now.
Me: Guilty.

Me: That last pic of you and the boys—I'm dying laughing. Look at all the mischief you still find yourselves in. None of you have changed a bit. Wow, so great to see all of their faces.
London: They say hello.
Me: Please tell them I said the same back.

London: You're going to give up that sunset for Amsterdam?
Me: I'm pretty sure the sun sets over there too.
London: See you soon, sweet girl.

"Damn it, you're sexy ..." Lance said as he walked into the bathroom.

My pulse was already rapid, as I'd been staring at Oliver's message that had just come in. But as I heard my husband, it increased even faster.

Slowly, I set my cell facedown on the vanity, trying hard to find my breath again, and I glanced up at Lance.

And when our eyes connected, what returned was the guilt I'd felt before, but there was something else as well. It was an excitement, and it was building just as fast.

Lance's eyes devoured me as he said, "I love you in red."

There were two neckties in his hands, and I could tell he had come in to ask which one to put on. He always wanted to coordinate, and he hadn't known what I was wearing to tonight's gala.

Now, he did.

And the heat from his gaze was burning my skin. "Thank you."

"You never wear that color."

I shrugged, feeling the tight, strapless dress pull at my chest. "I always worry it'll clash with my hair, and that alone makes enough of a statement."

"And tonight?"

I smiled even though it was almost impossible to breathe. "I'm feeling a little dangerous."

He set the ties down and came over to me. His hands gently pressed at my waist. "An hour—that's all they get of us. Then, we're coming home, so I can have you all to myself until you fly out tomorrow afternoon."

My skin was on fire, my stomach a mix of tingles and aches, and I wasn't sure which was worse.

"Baby ..." His eyes dropped down my body, his head shaking. "I'm one lucky man. You look so fucking beautiful."

I shook as I heard that word in my husband's voice, and it hurt in a way I hadn't expected.

And I hated myself for that.

I didn't know how to make this feeling go away.

How to make ... it stop.

How to make any of this stop.

But the one thing that felt right was to circle my arms around Lance's neck and whisper, "I can't wait until we're alone."

FORTY-TWO

Me: Landed. Love you so much. Call me when you wake up.

London: Are you back?
Me: Just had my first cup of Dutch pea soup. Mmm, so good.
London: Amsterdam missed you.
Me: I feel the same way ...

Lance: The sunrise I woke up to wasn't the same without you.
Me: Morning, my love.
Lance: Let's video chat when I get to the hotel in NYC. 8 p.m.
your time.
Me: Can't wait. xoxo

London: Sorry I had to go after your presentation, but I had another meeting. You did a hell of a job, gorgeous. They're enamored with you. It's great to see you get what you deserve. x

Me: I know you didn't have to be there, but thanks for taking the time to come. It meant a lot to see a familiar face in a very full crowd of strangers. I was nervous as hell.

London: Didn't look it one bit.

Me: :)

Lance: I just saw something on Madison Ave. and thought of you, so I bought it.

Me: Oh, yeah?

Lance: I'll give you a hint ... it's red.

Me: I can't wait to wear it for you. ;)

Lance: Eleven days.

Me: They're not going by fast enough.

"HELLO?" I answered, sitting up in bed after seeing *London* on the screen of my phone.

"Chloe fucking Kennedy."

My eyelids squinted shut, my head tilting back, and I let out the loudest laugh. "Oh, Jake. It's so good to hear your voice."

"What the fuck are you up to?"

I sighed, taking a look around my hotel room in Amsterdam. "I wouldn't even know where to start with that answer."

"Chloe, I'm asking what you're doing right now. Oliver and I are down at the pub, and I'm buying drinks. Come fucking join us."

Something tightened in my chest. "Jake—"

"I just flew all the way here from London," he said before I could get any words out. "It's been six years, Chloe. Meet us for old times' sake."

My eyes were shut again but for an entirely different reason.

I wasn't going to be alone with Oliver. Jake would be there, and we'd all have one drink together. Then, I'd come right back to the hotel.

This is innocent, right? Just old friends.

That was what I kept repeating in my head when I said, "Okay, I'll meet you. But just one drink, and you have to promise me that."

"Yeah, yeah," he replied. "I'll text you our location. Oliver says you'll be able to walk; it's really close."

"I'll see you soon," I said and hung up, dropping the phone onto the nightstand.

Once I'd gotten home from work, I'd changed into pajamas and climbed into bed. The days here were long and so tiring. But now, I stood in front of my tiny closet, trying to find something to put on with the limited options I'd brought with me.

I went with a pair of skinny jeans, a sweater, and knee-high flat boots, fixing my hair and makeup before I went back over to my phone and looked at the screen. There was a text from Oliver, sharing his exact location, and I knew just where the pub was located since I walked by it every day.

I slipped the phone into my purse, grabbed my key, and left the hotel. It was just after eight, and Amsterdam hadn't even gotten warmed up. The streets had a quiet murmur of traffic, the sidewalk almost sparse as I made it to the cross street. At the Stop sign, I turned and only had to go one block before I reached the pub.

And once I was inside, they were easy to spot because Jake shouted, "Chloe fucking Kennedy," across the entire bar.

I laughed as I made my way over, and Jake stood, greeting me halfway, giving me a hug and lifting me into the air.

"Looking fabulous as ever."

I giggled, squeezing him back. "God, do you men ever age?"

He set me down, his eyes giving me a once-over. "So fucking great to see you." He put his hand on my shoulder, clenching it before he brought me over to the table he shared with Oliver.

"Hey," I said softly as we walked toward each other.

Oliver's hand gently grabbed my waist, and he kissed my cheek, my body instantly filling with tingles. The leather and lust of his scent went to my nose, and I took the deepest inhale.

I'd missed his smell, and I had no idea what to even think about that.

"Thanks for coming," he said in my ear, his fingers leaving my waist as he pulled away.

"Jake wasn't going to take no for an answer," I responded, sitting in the empty chair as Jake called over a waitress.

"What can I get you to drink?" she asked as she stood next to me.

I saw they were having beer, and I answered, "I'll take the lightest lager you have on tap."

When she was gone, Jake looked at me and said, "All of us back together—who the fuck would have thought that was going to happen?"

I felt Oliver's eyes on me before I glanced at him and replied, "I certainly didn't."

Oliver continued to hold my stare. "I didn't either."

"Well, you know what? Maybe we should have," Jake said. "Because look at us right now—three motherfuckers drinking beer in Amsterdam like no time has gone by at all."

Except in my mind, a world had gone by in the last six years.

The biggest difference was the diamond sitting on my left hand right now.

The waitress dropped off the tiny glass of beer that wasn't much bigger than a shot glass—a way of drinking here that I was still trying to get used to.

"To old fucking times," Jake said as he held his glass in the air.

Oliver and I did the same, and as I took a drink, I looked at Jake. He still had black plastic-rimmed glasses, although they'd changed shapes since I last saw him, and he still wore just an old T-shirt, both of his arms now full sleeves of colorful tattoos.

"Are you doing good?" I asked him.

Jake wasn't the kind of guy who got serious too often, but there had been moments—like the time he'd told me how badly Oliver was going to hurt over me leaving—that I got to see the deeper side of him. But from the way Jake was looking at me now, I knew I wasn't going to see that side. Tonight was all about fun.

"I'm doing really great, lovely." He twisted the glass on top of the table. "I got myself a flat overlooking the Thames and a stable job in finance. Life is excellent. Well"—he lifted his beer and took a drink—"it would be a hell of a lot better if this one would come home."

"I'm perfect right here," Oliver shot back. "Your arse just needs to come and visit more often."

The waitress stopped by our table again and said, "Can I get you anything else?"

"A round of tequila shots," Jake replied. "And please make them extra cold."

"I have to be at the office by seven tomorrow morning," I

said to Oliver, my hand going to my forehead as I anticipated the headache I was going to wake up with.

He laughed. "Me too, sweet girl."

I didn't have a chance to respond before Jake was grabbing my attention. "One beer, one shot, and then I promise you can go to bed."

I smiled at them both. "We all know that's the biggest lie in the world."

The three of us couldn't stop chuckling because we knew I was right.

Five hours later—my phone showing it was well past midnight—I looked at Jake and said, "I told you so. Now, I need to get home before tomorrow turns into the longest day of my life."

Jake's expression turned sad, his hand clasping mine in a tight grip. "Sweetheart, you are going to be deeply missed." He kissed the center of my palm, his beer-soaked lips leaving a mark after he pulled them away. "Let's not go another six years, all right?" I nodded, and he held out his arms. "Get over here."

As I hugged him, memories of our time together began to fill my head, the partying and late nights and the laughs. It was only a semester, but we'd spent almost every day together, and we'd all been so close.

Once I'd left, everything had changed.

"So fucking great to see you." He kissed the top of my head. "Take care of yourself." I tightened my grip for a second longer. "And take care of him."

My arms loosened as I glanced up at Jake, our gazes holding while I took a step away from the table. "Good-bye," I whispered.

"I'll walk you out," Oliver said from behind me.

I grabbed my jacket off the chair and hung my purse across my body, and Oliver's hand went to my lower back as we walked to the front. He opened the door before I had time to reach for it, the wind hitting my face as soon as I stepped outside. And once I got out here, I saw it was completely different than when I'd first arrived.

Amsterdam felt alive.

"I'll walk you back," he said in my ear. He stared at me with a narrow gaze, breaking it for just a second to look at the commotion at his right and his left. "You're not going by yourself."

"I'll be fine." I lifted my hand to wave, and he caught it. And because I'd had the beer and tequila, my balance wasn't the best, and his gentle tug caused me to stumble back.

"Chloe ..." He caught me against his chest, his hands instantly cupping my face, thumbs grazing under my jaw, just like they always used to. "I've missed this, sweet girl."

I stared at his lips, remembering the way they used to feel and how they'd tasted and how I was able to close my eyes and see the details of his smile. How his presence had felt like the safest, warmest place in the world.

How that heat and protectiveness was seeping over me right now.

Oh God.

I tried to take a breath, and his scent grabbed ahold of me, a tightness now moving into my chest. "Oliver ..."

His mouth came closer, hovering in front of mine.

As I swallowed his air, feeling the heat come off his body, I could almost taste his skin.

And it was wrong.

But it was right.

And that thought was too much, yet it wasn't enough.

Everything inside my body hurt, and I was tingling and pulsing at the same time.

I couldn't find air, no matter how hard I tried, but there was an overabundance hitting my face.

I just couldn't.

I couldn't.

I couldn't ...

Oh God, no.

His lips were on me, and as soon as I felt them, I pulled my face away and breathed, "No ..."

But his hands didn't leave, and his grip didn't loosen. While my chest heaved, he continued to hold me and wouldn't let go.

"Chloe ..." he said again.

When he leaned forward, he didn't put his mouth on me but kept it an inch away. He stroked my cheek, staring at me in a way where I forgot we were standing on the edge of the busiest sidewalk in Amsterdam, six years later. And instead, it felt like we were standing just outside the airport, getting our chance once again.

But it was different this time.

I was different.

And while I got used to him being this close again, I took in his gaze, a place I used to want to live in forever. A place that was so comfortable, familiar, and the tightening slowly started to lighten.

"Sweet girl ..."

Closer.

Only air separating us.

I sucked in a mouthful. Holding it. Feeling the breeze move through my chest.

His mouth softly brushed mine once more, and a spark shot through me.

A warmth.

An energy I remembered and had missed.

I didn't fight the feeling in my body.

I didn't pull away.

I didn't think I could.

I reached forward, fisting his sweater in my palms, squeezing it with every bit of strength I had.

And when his lips grazed mine, they stayed there. His heat shot straight down my body, and I felt it in my toes.

"Oliver ..." I breathed, inhaling his scent as my lips parted, a name I hadn't said like this in so long.

A tremor moved through my chest, and I squeezed his sweater even harder, my mouth opening again for his tongue. His palms pushed into my cheeks, his body pressing into mine.

And I remembered.

Like his lips were whispering memories, I could recall every time they'd kissed me, and every feeling came back, every emotion filling me.

"Oh God." I quivered, and he was even closer.

The sweater was no longer under my fingers, and instead, I felt the rough, sharp whiskers of his beard and the way they were dragging across my face, my skin stinging ...

In a way it hadn't in a long time.

And just as that thought really settled, Oliver sucked my bottom lip into his mouth, his teeth lightly gnawing over it, gradually letting it go.

My eyes shot open.

The ice blue stared back.

And with it ... came a shock.

One that quaked through my entire body.

If I knew he wouldn't catch me, I would have started running, but the crowd was too thick, and Oliver was much faster than me.

My hand went to my chest, pushing against it to find air. "I have to go."

He must have sensed my urgency because he gripped my

hand and weaved us through the maze of pedestrians who were all partying at this hour. It was too loud to speak, too congested to walk side by side, so Oliver continued in front, and I squeezed his hand from behind.

And when I felt him stop, I looked up and saw we were several feet from the entrance of my hotel.

I released his hand and took several steps away, my heart beating so fast that I was sure it was going to explode. "Oliver ..."

He tried to come closer, and my palm went in the air to stop him.

"I can't ..." I breathed, but there was no air. "I'm married, Oliver. This is fucked. I can't do it. I love my husband, and I can't do this to him ... to us."

Pain shot through his eyes, and he went to reach forward again, but I stepped back.

"Chloe, I'm sorry."

I was putting more space between us, but as I stared at him, my chest was seizing, my throat closing. "We can't do this," I repeated again. "Not ever again. I don't know what the fuck I was thinking."

"Chloe ..." He was breathing fast, his eyes full of emotion. "I didn't mean for this to happen. I just ... fuck." He pulled at the top of his hair, teeth stabbing his lip. "I got caught up in the moment, and it's just so fucking hard to see you and remember that you're not mine anymore."

If there was any breath left, it was gone.

What was left was a feeling that was far bigger than me.

When he said my name, I didn't look over my shoulder. I just pushed my feet across the ground as fast as I could and hurried through the lobby to my room. Once I got inside, I stripped off my clothes, and I was naked by the time I got in the bathroom, turning on the shower as hot as it would go.

As I waited for the water to warm, I gripped the sink with both hands, letting it bear my weight, digging inside my body to find a calm.

To find a way to stop the tightening.

To make this all feel normal again.

To return to before.

But before was gone.

Everything I had known ... was gone.

When I went to swallow, I couldn't.

I tried to scream and had no voice.

I attempted to inhale and wasn't able to do that either.

Panicked, I looked up at the mirror, and I caught sight of the girl staring back at me.

The one with wild hair from the wind of Amsterdam and red eyes from the tears that were dripping from them.

And lips that, when licked, still had the taste of Oliver.

I didn't recognize her.

I didn't recognize me.

I ...

What the fuck did I just do?

FORTY-THREE

London: We need to talk.
Me: I'm not ready for that yet.
London: I'm here when you are.

London: You're leaving in four days, Chloe. I think we should
have a conversation before you go.
Me: I ... just can't.

London: I stopped by your office, and they said you already left
for the night. I wanted to see you before you flew back tomorrow.
Me: I went for a walk. I needed air.
London: Did you find it?
Me: Nope.
London: What time is your flight?

I STARED at Oliver's last text, my eyes stinging, fingers hovering above the letters to type a reply.

Once I left in the morning, I wouldn't be back for two weeks, and there were so many things I should say to him before I left.

But as I was tucked under the covers of my bed, looking out the window at the evening lights of Amsterdam, the thought of saying any of those things made me want to hide.

So did the thought of going home.

I turned my phone to silent and set it on the nightstand, and I covered my head with the blanket.

Me: *I'm coming over at 10. Don't ask. I just need my best friend.*
Molly: *You know I'm always here for you, babe.*

"Girl, what is going on?" Molly said after she opened her door and took a look at me. "Come here, honey."

She threw her arms out, and I fell into her embrace, squeezing her with every bit of strength I had left.

Strength that hadn't come from the two sleepless nights I spent in Boston and every minute since I'd been back with Lance.

Except these few seconds.

And I could finally ... lose it.

Oh God.

"I took out stuff for mimosas," she said, her palm rubbing circles between my shoulder blades, "but I think it's a vodka kind of morning." Her hand stilled. "Let's get you inside so I can funnel it in you."

She unraveled her body and clasped my hand in hers, bringing me over to the couch in the living room.

I pulled the stuffed unicorn beside me into my arms and held it against my chest as she went into the kitchen. "Where's May?"

She set two glasses on the counter, filled them with ice, and stopped pouring the vodka when she hit the halfway mark. As she carried the tumblers into the living room, she said, "She's at the park with my sitter, and they have plenty of cash to keep them busy for hours."

I held the drink in my palm, staring at the clear liquid, the ice bobbing over the top.

"Drink."

I slowly looked up at the sound of my best friend's voice, my lips trembling as our eyes connected, and I said, "Molly, I really fucked up."

She was sitting next to me, one hand on my arm, the other on my back again. "Start from the beginning, babe."

I nodded, but the emotion was already there, rippling in my throat. With it came a tightness that spread through my chest and traveled all the way to my stomach. And that was when the rawness started to eat away at me. "I would never do anything to purposefully hurt him ..."

She was searching my eyes, hunting for an answer, and I saw the moment it hit her. "Drink."

I felt the coolness of the glass between my lips as I swallowed.

"Now, tell me what happened."

I set the glass on my thigh, waiting for the acid to settle in my throat. "Oliver's old roommate Jake was in town, visiting from London, and he asked me to come out. God, it felt just like old times." The tears were brimming over my lids, falling straight to my chin. But they were so thick that I couldn't see my best friend's face. One I'd cried in front of for years, but this occasion felt so different. "Molly," I gasped when something seized my throat.

She gripped me even harder, speaking in my ear when she said, "We're going to get through it, just keep going."

There was no breath in my body, no air anywhere in this room, but somehow, I continued, "The three of us were at a bar, drinking. I'd been there for hours, and it was time for me to go home."

It all began to replay—the expression on Oliver's face as we'd stood outside the pub, the feel of his lips on mine, the roughness of his whiskers on my cheek.

"He kissed me, Molly." I swallowed and tried to open my lungs. "And I fought it. Oh God, I fought it." I wiped the tears only so I could see the truth in her eyes, so I could torture myself again over it. "But then I stopped fighting ... and I kissed him back." My chest was so tight that my words sounded like I was hyperventilating. "A few seconds was all it lasted, and then I freaked out, and he apologized."

She gave me a look, but I put my hand up to silence her.

"Before you say anything, we're both at fault." Tears were covering my lips, and I swiped my tongue across them. "I don't know what the fuck happened to me." The words were clenching my tongue, my throat, but I had to get them out. "I love my husband, Molly. I love him more than anything, and I don't know what to do."

She lifted my hand again, putting the glass to my lips. "Finish it."

The vodka burned all the way down, and I continued swallowing until there was only ice left. "What do I do?"

She was breathing so fast that I could see her fingers were white on my arm even through the tears. "Did you ever tell Lance that you work with Oliver?"

I shook my head.

Because I'd never expected ...

This.

"You've been there three months. If you tell him now, it's only going to make things worse, especially after what happened."

My stomach was churning, my mouth watering. "I know."

She was quiet for several seconds. "You know this is wrong; you don't need me to tell you that. I've never been the friend to judge you, and I'm certainly not going to start now. But, babe, there are obviously still feelings there, and you have to make a decision."

I could see the pain I was causing her, and I hated myself for it.

"Do you want to ruin your marriage and everything you guys have built together?"

"No."

It wasn't louder than a breath, but it was honest, and I could tell she'd heard me.

Her eyes turned more serious than I'd ever seen them, and her hands made sure my attention didn't shift anywhere. "Then, tell Oliver it was a huge mistake and that you were caught up in memories, but you've moved on with your life. Even if it hurts. Even if it's the hardest thing you'll ever have to do, you have to stop."

London: Talk to me, sweet girl.
Me: This is incredibly difficult.
London: It always has been for us.
Me: I feel like I can't breathe.
London: That's how I feel without you.

"Did you have a good time with Molly?" Lance asked as I walked into the kitchen of our condo, where he was working at the island.

Since I'd been traveling back and forth to Europe, he'd been doing more of that now.

Something I'd appreciated until I returned home from this trip and hated the feel of my own skin.

"It was good to see her," I said, putting on a smile as I went over to the fridge.

My hands were shaking as I grabbed the bottle of water, my legs feeling weak as I turned around, not realizing Lance was standing directly behind me.

I hadn't heard him.

Or felt him.

But now, he was reaching over my head, getting something off the shelf behind me, and as he neared my body, I did everything I could not to shake.

His arm dropped to his side, and his face came closer, the softness of his cheek brushing against mine. His lips moved to the corner of my mouth, and he whispered, "I love that I can do this anytime I want for the next two weeks." He gave me the softest kiss on my cheek before he walked back over to his laptop.

"Me too," I breathed, and I pushed my back against the closed fridge. "This is much harder than I thought it was going to be." I stayed there, frozen, unable to move because everything inside me was screaming.

"You look like you're still on Amsterdam time."

I glanced at my husband, not remembering when I had looked away. And my fingers squeezed the top of the bottle, the teeth on the plastic ring biting my skin. "I am."

"Go take a bath, baby. The jet lag should be gone by tomorrow."

I put on another smile, something I'd been perfecting since I'd been home, and I carried the bottle through the kitchen and into our bathroom where I turned the water on as hot as it would go.

FORTY-FOUR

"GOOD MORNING, GORGEOUS," Oliver said as he looked through the doorway of my office.

Even though this section of the building didn't have glass walls, I'd felt him in the air before I heard his voice.

I'd only been back in Amsterdam for less than twelve hours, and he was already consuming me.

But now that he stood here, our eyes connecting, my body responding like he was breathing over my naked skin, a wave of dread moved through me that was fucking fierce.

"Hi," I said softly, staring at a face that was so incredibly handsome that I had to force myself to look away. "I know we have to talk."

That was what I'd told him through text the day after my conversation with Molly, and for the rest of my time in Boston, I'd tried to keep things as short as possible with him. Because those two weeks home with Lance were everything I'd needed them to be. And when I'd gotten on the plane, I had returned to Amsterdam with a purpose.

To never see Oliver again.

Oh God.

His arms crossed as he leaned into the frame. "I'll be in the bar of your hotel at six thirty tonight."

His eyes told me he'd waited long enough to talk, and he didn't want to wait anymore.

"I'll be there," I told him.

His gaze narrowed just before he said good-bye and walked out.

Seeing Oliver this early in the day, knowing what I had to do tonight, made for an extremely long morning and an even more torturous afternoon, and I left work before I should have. I just couldn't take it anymore. And when I arrived in my room, I poured myself some champagne and soaked in my tub, hoping to find the calm I needed.

When my nerves were a little quieter, the water no longer scorching me, I got out and dressed in a pair of jeans and an off-the-shoulder long-sleeve shirt. I left my hair down in loose waves, only adding some lip gloss to my face.

I took a final look in the mirror, knowing the next time I was in this bathroom, my heart was going to feel much different than it did right now.

But I had to do this.

For Lance.

For us.

I swallowed, releasing the counter, and then I went downstairs to the lobby bar.

Since I was a few minutes early, I went up to the bartender and ordered a glass of champagne. As I watched him fill a flute all the way to the top, I said, "I'm going to charge it to my room."

"I'll keep your tab open."

I thanked him and took the glass over to a table in the corner. As I sipped, I scrolled through photos my friends had posted online, shots of them around Boston, having dinner, drinks—things I was missing.

Because I was here.

I wasn't halfway done with my champagne when I felt Oliver arrive. It was a heat that moved through my body, and my gaze lifted from my phone to search for him.

I didn't have to look far. He was walking past the bar and tables, heading straight for me. And with each of his steps, I saw the way his jeans hugged his long, lean legs, and when he unzipped his jacket, there was a light-blue button-down underneath that was the identical color of his eyes.

His trimmed beard grazed my cheek as he whispered, "Good evening, Chloe," right before he kissed the center of it.

"Hi," was all I could get out.

His scent was filling my nose, and I was taking in the feeling of his lips while my mind was burning with memories from our last kiss.

And it was those same thoughts that continued to haunt me as he moved to the chair across from mine and sat down. His arms leaned over the wood, bringing us closer.

Before either of us could say anything, a waitress appeared.

"Can I get you anything?" she asked.

Oliver ordered a local beer, and I agreed to a refill, mine being close to finished. Then, we were alone again.

Almost instantly, a smile spread over his face. "You know what I was thinking about the other night?" His hand went to his whiskers, brushing them with his fingertips. "The time we were at my family's cottage and you found that ancient cookbook that was my gran's."

I grinned as it all came rolling back. "Oh God, and I picked the recipe I thought was the hardest and bet that you couldn't make it."

His hands had expertly moved around that kitchen in a way I found so sexy.

As he laughed, a little bit of redness spread over the tops of his cheeks. "It was fucking dreadful. Worst meal I've ever made."

"It wasn't your best, I'll say that." The heat began to cover my face, and I couldn't move away from it, especially as his chin pointed down, and he was almost gazing at me through his lashes.

"It was a good semester, wasn't it?"

"The best," I whispered.

The waitress came to our table, and I downed the rest of my drink, replacing it with the new one she gave me.

And when she was gone, Oliver held his small beer glass in front of my flute and said, "To the city of hope."

I took a sip, watching him do the same. "That's what Amsterdam is to you?"

He set his drink down and leaned back in his chair, arms crossing over his chest. "Good things have happened to me since I moved here. I have a job I fucking love. I've met some really great friends." He dragged his bottom teeth over his top lip. "You've come into my life again."

There were words I had to say, promises I'd made to myself when I boarded the plane in Boston.

But now that I was here, the thought of speaking them hurt my heart so badly that I didn't want to open my mouth.

What I wanted was to spend more time with this man. To hold on to his smile for as long as I possibly could. To feel the sensation of Oliver under my fingertips.

"And you know what? I might even have you for a little bit longer if you end up renewing your contract," he continued.

I circled my hand around the champagne, pulling it to the edge of the table. "No one has said anything to us about that."

But during the flight over, my entire team had been speculating about whether it would happen and what they would do if it became an option.

"With the way you're performing, I promise, the in-house lawyer is already drafting a contract."

The booze was helping, but I could still feel the tightness in my throat. "I don't know what my life would look like if I stayed for another six months." My mind was a storm with questions.

"You'd just fall deeper in love with Amsterdam."

I felt the grin growing over my face, and I chuckled. "You think that's what would happen?"

His thumb slid down the side of the beer, reminding me of the way he used to rub my face. "You haven't fallen for it yet, sweet girl?"

That accent.

That gritty, growly voice.

I turned, glancing around the bar as though I would find the answer there, and when my eyes locked with his again, he said, "Outside those doors is the sexiest city in the entire world."

"You must be talking about the red light district?"

As he paused, I felt a flicker in the base of my stomach. "The red light district is what lights up Amsterdam, but sex is what keeps it on fire." His gaze dropped to my lips. "Have you seen any of the sex shows?"

"No." I crossed my legs under the table, the tingling working its way between them as I thought of what might happen during those shows. "I've walked through the area, but it was early in the morning during my workout, and there wasn't much to see at that time."

He watched me while he swallowed the rest of his beer, his thumb wiping his lips when he was done. "It's something you have to see."

"Then, I'll make sure it happens."

He moved his beer to the side, so he had enough room to lean on the table when he said, "Go and get your coat."

My eyes widened. "You're kidding. Now? But—"

"Chloe," he said before my thoughts ran wild, "let me show you a part of Amsterdam you're never going to forget."

My heart was pounding as I thought about the show and attending it with him and us spending more time together—things I'd never intended when I came to this bar.

"Stop thinking," he said, nodding toward the elevator. "Get your coat so we can leave."

Inside my head was the last place I wanted to be, so I pushed myself off the chair and said, "Be right back."

And there was a whole new energy pulsing through me as I went to my room and slipped on my jacket, adding more lip gloss before going back to meet him. When I reached the table, I saw the receipt was already there with some cash lying across it.

"Tab is closed," he said. "You ready?"

I didn't realize how close we were standing until he reached forward and moved a piece of hair off my face.

His touch sent more tingles through me, and I shivered. "Yes."

What I learned as we entered the notorious red light district was that walking there with Oliver and seeing it at this hour was an entirely different experience.

What was brown and gray during the day was lit with red at night, and the color stretched as far as I could see. It reflected off the water of the canals, shimmered over the black pavement, danced across our faces as we passed the red-lit windows. When the curtains were open, the most beautiful women dressed in lingerie were standing in front of the glass, their bodies speaking a language I understood.

And with every step I took, I smelled lust. It wasn't Oliver's cologne; this was from being surrounded by sex. But it wasn't just the act that I saw; it was also the hints, the whispers.

The secrets that were being left on these streets of Amsterdam.

And some of them were my own.

With Oliver's arm stretched across my back, holding me tightly against his body, his lips pressed to the shell of my ear, and he said, "We're here."

The entrance was large, a neon-pink elephant sign over the doorway.

I stood next to Oliver as he paid at the window, and then he handed our tickets to a bouncer. I had no idea what to expect when he brought us inside, but I was surprised to see it was designed like a movie theater with the stage in the front, curtain closed, and just enough light that I could see where I was going.

With almost every seat taken, the bouncer placed us on a bench in the front, and there was a low murmur from the crowd as the curtain slowly began to open.

Oliver's arm was around my shoulders, my body molded against him as I anticipated what I was going to see.

Slowly, the scene came into view.

Less than ten feet away was a woman completely naked on her knees, giving a man standing in front of her a blow job. Their eyes weren't on the audience. They were on each other—hands tangled, moans filling the air—and I didn't even think they knew we were here.

But I was close enough to see the details of their bodies, the wetness her mouth left on his cock, her fingers as she rubbed her pussy. Each time she brushed across her clit, she bobbed her mouth deeper to meet him.

She was enjoying this.

So was I.

And something inside me erupted, and my entire body was breaking out in a sweat.

"Now, you feel it," Oliver breathed over the side of my face as though he had sensed it too.

Spit began to gather on the corners of her mouth as she took in more of him, and he rewarded her with a second finger.

I felt myself wiggle over the hard wooden bench. "Oliver ..." I didn't know why, but I had the strongest urge to sigh his name from my lips.

Before I took my next breath, his hand was grabbing mine, and together, he slid them between my crossed legs. And when he felt the heat that was waiting for him, he growled.

Seconds later, the man on the stage pulled his dick out of her mouth with a pop, and he laid her down on a mattress, got on his knees, and positioned his face between her legs. While he held her gaze, a look passing between them that the entire audience could see, his tongue flattened, and he licked the whole length of her pussy.

My hands circled around Oliver's wrist, and I moaned, "Oh my God."

When he put a finger inside her, she let out a scream that vibrated past each row. I could see the wetness on his finger as he was pulling it in and out, the tip of his tongue flicking against her clit.

I could feel both ... as though it were Oliver doing it to me.

Unexpectedly, the curtain closed, and the room turned dark again, soft voices misting through the theater like fog.

I felt Oliver's eyes on me, and I gradually glanced at him, my chest heaving, sweat beginning to seep through my pores.

"Do you want more?"

I didn't know what he was asking, but my answer was, "Yes."

His fingers stretched in a little deeper, the tips of them

moving toward my center and back as the curtain started to open again. For this act, a woman sat on a blanket with her legs spread, holding a vibrator against her clit. Her head was back, eyes closed. Every breath of hers filled the silence, so I could sense what was spreading through her body, what was building.

My clit felt like it was vibrating, the intensity of her screams moving through me.

I was already so warm, but I needed more and leaned my face into Oliver's neck. I just wanted closeness. To feel him. To remember what it was like to have him as mine.

And it was wrong.

I felt that in the most powerful way.

But it also felt right, and that was what pushed me to graze my nose up to his ear, inhaling his scent.

The higher I got, the deeper his fingers dug until he said, "I bet you're so fucking wet right now."

Oh God.

I was trembling. A need running through me. Emotions darting in all directions that I couldn't begin to process.

"Do you want more, Chloe?"

The woman on the stage was having an orgasm; I could hear her hips rocking out every wave.

"Yes," I breathed against him.

His hand went to my face, thumb stroking my chin. "You're sure? Because once we do this, there's no more ignoring me."

"I know." I filled my lungs. "I don't want to ignore you anymore."

His hand was on mine, and we were out of our seats and leaving the theater. As we hurried to my hotel, I didn't pay attention to the characteristics of the red light district, like I had on the way in. Because as Oliver weaved us through the packed sidewalk, I only noticed him.

And when we reached my hotel, I handed him my key, and

he led us to the elevator and down the hall. Once my door was open, his hands were on my waist, tearing off my jacket. My shirt came off next, and he moved me to the wall by the couch. As soon as I was against it, his mouth was on my neck, sucking bits of skin as he lowered to my breasts.

"Chloe ..." he groaned, ripping the lace of my bra to take a nipple into his mouth, biting, flicking the end with his tongue.

"Fuck!" I screamed, my hands rolling over his head, fingers gripping his hair.

Each time his mouth moved to the other breast, he pinched the nipple he'd left behind, making me cry out from the pain and moan from the pleasure at the same time.

"Do you know how long I've thought about doing this?" He took a nipple between his teeth, biting the end. "How I've thought of nothing but how badly I want to taste you and feel you and hold you and make you come."

He had the button of my jeans open, the fly down, his mouth leaving my breasts so he could tug my pants off my body. As I stood in front of the wall in just a pair of panties, a smile came across his lips.

"My sweet fucking girl is being so naughty tonight."

There was a hunger, a pulse.

Need.

And they owned me.

Oliver stayed on his knees, hands gripping the outside of my thighs as he looked up at me.

Two small steps separated us.

That was all.

And his mouth would then be on me.

As he gazed into my eyes, the ice blue staring back, his lips parted, fingers dragging down the corners of my panties. And when the material hit my bare feet, he looked between my legs and groaned, "That fucking pussy."

But he didn't close the gap between us.

He was waiting for me to do that, to surrender my body to him, because he needed to know I wanted it as much as him. I took a step and paused, needing that moment of hesitation, and I looked at the wetness on his lips and the hint of his tongue. I then took another, setting myself over his mouth.

His nose pressed into the top of me, and I felt him inhale. "You smell so fucking good ..." He took another long, deep breath. "Jesus, I fucking missed this."

Just as I grabbed his hair, he swiped my clit with his tongue, and I screamed, "Oh my God!"

He was licking up and down, and I was contracting beneath him, especially when his two fingers slid inside me and my back slapped against the wall.

"Yes," I moaned, squeezing his hair, my hips beginning to move with him.

His tongue was flicking me harder, faster, and then I felt something foreign.

Something I'd never had before.

It was his finger circling my other side, a place that hadn't been explored before, and while his tongue danced against the most sensitive part of me, he spread the wetness from his mouth. Once I was soaked everywhere, he was rubbing that back entrance, awakening it until just the tip of his finger was inside.

"Oliver." I quivered, the fullness taking ahold of me, shooting through my stomach.

In there was a build. I felt it instantly. Between his tongue and fingers, I was to the point where an orgasm was just licks away. And as it neared, I began to buck against his mouth. "*Ahhh.*"

"Come on my face, Chloe."

His fingers began to move harder, deeper, and when I felt

the roughness of his whiskers, I glanced down, seeing his icy-colored eyes.

And in this moment, I knew I was looking at the man I never stopped loving.

With that thought came a ripple of shudders that shot through my stomach. My hips pumped as he licked, the orgasm moving its way through my body. And when I stilled, he lifted me off the wall and carried me to the bed.

"Fuck, Chloe, I don't have a condom," he said as he set me on the mattress.

I didn't either.

"Are you safe?" I asked, feeling like it had been only seconds before when I asked him this the last time.

"Yes, I'm clean. You know I would never do anything to harm you."

I reached for his belt buckle as I said, "I'm on birth control," and I opened the leather strap and unzipped his jeans.

There was nothing romantic in the way Oliver kissed me, the way I was grabbing at his clothes and pulling them off. This was urgency, and I couldn't stand that something was separating him from being inside me.

When I got him naked, I backed up on the bed, moving closer to the pillows to get a full view of his body. "God, you're sexy," I groaned. I remembered each edge and plane so well, but it seemed time had only made them more defined.

He climbed on the bed, and my legs surrounded him as I felt the bareness of his cock at my entrance. It was sitting there, just taunting me, knowing how badly I wanted it.

"Oliver," I moaned, trying to take more, but he wouldn't give it to me. "Please," I begged. In one second, he was buried inside me, and I was pulsing around him, shouting, "*Yesss.*"

"Fuck," he breathed over my lips. "It feels like I never left."

Oh God.

He tilted his hips back and thrust into me, working into a rhythm that only lasted a few seconds before he was lifting me off the bed, and I was back on the wall. Oliver was using the wall to hold my weight, pulling back to his tip and driving into his base.

"Yes," I cried, my pussy convulsing from the friction.

More sweat was bubbling on our skin, and I could taste the saltiness of it as I licked his neck.

Each grind caused the plaster to burn my back, but the pain didn't make me want to stop. It made me want to yell, "Harder," as my body began to cry for a release.

But he didn't allow for it to happen because he was moving me again, and we were on the bed once more, Oliver placing me on my knees. I crawled forward, and before I reached the headboard, he was behind me. In one stroke, he was fully inside me.

"*Ahhh*," I grunted and then again when his hand touched my clit, rubbing it back and forth as I arched my back to meet him.

His speed was fast, intense.

Each drive bringing me that much closer.

"Not yet," he warned, his other hand biting my hip. "I've waited six long years to be inside you. I'm not ready for this to be over."

He was leading me so close to that edge, and every time I neared the peak, he slowed, and I would return to a simmer, my body having to build all over again. Just when I didn't think I could take another second of the tease, he was putting his back to the headboard and steering me on top of him.

"I want to watch you fuck me," he said, his gaze dipping down my body as his hands guided me over his crown. "Take all of my cock, Chloe."

I lowered, feeling every inch fill me in a way that made me stop breathing.

"Now, ride me."

With his finger on my clit and my arms wrapped around his neck, I rose over his shaft and dropped as I pressed my lips to his, and I took all of him in.

Every part.

"Oliver," I breathed, squeezing his shoulders.

His teeth were on my nipple now, eyes locked on mine.

"Bite it," I begged, remembering the look on the girl's face tonight when the man's fingertips had practically done the same to her.

When his teeth chomped down, I shouted, my back arching, and it made me ride him faster, my speed only increasing the more he rubbed my clit.

I couldn't stop the build.

"Kiss me," I pleaded, looking down as his mouth moved to my other breast.

He saw my need, and he was ravishing my lips, a rawness building inside me, moving through me so fast. And I could tell he wasn't far behind because he was using this sharp, fierce drive that could only come after six years of waiting to come inside me.

I understood exactly how that felt.

And I welcomed it.

"Come," I growled as his pants hit my lips.

That was all it took for both of us.

Blow after blow of pleasure tore through me, and I screamed his name and heard, "Chloe," at the same time.

We were shuddering together, our bodies locked, fingers desperately gripping each other's skin. And while the most satisfying sensation spread through me, I felt him empty himself inside of me.

I clung to his neck until our bodies stopped moving, our lips pressed together, air mingling. "Oliver ..."

His nose was rubbing against mine, the dampness of our skin making us so slick. "I'm so fucking crazy about you," he whispered softly, and I remembered the first time he'd said that to me.

I squeezed him inside me, not wanting to let him out, and I breathed, "I feel the same way about you."

"Good morning, sweet girl," Oliver said as he kissed me on the cheek.

My eyes flicked open to see him sitting next to me on the bed, dressed in the clothes he'd worn last night.

"I have to run back to my place and shower for work." He kissed me again, leaving his lips there for much longer. "I'll see you in a little while."

"Mmm," I groaned, grabbing his hand so he wouldn't leave. "You want to meet for coffee?"

He smiled, his fingers now rubbing across my chin. "I would love that. I'll text you in a little bit."

He kissed me once more, and after I watched him walk to the door, I hurried out of bed and searched the room for my purse, finding it near the entrance. I grabbed my phone from the inside, and the first thing I saw was a text from Lance.

Lance: Looks like you're already asleep, baby. I'll try you again when I wake up.

Every memory from last night began to replay in my head. The sounds. Tremors.

What it'd felt like each time I came.

And not one of those orgasms was from my husband.

They were from my first love.

And now ... I was a cheater.

An adulteress.

But really, what I was deep down inside was a woman completely in love with two men.

Me: I hope you're having the sweetest dreams. I love you.

I set my phone on the nightstand, and I walked to the shower, where I knew the water would never be hot enough again.

FORTY-FIVE

AS I THOUGHT of the photo Oliver had sent me this morning of himself, a smile moved across my face, and I stepped out of my closet and into my bathroom, not realizing Lance was standing just a few feet away.

My heart seized, my grin changing for my husband, and our stares connected in the mirror.

"Hi."

His eyes slowly dipped down my body. "I loved waking up to you this morning."

"I'm happy to be back," I said, still wearing my grin as I searched for my breath.

I walked to the vanity and grabbed my diamond studs.

A gift for our first wedding anniversary.

While I was screwing in the back to the first earring, my stomach tightened as I recalled the moment when Lance had gifted them to me in Florida. And just as I was sliding in the second diamond, he came up behind me, hands crossing over my stomach.

His face dived in my neck where he inhaled. "You smell incredible."

I laughed as his nose grazed a sensitive part of my skin. "If you wrinkle me, you're dead."

Both of us were in black suits, but mine was with a teal lacy shell and dangerously high heels, and his was with a crisp white button-down and a red-and-black-striped tie.

"But you know I love to iron," he growled. "What time will you be home from work tonight?"

I shook my head, fixing my hair now that my jewelry was on. "Hopefully not too late."

"I can always have Anthony pick you up at the office and take you straight to the restaurant."

I paused, dropping the large curls I'd been fixing around my face. "What restaurant?"

"Mistral."

I turned toward him, the reflection in the mirror not showing me enough. "You mean tonight?"

He searched my eyes before he said, "Yes, we're having dinner with Marshall and Molly."

My chest began to tighten, my heart pounding so fast that I couldn't breathe. Everything hurt, and it was moving into my throat like a bull coming out of the gate. "Why would you schedule that?" I snapped.

His hand moved to my shoulder, rubbing into the muscle. "Chloe, we've had a standing reservation for the last Thursday of every month for two years."

Even though we texted every day and we'd spoken a few times, I didn't want to see Molly. I hadn't since our talk. I just wasn't ready because I knew all she'd have to do was look at my face, and she would know what was happening with Oliver.

And the idea of seeing her with Lance ... I just couldn't handle that yet.

Especially because I'd practically moved in with Oliver since the morning after the sex show.

I stared into Lance's navy eyes and replied, "I'm too exhausted to do anything."

"We'll get you to bed as soon as we get home from dinner."

My brows rose, the gate opening in my throat. "I'm certainly not going to do that because I'm not going to dinner."

"Chloe ..."

A weight was pushing on the center of my chest.

It was almost unbearable.

And it was making my entire body shake.

"Lance, why wouldn't you confirm with me first?" My voice was rising, and I couldn't stop it. "You know how tired I've been, my God."

He laughed as he stared at me. "Don't you think you're being a little unreasonable? You've never passed on a night out with Molly—ever."

His laugh set me off even worse. "I'm so fucking burned out; I can't even see straight. How dare you call me unreasonable."

"Baby"—his hands went to my cheeks while my chest heaved—"what is going on?"

What is going on?

I was losing control and taking it out on him.

And I knew how wrong that was, but I couldn't stop.

"I'm so stressed ..." I whispered, the tears immediately forming in my eyes, pooling quickly, and brimming over my lids. But Lance was there to catch them before any hit my lips. "I have this huge presentation tomorrow morning, and today's the run-through. I'm sorry; it's not good for me to go out tonight."

I saw the concern pass over his face.

"Don't worry about it." He pressed his lips to mine and

added, "I'll take care of it." He searched my eyes one last time, holding my face even tighter. "We'll have a quiet night in."

A knot wedged in my throat, stabbing me as I said, "Thank you."

He kissed me once more before he left the bathroom, and I went over to the sink, turning on the water, but I didn't stick my hands beneath the stream.

I didn't even look at it.

I just needed the noise before I completely lost my fucking mind.

I concentrated on the sounds, the drips, the splashes, and somehow, I was able to calm my heart down and find my breath. And I straightened my suit jacket and skirt and made my way out of the master suite.

I was halfway to the kitchen when I heard Lance on the phone, saying, "We're not going to be able to make it." He paused. "Chloe is exhausted from the trip, and she has an important presentation in the morning she has to prepare for." I stayed by the wall, listening, assuming he was talking to Marshall. "The traveling is hard on her," he said, and then, "Sounds good. I'll see you at work."

I filled my lungs as deeply as I could and continued walking, our eyes locking as I made my way into the kitchen.

"I called Marshall about dinner. He understood and said maybe we can do it next week." He took half of a grapefruit out of the fridge and a spoon from the drawer.

"I'll make it up to them."

He took a seat at the bar across from me, and just as he scooped out the first section of fruit, a text came through my phone. Since messages no longer showed on my screen—something I'd programmed a few months ago—I had to open the Messages app to see the text.

Molly: You're canceling dinner?
Me: So many late nights and early mornings trying to get this
brand launched. I'm just exhausted, Molly.
Molly: Okay. Miss you.
Me: xoxo

I glanced up from my phone, seeing his eyes on me, and said, "I'm going to be late for work." I walked over to his side of the counter and put my arm around his shoulders, pressing my lips against the softness of his cheek. "I'm sorry." I took a breath, keeping my lips on him. "I'll see you tonight."

His hand brushed across my waist. "Have a good day, baby."

"This is amazing," I groaned as I chewed the Mongolian beef with scallions that Lance had picked up from Chinatown after work.

He'd also brought home an order of braised eggplant and sweet and sour pork, and those were just as delicious.

"These are my favorite kind of nights," he said as he reached across the table, spearing the broccoli that I'd left in a pile on the side, "when we get to stay in and have time together." He watched me with the biggest smile, his jeans and untucked button-down looking so sexy on him.

"Mine too."

There were many things I was unsure of, but as I stared at my husband sitting across from me, there was a feeling that consumed my chest.

It was love.

And in that moment, I knew without a doubt in my mind that I couldn't hurt this man.

FORTY-SIX

"TODAY, you're going to fall in love with Amsterdam," Oliver said as he kissed across my cheek. His arm wrapped over my shoulders as we walked away from my hotel, enough distance that my coworkers couldn't see us.

A tiny bit of sun was peeking through the clouds, and it was dancing in my eyes as I gazed at him. "You're going to make sure of that, huh?"

He nodded. "I promise, sweet girl."

"Are you going to tell me what you have planned?"

He smiled as he turned us right, and we headed down this long section of the canal where the small bridges crossed to our left, connecting us to the next street. Knowing I wasn't going to get an answer, I clasped my fingers through his.

The only thing Oliver had told me about today was that he wanted me to dress warm. Under my jacket, I was wearing my thickest sweater, and there were UGGs on my feet. As we walked over the dark brick pavers of the sidewalk, I leaned my face into his shoulder, smelling his familiar scent, and I opened my eyes to what was before me—the most beautiful homes lining the canals and people riding their bicycles along the side-walks and banks. There was the scent of food lingering in the crisp, cold air. I squeezed him a little harder and glanced at his profile. My heart clenched, and I knew there was nothing he could show me in this city that would be more beautiful than him.

Our eyes connected, and his lips gently pressed to mine.

"Just down here," he said when he pulled away, and he led us to the side of the closest bridge and to the dock that sat at the base of the water.

A boat was parked at the end, the captain standing outside, facing us.

"A canal cruise?" I asked Oliver as we stepped onto the dock.

"Best way to see the city."

I smiled, thanking him, and he released me just as the captain took my hand, assisting me down the three narrow steps of the boat.

He said, "Welcome," once I was inside. He pointed toward the rear and added, "Food and refreshments are in the galley. Make yourself at home."

As Oliver came in behind me, I stopped in the center of the cabin, where there were finger sandwiches, quiche, fruit, and a vanilla cake with strawberries. To the side, chilling on ice, was a bottle of champagne.

"It's beautiful," I whispered when his fingers touched my waist. I turned around to face him, my arms circling his neck. "You're amazing."

His hand dropped down my back, squeezing my ass before he gave it a light smack. "Take a seat. I'll pour us drinks."

Still grinning, I went over to the cushioned bench that ran the whole length of the galley and sat in the middle. I watched him pop the cork off the bottle and pour some of the bubbly into glasses. When he came in next to me, he handed me one.

"What are we toasting to?"

"Contract renewals." He smiled, his eyes smoldering. "And to you loving this city of hope."

"Cheers," I whispered, and I brought the drink to my lips.

As the engine began to hum and we pulled away from the dock, Oliver's arm went around my neck, and he settled my back against his chest. The wind howled as it came through the thin windows of the boat, blowing my hair, and I understood why he'd asked me to bundle up.

We weren't more than a few blocks away when he pointed at a building. "Do you remember eating there?"

My eyes followed his finger, and I recognized the stone entryway and the beige sign from my last trip to Amsterdam. "Those truffle fries," I groaned.

"That restroom stall," he moaned back.

I laughed, clinging my fingers to his elbow as it rested over my breast, and I thought of when he had taken me into that restroom. We'd snuck off between our appetizers and the main course, and then we'd straightened our clothes and went back to our table like I hadn't cried out an orgasm in the men's room just moments before.

Oliver's lips moved to my ear, and he said softly, "You could have this for another six months."

He was referring to the contract renewal I'd received. The offer was almost identical to the one I had now, except the pay was considerably higher. Since each member of my team was given the same amount, we'd been discussing the details together at work.

"It would be lovely," I replied, staring out the window as we glided over the water, through the narrow waterway.

"With your last trip scheduled for next month, I suspect you have to make a decision soon?"

I nodded against his chest. "I do."

I couldn't believe I was at the five-month mark already and how much had happened since I signed the first contract.

How I was in this boat right now with Oliver, and just days ago, I had been in Boston with Lance.

How Oliver had spent the night in my bed last night, how Lance and I had been talking about spending my birthday in Florida.

How Amsterdam was absolutely perfect with Oliver.

And Boston was perfect with Lance.

But I knew I had to make some decisions soon even if they were going to be impossible. I just couldn't keep going on like this. My mind was constantly a mess, and it wasn't fair to both of the men I loved.

I sat up and took one of the small sandwiches off the plate, biting the end before holding it up to Oliver's mouth so he could eat the rest. As I was reaching for a strawberry, I felt my phone vibrate multiple times, letting me know several messages had come through. I turned my body just a little to access my back pocket, where I kept my phone, and entered my password. When I clicked on my texts, the first message that came up was from my husband.

Lance: Ten days, baby. Miss you.

I stared at his words, swallowing, trying to fill my lungs as I heard, "Sweet girl."

Slowly, I glanced up and stared at the icy-blue eyes that were gazing into mine, and I begged for some breath before I said, "Yes?"

"Can you grab me a napkin?"

I tried inhaling again and searched the table, handing him a few paper ones that I'd found. Then, I put my phone away and added more champagne to my glass, leaning into Oliver's body again.

"How about some cake?"

I shook my head. There was no way I could put food in me. "I'm not much of a cake girl."

He hugged me against his chest as we slowed under the bridges, and I listened to the captain point out several of the historic landmarks as I tried to clear my mind.

"I'll get you some chocolate chip cookies," he said when the captain finished. "I know a bakery that's not far from where we're docking." He kissed my cheek, and I felt a wave of heat move over me. "The owner is British and makes the best sticky toffee pudding."

I wrapped my fingers around his arm. "I'll have to try some."

"We'll get some hot chocolate too. It's fucking divine there."

A memory flashed through my head of Vail and the candy store Lance had sent me to.

The place where I had found magic ... in Lance.

And now, with my back to Oliver, I was staring at Amsterdam, and there was a tear rolling down my cheek.

Oh God.

FORTY-SEVEN

Molly: It's been a few days ... are you alive?
Me: So slammed at work but still breathing. Thanks for
checking on me.
Molly: Can we go back to being besties, or are you still avoiding
me?
Me: LOL. I can't even with you.
Molly: I miss you.
Me: So much it hurts.
Molly: Girls' night when you get home? I'll send the boys to
something sport-ish, and May will go to Marshall's parents'
house.
Me: Sounds like a date.

"CHLOE," Marshall said as he was getting off his elevator into the lobby of his building. "Welcome home."

"Thank you." I smiled, and we kissed each other on the cheek. "Lance is super excited about the game." I nodded toward the front entrance where my husband was waiting for Marshall outside in the backseat of his SUV.

"Same." He laughed, pointing toward the ceiling. "She has enough food in the condo to feed the whole building."

"That's our Molly." I continued to smile while I walked into the elevator and he stepped out.

"It was really good to see you, Chloe. The four of us are overdue for our Mistral date."

"Yes, we are, and I can't wait. Have a good time tonight," I said, and the door began to slide shut, my hand going in the air to wave good-bye.

I'd been home for three days, and the thought of this visit had been eating at my stomach from the second I landed in Boston.

Yet I desperately wanted to see my best friend.

I just didn't want her to see me.

Because even though I could hide what I was doing from the rest of the world, including my husband, Molly was the only person who would see straight through my lies.

And that was something I just wasn't ready to face.

But now, the elevator was opening, and I was moving down the hall, gently knocking on their door. I sucked in my breath, and as it opened, a face I knew so well came into view.

"Hi," I said, the sound of my voice surprising me.

She said nothing; she just stared back.

And then I felt it—the moment she saw the truth and when it all settled inside her.

"Molly ..."

She smiled wide, not showing any teeth, and she opened her arms and pulled me against her.

At first, it was just a hug where she was squeezing the hell out of me. But then it became so much more when I realized just how badly I needed my best friend's arms around me.

"Don't let go."

"I won't, babe." She strengthened her grip. "I'll stand here all night if you need me to."

The tears were there before I even took a breath, the weakness moving through my body, turning all of me numb.

"Now, I know why you've been avoiding me." She clenched my shoulders. "I mean, let's face it; I knew before. But now, I really know."

I clung to her even tighter, remembering the last time I had been here when I held her almost the same way. "Let's go inside before your neighbors know how much of a mess I am."

She slid her arm around my waist and led me into her condo while I wiped my face with both hands, still not getting all the wetness.

"Here." She handed me a tissue when we got into the kitchen. "And take this too," she added, sticking a tumbler between my fingers that I assumed was vodka on the rocks. "Now, let's get cozy." Her hand was back in mine, bringing me to the large sectional in the living room, and then she spread a big, fluffy blanket over us.

I held the drink in my lap, trying to find a place to start, words that could accurately describe this new place I was in.

But when I looked up at Molly, I had nothing. And not a single syllable came from my mouth.

"I'm your person," she said softly, the pain visible on her face. "And you completely shut me out."

Oh God.

I'd already fucked up so much.

It killed me that this situation had now affected her and our friendship.

"I didn't want to have this conversation, Molly." I swallowed, the vodka burning in a way that I had to wait several seconds before I could speak again. When I looked at her, a pain began to gnaw through the center of my chest. "I didn't want to admit the truth to you."

She reached across the couch cushion, her fingers now rubbing my shoulder. "Of all people, I should be the one you can admit anything to. Always. But, Chloe, you can't keep going on like this."

"No." I felt my chest heave, as I'd been thinking the same thing for days. "I can't."

"Do you love him?"

Silence passed between us as she waited for an answer.

And it hurt like hell, but I had to tell her the truth.

"Yes." A sob blasted out of me. "I love him."

"What does that look like? Long-term, I mean. You live here, and he lives there. He comes here and gets a green card? Or you get a work visa, move your whole world to Europe, and live happily ever after?"

I took a breath. "I don't know."

"You have to know, Chloe. You have to have a plan because, no matter how you work this out, someone is going to get hurt."

The spit began to thicken in my mouth. "I have options."

"Like what?"

I knew she wasn't going to want to hear this, but she needed to because it was a strong reality.

"I can extend my contract, and it's something I've really been considering."

"What?" Her voice was rising fast. "Have you literally lost your fucking mind?"

I squeezed the cold glass in one hand and the blanket in the other as I cried, "I don't know what you want me to say."

"Chloe ..." Her fingers were clamping down on my shoulder, her tone getting even stronger. "I want you to say you're going to stop playing house with Lance while you're in Boston and you're going to stop playing house with Oliver while you're in Amsterdam and that you're going to make a goddamn decision."

"Molly ..."

"You have a life here." Her back straightened, her stare narrowing. "You have a husband who would give up his business, houses, and probably every dollar to his name just to be with you. And you have the most beautiful life that the two of you have created together—a life every person I know would die to have." She paused, and it felt like my throat was going to close. "Are you going to give all of that up for Oliver? The man you dated for just a semester when you were twenty-one years old? Who you only spend two weeks a month with?" Her fingers lightened, and I wished they were gripping me again. "What's it going to look like when the honeymoon wears off and things get tough between you and Oliver? You already know how incredible your life can be with Lance, but can you say that about Oliver?"

The silence came again.

It was so thick that it took my breath away.

"Fuck," I cried, my hand going over my face.

I needed the darkness, a minute just to myself because what was happening inside me wasn't normal.

Not with the amount of guilt I was bearing from what I was doing to both of these men.

When my palm finally dropped to my lap, I stared at my best friend again, and in the softest voice, she said, "Babe, I love you, but you have to tell me how you see this ending."

I glanced away as an image of Lance came into my head. It was of us kissing before I'd gotten out of the SUV tonight and another one of us making love in the shower just a few hours ago.

I thought of Oliver, the texts we'd exchanged today, the way he had taken my body the morning of my flight.

I stared back into her eyes, giving her as much of my truth as I could. "I don't know, but when I figure it out, I promise, you will know." I reached forward, putting my hand on her arm. "Can you accept that for now? Because, Molly, it's honestly the best I have at this moment."

She didn't say anything; she just pulled me into her arms, and I hugged her right back.

"Are you hungry?" Lance asked, his fingers linked through mine as we walked down Boylston Street, passing some of our favorite restaurants.

"I had a huge breakfast," I replied, sliding to the side to avoid a large group of pedestrians. "But I could eat something small."

"We could grab ..." His voice trailed off, and I glanced toward him to see where his attention had gone. He was staring at the store window we were walking by and said, "Come look at this," bringing me over to the glass.

The display was for a baby boutique, filled with tiny outfits and adorable accessories.

"That one," he said, pointing to an outfit in the back, which was an infant bikini, hat, and sunglasses. "For when we're in Siesta Key."

In the window, I was able to see my husband's reflection, the smile on his handsome face as he looked at the clothes and hats and bathing suits for babies.

There was so much love in his eyes.

And it was for a family we'd been talking about starting for the past year.

His reflection began to shift as he moved behind me, pressing his hands against my stomach, lips close to the back of my ear. "Since you're not renewing your contract, we only have one more month to go."

As I stared at the clothing display, my eyes closed, a shudder trickling through my body.

"Can you imagine what our baby is going to look like?" His voice was so soft now; I almost didn't recognize it. "I wonder if our little girl will have your wild red hair or if our boy will get my eyes." He breathed against the side of my face. "Chloe, I'm ready to start the next chapter in our lives."

I felt the tears leave my lids as I opened my eyes. Not afraid of Lance seeing me cry, I turned around and hugged his waist. The expression I had seen in the reflection of the window was the same one I was looking at now.

I closed my eyes once again, holding my lips so close to his, and I whispered, "I love you," right before he kissed me.

After spending the day walking around our neighborhood, shopping in several of the new stores, Lance and I came back home.

We were standing in the kitchen, his eyes on his phone, when he said, "I have to return a few of these emails before dinner."

Relief flooded through me as I smiled for my husband and said, "I'm going to take a quick shower, then."

And once he kissed me, heading for his home office, I went into our bathroom and locked the door behind me.

As I stripped off my clothes, leaving them wherever they landed, I avoided the mirrors.

I didn't even glance down to look at my own skin.

When I reached the shower faucet, I turned it to the hottest setting. Then, I walked straight in until my back hit the wall, and I slowly slid to the floor. I tucked my knees to my chest, and I held myself in the tightest ball while the freezing water pelted my face.

And while I waited for it to warm, my mouth opened, and this time, it wasn't silent screams that came out.

It was sobs.

FORTY-EIGHT

"I'M GOING to need your signature at the bottom of each page," Sven, my manager, said as he pushed a stack of papers toward me.

"No problem," I replied, my eyes falling onto the first lines, lifting the pen off his desk.

I knew what the contract said; I'd read it many times. I even knew the places I needed to initial, sign, and date—doing all three before I returned it to him.

He carefully checked each sheet, and then our eyes connected.

He stuck his hand out in the air for me to shake. "That looks like everything." He nodded to confirm. "Have a safe trip home, Chloe."

"Thank you." I released his fingers and made my way out of his office and down the hall, stopping at my desk to grab my things before I left.

These past two weeks in Amsterdam had gone by so quickly that it felt like I'd just gotten off the plane. But as I'd learned during my semester in London, time was something I couldn't slow down. So, I had taken in every moment I had with Oliver.

And now that it was the last evening of my six-month contract, I would be flying home tomorrow. I left the office and went straight to my hotel where he was waiting for me.

Just like we were in college all over again, he stood in my tiny kitchen, making us dinner.

But now, six years later, we were different people.

We'd just found each other again.

And, God, did it feel right.

"Hungry?" he asked.

I wrapped my arms around his neck and squeezed him tightly against me. "Starving."

"Good. I made a lot."

I kissed him, and as his lips parted, I felt the smallest touch of his tongue. And I breathed in his scent and held it inside me.

"Oliver ..." I moaned softly.

His beard brushed over my cheek, and I took in the sensation, the warmth that he passed on to me.

He stayed just like that for several minutes until he leaned back to look at my eyes. "I'm going to feed you and then make love to you since it's going to be six weeks before I get to do either again."

I shook my head, the emotion starting to come to my eyes. "Both sound delicious."

"Sven thought he was doing the American team a favor by giving you a longer break at home." His gaze dropped to my lips. "But these six weeks are going to feel like an eternity."

Tears were already in my eyes, and when I nodded, they loosened. Oliver was on them immediately, wiping them before they fell.

"You're so sweet, and I'm so lucky," I whispered. "I have no idea what I did to deserve you."

He kissed the tip of my nose, across my lips, and over each cheek. "I'm the lucky one." He then rubbed his beard over my skin as though he knew I needed all the extra roughness I could get before my flight tomorrow. "I made my mum's spaghetti." He paused, and I saw the pain in his eyes over her passing. "I know you remember that dish."

"I knew I smelled that yumminess when I walked in."

"I'll get us some plates."

His hands dropped from my body, and he reached into the cabinet, bringing two dishes over to the stove where he put pasta into each. He then placed them on my table, adding garlic bread to the plates.

Before I even sat down, I knew he had poured us champagne, and there were probably cookies for dessert. "Thank you," I said, staring at his mom's specialty. "You know how much I love when you cook."

"You inspire me to want to spend more time in the kitchen."

I grinned as I took my first bite, savoring the hearty flavor of the Bolognese. "You're an exceptional chef, Oliver." I swallowed and took another bite, my eyes closing as the taste melted on my tongue. "Don't ever stop cooking."

When I looked at him again, I saw his beard had grown a little wilder. I loved this length and the way his hand brushed over the bottom of it after he chewed.

As he noticed me staring, he smiled. "Six weeks is a fucking eternity." Hearing him repeat it only emphasized how hard this was going to be. "But then, at least we have another six months together." He took several breaths. "I'll take any time I have with you, but you know ... you're going to have to make a choice soon, sweet girl."

"I know." I stuck the fork into the mound of pasta and kept it there. "Time has certainly never been in our favor, has it?"

"Not since I met you." He licked the sauce off his lip. "Always slipping away every time I try to grasp you."

I left my fork and reached for my napkin. "That's because I'm not good at good-byes."

"We've had a lot of them." He took a long drink of his champagne. "I hope, one day, we'll have forever, and I won't have to say good-bye again."

I glanced out the window, the one that was letting in a breeze of Amsterdam and said, "Hope." I then took in the deepest breath before turning toward those icy-blue eyes. "This is the city for it."

His gaze deepened. "My sweet, sweet girl."

Knowing there was no way I could put another bite in my mouth, I rose from the table and straddled his lap. My arms circled his neck, my lips gently pressing to his.

From the moment Oliver had first kissed me in London, I'd felt this wave of warmth pass through me, an intensity that started in his fingertips and traveled through my whole body. The closer we got, the deeper I fell, the hotter his heat became. So, as he kissed me, his fingers touched my face, cupping it in a way that was so original to him, and I was scorching.

But tonight, there wasn't an urgency in his movements. What he gave me was a slow, building passion that wrapped around us, holding us to this moment forever.

"Chloe ..."

He began unbuttoning my shirt and lifted it over my head before he carried me to the bed and pulled off my pants and undergarments. While he was taking off his clothes, I backed up to the headboard so I could watch him. With each piece he removed, memories burned into my mind of the times I'd kissed those exact spots, when I'd run my fingers across them.

"Sweet girl," he hissed as he joined me on the bed, sliding between my legs.

He didn't wait for the tease. He made sure I was ready—and I always was with him—and then he was thrusting inside me.

In one, long, deep, powerful stroke.

"Oh God, yes," I moaned, my head falling against the pillow. My legs circled his waist, keeping him as close as I could. My arms stayed tightly wrapped around his neck, and while he moved in and out of my body, I kissed every bit of his skin I could reach. I passed along the edge of his neck, traveling to his ear and down his chest. "Oliver ... I love you."

My breath came out in pants, each pump of his hips almost taking the air out of me.

We were suddenly moving, and he was lifting me on top of him, setting me on his lap, giving me the view I'd wanted all along—nothing but his handsome face.

While our chests were pressed together, mouths locked, I lowered my body, taking in every inch of him. When I got to the base, I hugged him to me, pulsing as I kept him inside me. And gradually, I began rocking over him, our limbs staying tangled, mine finding a home nestled with his.

"I love you," I heard.

I gasped at the way his words floated down my throat, and I held them in my chest.

As my hands settled over his shoulders, his went to my face, thumbs on my jaw, and I found that rhythm we both needed. The pace that caused his grip to tighten, forcing a build through my stomach, and when I neared that place I couldn't return from, my eyes opened.

"Oh God." I quivered over him.

His thumbs were at the corners of my mouth. "Kiss me."

I did, and that was when I completely lost it.

An orgasm started at my core, tearing through my chest,

rippling up to my fingertips where I was holding him so close that there wasn't even breath between us.

I felt him come just seconds behind me, his hips giving several hard thrusts, meeting me while I rocked over him.

His hands almost squeezed my face as he emptied himself and moaned, "Chloe."

When we both stilled, we stayed there in sweaty arms and exhales, and there were even tears while we held on to each other in a way where love couldn't escape. It stayed just between us, in the windy city of Amsterdam, where it belonged.

And after I spent the night in his arms, Oliver got into a taxi with me. Once we arrived at Schiphol Airport, he had the driver park along the curb of the departure gate.

I stood on the curb, like I had six years ago, while Oliver got my suitcase out of the trunk. I watched his hands work as expertly as they did in the kitchen, lifting the heavy bag as though it were flour. I watched the way his face smiled as he looked at me, moving closer until his palms were on my cheeks.

"Mmm," I breathed, turning my face so I could nuzzle into his hand.

He said nothing as he stared at me. Once again, our time was limited, as we knew the taxi couldn't stay parked there forever and I had a flight to catch.

But Oliver took these moments to really look at me, and he finally said, "Six weeks."

I nodded, and the first tear dripped.

"I know that feels like forever, sweet girl."

He pulled me against his chest, my cheek now resting over his heart, and I heard the way it was beating for me.

Beating so fucking hard.

"I love you," I whispered. I reached for his sweatshirt and held the material between my palms, squeezing it into me, my nails stabbing it as hard as I could. "You know I hate saying good-bye, Oliver."

He looked at me, his thumbs swiping under my eyes. "We don't have to." He pressed his lips to mine, his breath filling my lungs before he pulled away and said, "Because even if it hurts ... you're going to come back to me, and we're going to start making plans for our future."

"One day, I hope the hurt will finally go away," I said so softly.

He gazed down at my lips before he briefly kissed them. "I love you," he finally replied, the words hitting my face, slipping inside my mouth so I could swallow them.

And once I did, I smiled at him and breathed, "You're so perfect." I wiped my face with the back of my hand, my chest making it impossible for the tears to stop.

I took a step back, and our arms stretched. And even though I had the suitcase handle to hold on to, I still couldn't let go of him.

"You know what I'm going to do, sweet girl ..."

More wetness hit my cheeks when I nodded. "You're going to watch me walk away."

"Yes."

Once again, I didn't think the tears could stream faster at how much this man loved me.

My foot felt like it weighed a million pounds when I lifted it over the pavement to take a step, our arms extending to the point where our fingers could no longer hold on.

And they broke ...

I took a final look, and then I put my back to him and hurried inside.

It was the only way, or I wouldn't go.

Once I was in the terminal, I rushed past the crowds to the glass window that overlooked the outside. From here, I was able to see Oliver. He was standing where I had left him, still staring at the entrance as though he was visualizing me move through it one last time.

Then, he got in the taxi and shut the door.

As the driver pulled away, my hands slid down the glass, and my ass hit the ground. Sobs racked my body while I tucked myself into a ball, rocking over the airport floor.

When I was finally strong enough, I took out my phone and pulled up my messages, finding the one I wanted. As I sobbed with the rest of the emotions I had left in me, I started to type.

Me: I'm coming home. xo

PART FOUR

A love ... that never ended.

FORTY-NINE

OLIVER

"WHAT IN THE fuck are you still doing here?" Jake asked as he popped his head into my office. "Don't the important people get to leave early?"

"Then, we'd both be gone," I said, laughing at my best mate as he sat in the chair in front of my desk. My eyes were on the T-shirt he wore, and I remembered when we'd grabbed it after a concert at The O2 when we were back in London, visiting family. "Do I need to give you a pay raise? Your shirt has a goddamn hole in it."

He looked down, shaking his head. "It's fucking Noah," he said, referring to his nine-year-old. "Emma's been teaching him to do the laundry, and there're rips in everything. I don't know why my wife thinks it's such a good idea for this to be his chore if everything I fucking own is ruined." He smiled as he adjusted himself in the chair. "Good thing I work for the largest travel booking site in the country and you can afford the pay raise I'm going to hit you up for."

I turned my chair, my hands leaving my computer, to face

him. "You're my CFO. If you want a pay raise, you know how to make it happen."

We were both laughing when there was a knock at the door, and our assistant walked in.

"Should I come back?" she asked, glancing between her bosses.

"No, no." I waved her over.

"I wanted to give you this before I left." She held up a folder and then set it on my desk. "It's the list of interview questions that the station sent over. I printed them out so you can prep."

"Oh, I'll take that," Jake said, snatching the folder before I could grab it.

"I'm going to call and have your dinner delivered," she said. "Would thirty minutes be all right?"

Knowing there wasn't anything in my fridge at home, I thanked her and followed it up with, "That's perfect." When she left, I glanced over at Jake. "How do they look?"

He got up from his chair, reading as he walked to the window. When he returned to my desk, his grin gave me my answer, but he still said, "You're going to have fun with some of those." He took a few steps toward my door. "See you in the morning?"

"You bet."

Once I watched him leave, I opened the top of the folder and began to go over the questions.

The interview was for the largest business publication in Europe, and they had named me as the highest-earning CEO of the year. The feature would stream live for sixty minutes. It would also include a pre-taped segment, which had filmed at my office, to show all aspects of the business I'd built in Amsterdam after resigning from International Bookings ten years ago.

As I got further down the list, I realized what Jake had meant.

Oliver Bennett, at fifty years old, you're officially Amsterdam's most eligible bachelor. Has there never been a leading lady in your life?

The question had no relevance whatsoever to my company, but I understood their interest. How could someone my age, with my success, never settle down? It was actually something I was asked often, but the answer I gave was never honest. The one I would give during the interview wouldn't be either.

Because no one in this world needed to hear that I had been in love two times in my life and both were with the same woman.

The first was when we had been just kids, and as much as I'd wanted to tell that gorgeous girl not to leave London, I couldn't. I wasn't going to be the man who had taken her virginity and her future. I couldn't live with that kind of guilt. The only thing I could do was let her go.

It was the hardest thing I'd ever done. Nothing made me move on. And I never really settled down, partly because I was young and having such a blast with my mates. And partly because Chloe was the girl who had come into my life and turned it upside down.

And then six years later, when the European managers had been forming their US teams, I had seen Chloe Kennedy Hamilton on the list, and every memory I'd tried to let go came rushing back.

I had to have her in my life again.

I didn't know how much of her I would get; the name change told me she was married. But there was a reason we'd been brought back together, and I had to find out what it was.

I had no expectations when I met her in that corridor. I just wanted to be near her one more time, and if her presence was all I got, I would take it.

But slowly, that sweet girl began to let me in more, and it was like the six years we had been apart had never happened. And she slid into this pattern of traveling home to her husband and spending the rest of the month with me.

All I wanted was what we never got a chance to have the first time.

The possibility of a future.

And those six months ...

They were so fucking hard on her.

They were so fucking hard on me.

But they were a gift, and we both knew that.

And we had known when she came back for her second contract, she was going to have to make a decision.

I walked over to the window, pushing my palms on the glass, looking over this city that had always been so hopeful for me, and I remembered when I'd watched Chloe walk into the airport in Amsterdam.

That evening, I'd waited for a text, telling me she had landed.

I got nothing, and she didn't reply to any of the ones I'd sent her.

Because of her husband, I agreed I would never call, and as much as it hurt, I wouldn't break her trust, so all I could do was wait.

Every fucking minute was tortuous.

When Monday morning came and I still hadn't heard from her, I went to Sven's office and asked if he'd been in touch with the American team to see if they had arrived. I'd tracked the flight, so I knew the answer already, but he assured me everyone was fine. I then asked about Chloe specifically, and he told me that on her last day at the office, right before she left for the evening, the contract she'd signed was actually for termination. She'd canceled the six-month extension and discontinued her employment.

In that moment, I knew ... she'd made her choice.

I didn't hate her.

I could never hate her.

I always knew there was a possibility she wouldn't choose what we had.

Maybe there were signs that I'd missed from that night. Perhaps I should have known she wasn't ever going to come back to me. That on the curb, outside of departures, was the last time I would ever get to kiss Chloe.

But when I thought back to that memory, I didn't look for the holes. I just recalled the love that was in her arms when she held me and what it felt like to have her in my hands.

Those were the things I focused on.

And all these years later, I knew she still had love for me because she never unfollowed my social media page and she never kicked me off her private one.

In my heart, that was her way of making sure I was okay.

For a long time, those pictures of her were what got me through it; they were the only things I could hold on to. And I used them as a window into her life where they answered questions I would never get to ask her.

Fuck, there were some big moments.

I got to see her body grow each time she was pregnant—the first two with boys and the last, she'd finally gotten her girl with red hair. I watched her children age and go off to school and Chloe's family take holidays with Molly and her husband and kids. Even now, it looked like the two best friends still got together for drinks every week.

My God, she's a beautiful mum.

As that thought gripped me, I walked over to the bar in my office and grabbed a beer out of the fridge, bringing it up to my lips and swallowing until it was gone.

When I set the bottle down, I took out my phone and pulled up my photos, finding the same one I always looked at every time I needed her.

I'd taken the picture in a pub in London, the night Jake had sung to her from the top of a table.

That was almost thirty years ago, and we had been so young and in love.

Blind to the pain that was waiting for us in the future.

But those months were real, and so were the ones in Amsterdam.

As I looked back at my life, I could say it was wonderful. There had been many women. Lots of smiles. Hours of laughter.

But at this age, I could say I'd never had anyone like her.

She'd once told me she hoped the hurt would finally go away.

After watching her leave me twice, I didn't think it would.

And, damn it, sweet girl, it never did.

AUTHOR'S NOTE

When the idea for *Even If It Hurts* came to me, I knew it was going to be an extremely challenging story to write. If you've read me before, you know I don't shy away from sensitive topics, but after penning twenty-five books, I can say, this was the toughest and the hardest.

You see, when I craft stories, I become the character. I live their pain and sorrow, and I experience life through their eyes. The emotional upheaval it took to put myself in Chloe's shoes was one I hadn't expected or prepared for. I can assure you, I went through many boxes of tissues while writing her journey with Lance and Oliver.

If you follow me on social media, you've seen lots of pictures of my husband. What most of you don't know is that we've been together for nineteen years, college sweethearts who were absolutely crazy about each other, much like Oliver and Chloe. Because of my experience with falling in love, I'm fascinated with the concept of first love. I wanted to explore what it would feel like to lose that love over an uncontrollable circumstance and what it would look like if he came back into your life at a different time, place, and under much different circumstances.

I know *Even If It Hurts* is a hard limit for many of you, but I hope you can close this book and feel every emotion I weaved into this story and every tear I shed. I hope you'll feel the love that Chloe had for Oliver and Lance. And I hope that somewhere on those final pages, you were able to find some forgiveness for Chloe, a woman lucky enough to be loved by two of the most amazing men ever.

xoxo,

Marni

ACKNOWLEDGMENTS

Nina Grinstead, there are no words for this one. Our baby forever. Love you so, so, so much. Team B.

Jovana Shirley, with every book, this statement only becomes truer—I wouldn't want to do this with anyone but you. I treasure you and the love that you give my books. Love you so hard.

Hang Le, my unicorn, you are just incredible in every way.

Judy Zweifel, as always, thank you for being so wonderful to work with and for taking such good care of my words. <3

Chanpreet Singh, thanks for always holding me together. Adore you, lady. XO

Kaitie Reister, I love you, girl, so hard. You're my biggest cheerleader, and you're such a wonderful friend. Thank you for being you.

Donna Cooksley Sanderson, thank you, thank you, thank you—for a million and one reasons. I love you so much and I cannot wait to hug you again. xx

Nikki Terrill and Andrea Lefkowitz, you girls are my soul sisters. Thank you will truly never be enough.

Kimmi Street and Crystal Radaker, my sisters, I love you more than love.

Ratula Roy, words will never do justice to how much I love and appreciate you. You mean everything to me.

Ricky, my sexyreads, I love you.

Julie Vaden, as always, thank you for letting me pick your brain. You're the best. XO

Extra-special love goes to Hilary Suppes, Kayti McGee, Chris Fletcher, Elizabeth Kelley, Jennifer Porpora, and my group of Sarasota girls, whom I love more than anything. I'm so grateful for all of you.

Mom and Dad, thanks for your unwavering belief in me and your constant encouragement. It means more than you'll ever know.

Brian, my words could never dent the amount of love you give me. Trust me when I say, I love you more.

My Midnighters, you are such a supportive, loving, motivating group. Thanks for being such an inspiration, for holding my hand when I need it, and for always begging for more words. I love you all.

To all the bloggers who read, review, share, post, tweet, Instagram—Thank you, thank you, thank you will never be enough. You do so much for our writing community, and we're so appreciative.

To my readers—I cherish each and every one of you. I'm so grateful for all the love you show my books, for taking the time to reach out to me, and for your passion and enthusiasm. I love, love, love you.

MARNI'S MIDNIGHTERS

Getting to know my readers is one of my favorite parts about being an author. In Marni's Midnighters, my private Facebook group, I post covers before they're revealed to the public and excerpts of the projects I'm currently working on, and team members qualify for exclusive giveaways. To join Marni's Midnighters, click HERE.

ABOUT THE AUTHOR

USA Today best-selling author Marni Mann knew she was going to be a writer since middle school. While other girls her age were daydreaming about teenage pop stars, Marni was fantasizing about penning her first novel. She crafts unique stories that weave together her love of darkness, mystery, passion, and human emotions. A New Englander at heart, she now lives in Sarasota, Florida, with her husband and their two dogs. When she's not nose deep in her laptop, working on her next novel, she's scouring for chocolate, sipping wine, traveling, or devouring fabulous books.

Want to get in touch? Visit me at...
www.marnismann.com
MarniMannBooks@gmail.com

ALSO BY MARNI MANN

STAND-ALONE NOVELS

Even If It Hurts (Contemporary Romance)

Before You (Contemporary Romance)

The Assistant (Psychological Thriller)

When Ashes Fall (Contemporary Romance)

The Unblocked Collection (Erotic Romance)

Wild Aces (Erotic Romance)

Prisoned (Dark Erotic Thriller)

THE AGENCY STAND-ALONE SERIES—Erotic Romance

Signed

Endorsed

Contracted

Negotiated

THE SHADOWS SERIES—Erotic Romance

Seductive Shadows—Book One

Seductive Secrecy—Book Two

THE PRISONED SPIN-OFF DUET—Dark Erotic Thriller

Animal—Book One

Monster—Book Two

THE BAR HARBOR SERIES—New Adult

Pulled Beneath—Book One

Pulled Within—Book Two

THE MEMOIR SERIES—Dark Mainstream Fiction

Memoirs Aren't Fairytales—Book One

Scars from a Memoir—Book Two

NOVELS COWRITTEN WITH GIA RILEY

Lover (Erotic Romance)

Drowning (Contemporary Romance)